About the Author

Martha Conway is the author of *12 Bliss Street*, which was nominated for an Edgar Award, and *Thieving Forest*, which won the North American Book Award for Best Historical Fiction. Her short stories have appeared in *The Iowa Review*, *The Carolina Quarterly*, *The Massachusetts Review*, *Folio*, and other journals. She teaches creative writing for Stanford University's Continuing Studies Program and UC Berkeley Extension. Born in Northern Ohio, she now lives in San Francisco with her family.

David —

SUGARLAND

A Jazz Age Mystery

Enjoy your trip back to the Roaring Twenties!

Martha Conway

Martha Conway

Noontime Books
San Francisco, California

Noontime Books
San Francisco, California
info@noontimebooks.com

Publisher's Note: This is a work of fiction. Names, characters, places, and incidents are a product of the author's imagination. Locales and public names are sometimes used for atmospheric purposes. Any resemblance to actual people, living or dead, or to businesses, companies, events, institutions, or locales is completely coincidental.

Cover Design by Kit Foster

Ordering Information:
Quantity sales. Special discounts are available on quantity purchases by corporations, associations, and others. For details, contact the address above.

Cataloging-in-Publication Data

Conway, Martha, author.
     Sugarland : a jazz age mystery / Martha Conway.
     pages cm
     ISBN 978-0-9916185-3-8
     ISBN 978-0-9916185-5-2

     1. Women jazz musicians--Fiction. 2. African American women musicians--Fiction. 3. Jazz--Illinois--Chicago--Fiction. 4. Prohibition--Illinois--Chicago--Fiction. 5. Murder--Fiction. 6. United States--Race relations--Fiction. 7. Chicago (Ill.)--Fiction. 8. Detective and mystery fiction.   I. Title.

    PS3603.O565S84 2016   813'.6

Printed in the United States of America

SUGARLAND

1

Hoxie, Illinois, 1921

AT TWO IN THE MORNING the trains were stopped for the night, and the old wooden depot, manned only during the day now that the Great War had ended, was deserted.

Eve could see her breath in the cold January air as Gavin Johnson helped her up the last step of the empty train car. Then he jumped up himself. He moved closer and she smelled whiskey and something musky he'd splashed on his face. He pressed her against the rail and began to kiss her with lips cold at first but getting warmer. That was all right.

She turned her head and kissed him back, a feeling of steam moving up through her body. The night was so still it was like a creature holding its breath. She pulled away for a moment. "How'd you get a key to the train car?"

Gavin just laughed. "Let me put out the light." He opened his lantern's tiny glass door to blow out the flame, and in the darkness Eve followed him into the empty car.

Her blood was still warm from the corn whiskey she had drunk with the boys after the show, and she felt a little lightheaded. Here she was with a handsome man late at night, alone, her heart beating hard. Before her the rows of worn velvet seats were like people turning their backs. For some reason this excited her more.

"Nice at night, dontcha think?" Gavin asked, taking her hand. With his other hand he touched the soft fold of her dress at the collar. Then he began to unbutton her coat. They were in the Entertainers' car, the special train car they all traveled by and even slept in if there weren't any colored hotels in town. Jimmy Blakeley and His Stoptime Syncopaters, they were called, with Gavin Johnson on tenor sax and Eve Riser on piano. Everyone in the band was young and excited, and Eve felt young and excited just being around them. But sometimes it got lonely going from place to place without resting.

From the window Eve could see the empty depot house. Gavin touched the side of her face and she closed her eyes.

Oh she should know better all right. But she was feeling so good, she had played so well that night, really found her way into the music. Also that afternoon she had started a new song—"Sea Change," she would call it. The first four bars were a gift, just appearing in her mind as she walked back to the hotel from the drug-store, and they still looked good even after she'd written them down. Eve had learned always to travel with a notebook—she had four songs published already under the name E. R. King—and a one-pound bag of sugar. She liked coffee very sweet and some places didn't offer you even a spoonful.

He kissed her neck and her collarbone. Her throat was dry and she opened her eyes. "Hold on," she said, and went down to the other end of the car, to the tin cup hanging by a nail above the faucet.

"Spigot won't work," she said, turning it round. It was so loose it spun in her fingers.

"You don't need any water," Gavin told her.

He came up behind her and replaced the cup on the nail. Her hand was still out like it was holding something invisible, and he took it and pressed his thumb to her palm. Then he folded her in his arms. It was hardly warmer inside the train than out and she pressed against him too now, wanting to feel every inch. Gavin spread his overcoat on the floor and Eve let him guide her down onto the aisle, a hard space meant for feet. After a while his kisses became firmer and deeper like now they had really started, they were really going somewhere now.

She felt his hands behind her neck, fumbling with the buttons of her new dress.

"Gavin," Eve said.

"Shh, angel girl. I got us all covered."

She let him undo the buttons. She'd been on the cir-cuit six months now. Six months of playing different pianos all in need of tuning, of fending for herself, of shooing off managers who said come on back to my office and I'll show you something I know you'll like. Eve was tall and dark-skinned with widely spaced eyes and low, prominent cheekbones. Her great-grandfather on her father's side was a Shawnee Indian—where she got her cheeks from, her father always said.

Some of the boys in the band called Eve beautiful but she didn't know about that. What she cared most about was her music. The horn players liked to start off with notes so strong and high you thought there was nowhere else to go, challenging Eve to follow. She always did. She thought of them as brothers, the teasing variety. But then Gavin came in halfway through their tour, a fine-looking man with deep brown eyes and a complexion her grandmother would call Georgia brown. At first Eve thought he was just another alligator with his little straw boater and his silk tie and his fine boutonniere pin from one of his daddy's social clubs, but it turned out he was there to play second sax. He called her angel girl and brought her coffee in the mornings. She was tired of being lonely. She liked his sloping smile.

Gavin got her last button unbuttoned. The moon shone through a window behind him, his eyes dark liquid drops in dark hollows. He pulled her dress down to her shoulders and kissed her collarbone again.

"Beautiful," he said.

"I should say," said a deep voice behind them.

Eve shot away so fast her head knocked into the leg of one of the train seats, and the sudden throb made her reach back to touch the spot, causing her dress to fall farther. She quickly pulled at it with her other hand.

"Don't stop," the voice said.

Eve looked up. A man was looking down at her. A white man.

"What the—? Why you here?" Gavin said, getting to his feet. Eve moved behind him. "The meeting is set for tomorrow."

Eve tried to stand and found that her legs were shaking. She was confused. Gavin knew this man? Why would he have a meeting with a white man from— where were they now, Hoxie? A little town south of St. Louis, where she was fairly sure Gavin had never been before. She held on to an armrest, crouching in the aisle.

"Saw the light from your lantern," the man said. "Thought plans had changed."

She could hear the leer in his voice. With one hand she reached behind her and tried to button her dress's top button.

"Don't you move," the man said. When Eve looked up she saw he had a gun. She fumbled harder with the dress button.

"I said get your hand down." He pointed the gun at her.

Gavin put up his arms. "Now calm down, calm down, let's talk all this over."

"I don't mean to talk," the man said.

"You and me have some business tomorrow. Let's not upset that."

The man cocked his head. He was younger than he first looked but with an older man's thick build and stomach. Dressed like a farmer with heavy brown boots and the smell of straw about him. Wearing a hat you'd only see in the country.

"Man can have more than one kind of meeting," he said. He was looking at Eve.

Eve stood up behind Gavin, her hands holding her dress up as high as it would go. "Don't you start thinking you have business with me," she said. Her legs were still shaking.

"Hush," Gavin told her.

But the man laughed. "I like a girl with some life."

"Let's go outside," Gavin said to the man. "We can talk about this. We don't want anyone upset. Especially folks in Chicago—you know what I'm saying."

"Why would folks in Chicago be upset?"

"If they don't get what they paid for."

"It's not me they'll be looking for," the man said.

"Oh I think it is," Gavin said. "Say I come to find I can't trust you."

The man looked at him, glanced at Eve, and then looked back at Gavin. "Well, you know. I could call off the deal myself. Our Chicago friends wouldn't like that, either." He waved the gun a little, reminding them all of its presence. There was a slight slur to his speech that Eve hadn't noticed before. "Five minutes outside with the girl," he said. "Then I'll leave."

Gavin pressed Eve farther behind him. "You swear, just five minutes?"

"Gavin!" Eve said.

The man started backing up the aisle still pointing the gun. Gavin took hold of Eve's arm.

"No I will not," Eve said.

Gavin pushed her in front. "Don't worry," he whispered. But his voice sounded scared.

The man tripped a little and then righted himself. "What'd ya say?" That slur again.

"I told her not to worry," Gavin said. "You won't hurt her. Am I right? Watch it now, there's my lantern right there on the step. Here's the girl."

By now the man was out on the little balcony. He held out his arm for Eve and at the same time looked down on the step for the lantern, and Gavin took that moment to pull Eve back, slamming the heavy train door shut. From the other side they heard a kind of roar.

"Is there a bolt?" Gavin asked with his shoulder to the door. His breath came out in a spurt.

The man shouted a curse, then a string of curses.

"Pull up the handle—that locks it," Eve told him. She had once locked herself in by mistake down in Georgia when they had to sleep on the train.

A gunshot sounded.

"Christ!" Gavin said. He pulled himself away from the door and Eve moved quickly to the other side of the train. "Am I shot?" he asked.

"Open that door! Open it!" the man was shouting.

Gavin pulled the last window down a crack. "Go away and come back tomorrow!"

"I ain't leavin' this train car!"

"Oh Lord," Eve said. She looked out the window. "He's coming round the side."

Gavin pulled something out of his coat pocket—a pistol. He wedged it in the window crack.

MARTHA CONWAY

"You had that all along?" Eve couldn't believe it.

"I wasn't going to let you out there with him."

That's not what it sounded like to me, Eve wanted to say, but she kept her mouth shut.

"I have a gun here," Gavin called out to the man. "You go on home!"

Another gunshot sounded and the window next to Gavin broke.

"Christ!" he said again. "The man is drunk."

"I could've told you that," Eve said. She crawled across the aisle to the other side of the train, surprised that as scared as she was she could still be mad. When she looked over Gavin was pointing his gun out the window again. "Gavin, don't!"

"I'm just going to scare him into leaving." He pulled the trigger. The gun made a weak noise as it fired, like a toy. Outside, the man only laughed. But even so a dark feeling came over Eve, like a warning.

Gavin pulled the trigger a few more times. Pop. Pop, pop.

Eve held her breath so she could hear better. The man wasn't shouting or laughing now. That was bad. After a minute she crawled across the aisle and pulled herself up to look out the window. The moon was on this side of the train, which was unfortunate because it meant that she could see clearly the man's fat, unmoving shape on the railroad ties below. His neck at an unnatural angle.

"Lord Jesus," she said.

· *8* ·

Eve had never seen the sea—she was from Pittsburgh—but she understood how something could ebb away while you watched. People got lynched for just being near a dead man, let alone the ones who did the killing. She couldn't stay in this town one more minute, and neither could Gavin.

As she looked down at the man's body sprawled on the ground she put her hand on her coat, near her heart. No question—dead. "Got him clean through the eye," she said. Gavin had come outside with his pants still half-unbuttoned, and he fumbled a little with the top one.

"I just wanted to scare him away," he said again.

Eve let out a breath she could see in the night air. "Well, he went."

She was cold but her palms were wet and her heart was beating right out of her body. Only last month two black men in South Carolina were killed for giving a robber a room for the night, and one of them had his feet roasted in a fire before he was shot. Hoxie was a small town, too, and it was worse in small towns. No, they couldn't stay here even just to finish out the gig.

Gavin turned and kicked up some gravel. "We got to get him away." His breath had a sour, scared smell.

"Get him away?"

"To the woods."

"And how do we do that?"

"Just, I don't know, drag him over. Come on."

They tried, each to an arm, but the man was as heavy as a hundred-year tree. After a few feet they stopped. Gavin took off his hat and mopped his brow. "Let me think." He looked back again at the empty depot house. Eve was thinking, even if we get him to the woods then we have to bury him, and how do we do that?

"Wait a minute. Wait now. I have an idea." Gavin looked around. "Help me pull him to that tree there."

There was a sapling at the end of the siding. "That tiny thing?" Eve asked.

With a grunt Gavin bent over the man. He blew tenor like a long breathless kiss, but he was small and not very muscular. Also, Eve had to admit, a bit of a dandy. Back in Chicago he was known as the Saint because he always dressed like he was going to church, and Eve noticed that even now he was careful with his pants.

She stepped backward over weeds trying to keep her grip on the dead man's arm. Beside her Gavin kept huffing, and twice he nearly fell. Hard to believe he'd been a soldier. He'd told her that he played sax in one of the Pioneer Infantry Bands during the war, and that even though he was shipped overseas he never saw the inside of a trench—Gavin claimed they just played ragtime all day long and drank hot chocolate. Never once shot a bullet, she suspected, until now.

They got the body over to the tree and propped him up against it, like the fellow was just resting a minute. Off in the woods a hoot owl called but nothing answered.

"Got anything black?" Gavin asked Eve. "Like a ribbon or something?"

Eve thought. "Some black lace I used when I hemmed up my dress."

"Give it here."

"No I won't. My dress'll come all undone."

Gavin's voice rose. "I'll get you a new dress! Now come on."

Eve turned up the bottom of her dress and bit the thread end of the lace off, then began pulling at the lace and the loose thread. How long did they have until the sun came up? She had to get back to the hotel, get her things, get gone. The hem of her dress started to fall.

"Here," she said, giving the lace to him.

"That's the one. Now ..." Gavin looked around. "You see any flowers near here?"

"In January?"

"All right then, what. Let's see." Gavin found some tall dark weeds and pulled them up by the neck. "Here." He wound the black lace around the clump like it was a bouquet, tying and then retying the bow.

"What's that supposed to be?" Eve asked.

"Look like the Black Hand Society done it."

"The Black Hand Society! No one believes that old story."

"Sure they do. Anyhow, man's a moonshiner. Sells off his crop to gangsters so they can make whiskey. Everybody knows that." He started buttoning up the man's coat. "They'll say he had it coming."

Eve stiffened. "You involved in that business?"

"Me?" Gavin scoffed, holding up his thin arms. Not really an answer, Eve thought.

"Listen to me now," he went on. "I'm going to give you some money and a letter. You deliver all that to Mr. Rudy Hardy—he's a white man in Chicago. I'll give you a telephone number where you can reach him."

"And where will you go?" Eve asked, trying to think what towns were nearby.

"Back to the hotel. I mean to stay with the band."

Eve was astonished. "But the sheriff'll come! They'll kill you!"

"If I run, they'll know it's me. You're a woman. We'll say you got a telegram late last night from your sister in Chicago. She's singing for Henry James now, ain't that right? We'll say she telegrammed over, calling you back."

"I don't know."

"You got to, Evie! Else I'm really in trouble."

"Lord," Eve said again. Was the sky getting lighter? The dead man sat crazily against the slim tree with his coat buttoned up to his chin. His face with the one eye running blood reminded Eve of a dead owl she'd once seen with its eyes pecked out—it had been sick with something, and the little birds just pecked and pecked its eyes till it died.

Gavin pulled a clean white handkerchief from his pocket, took off his hat, and wiped the inside brim. Then he went through the heavy man's pockets. Even hares leap on dead lions, her grandmother used to say, and here it was played out before her. After a while Gavin counted what he'd fished out, and added a thick fold of bills from his own pocket. He held the whole wad out to her like it was poison. His hand was shaking. Eve folded her arms and took a step back. This was not a good plan.

"Go on, take it. I'll write a letter explaining everything. You can carry that along with the money."

She shook her head.

"You'll be all right," he said.

2

THE TRAIN TO CHICAGO, a regular passenger train, would take most of eight hours. In her suitcase Eve had all her clothes and shoes, her notebook, a half-empty bag of sugar, and a loaf of bread. She also carried a bag with some sausage ends and a jar of pickled hot peppers called birds' eyes that Jimmy Blakeley's aunt had sent over from New Orleans. Jimmy gave her the whole jar, saying, "It's a long ride."

But she was used to long train rides—she'd been riding in the Entertainers' car these last six months, and when she was a child she traveled around Pittsburgh every weekend in open trolley cars playing at Sunday picnics and parties with her father. Eve was born Eve Louise Riser into a family of musicians. Her mother had studied music at Fisk University and her father led a brass band well-known in Pittsburgh—two trombones, three trumpets, two drummers, a clarinet, and a peck horn.

Everyone in her family could play at least three different instruments. Her brother Kid made his own drum fashioned out of a wooden fruit crate, two hubcaps, and a tin pie pan. When he was fifteen he entered a contest for a music scholarship playing the violin, and when it was over the judge told him he would have won for sure if he hadn't been colored. That tore him up so much that he broke his violin into pieces and never played again. Now he was a barber in McKeesport.

Eve could remember her father dancing in the dusty road outside her house in the summer with some other men when their day jobs were done. When they played for processions they wore solemn, hook-eye black suits with stand-up white collars like a marching band of priests. After Eve's mother died—Eve was six—her father married a woman who drank too much and took in laundry. In that order. Eve's new stepmother had one sweet, light-skinned girl named Eulalie, whom everyone called Chickie. Chickie's father was white and that was all anyone knew about him.

Eve loved Chickie as soon as she saw her, although up until that very minute she had decided to hate her. A sweet-tempered girl, that was Chickie, who might seem a little slow until she came out with a sudden, shrewd remark that made you wonder if all that slowness was an act. She was only ten months younger than Eve and they always shared a bed, staying up late to talk about their plans for getting away. They wanted to perform. They wanted to be famous. Chickie had a beautiful voice, and Eve could play banjo, trumpet, and baritone horn. But what she was best at, what she loved, was the piano.

When Eve got to the station it was not yet six in the morning. Everyone was in a turmoil about the dead man found near the tracks.

"Right by that tree," she heard a man on the platform say. "A bouquet of flowers in his lap. That's got to be a message."

She tried to keep her expression neutral, but she felt stiff and afraid. On the far end of the platform a boy was selling dried fruit and candy. She asked him would he sell her one of his empty baskets, and he said that he would.

It was bright out but cold, and the wind was starting to come up. Eve put her food in the basket and covered it with a large clean handkerchief. She put the letter and the wad of money that Gavin had given her into the basket too, and then on second thought took it out again and put it back in her handbag. The money was folded up into her old black coin purse, the sateen smoothed almost to threads. The purse bulged significantly.

As she picked up her suitcase and started to climb up into a car, an attendant rushed her back out.

"Colored car's up behind the locomotive," he said.

It was an old wooden car with a coal stove for heat. Eve found a place up in front near the stove. A couple of white men were smoking in the rear, since it was also the smoking car.

Mr. Rudy Hardy in Chicago, Eve reminded herself. She took the coin purse out of her handbag and put it in the bottom of the basket while she kept an eye on the platform. After about a hundred years or so the train whistle blew, and a porter clanged their car door shut. The train started up with a groan like it was waking irritably from the dead, and began moving down the track.

Eve took out the coin purse and held it in her hands. She hadn't counted the money, and now she wondered just how much there was. As the train swayed and picked up speed she tried to make her heart stop beating so hard just by telling it to. The guards on the platform talking about the dead man also talked about the Black Hand Society—maybe Gavin's trick had worked. No one was looking for her. Still, she wanted to be as far away as she could be.

She put the coin purse back in her handbag and took out the bread and sausage ends from the basket. She wanted to count the money but that would be crazy. One of the smokers was sitting in the row behind her across the aisle, reading a newspaper. He lit up again, not bothering this time to go to the back of the car.

It was noisiest here behind the engine and cinders flew up against the windows, which meant you couldn't open them to get some air. Eve finished up the sausage and half the loaf, and then tidied the basket. For a while she read someone's discarded paper—two players from the Black Sox trial last summer were trying to get reinstated in baseball, and the price of bread had fallen a little at last. Maybe these hard times after the war were finally at an end. Now that would be good. But after a while something came over her—a feeling like she was being watched. She made herself turn another page of the paper. At last over the engine noise she heard movement behind her. She turned around to watch the smoker as he left the car, a cigarette still burning in his hand. Just before he left, he threw the butt on the floor and stepped on it.

Her fingers relaxed a little. Well, in Chicago she would be with Chickie again, that was one good thing. Maybe Chickie could even get her a job. Chickie was singing with the Henry James Band at the Oaks, a good band at a good club. Everyone came to hear her. She had a voice that caught people's attention, like something wild that had just been caged. Chickie was beautiful too, tall and regal, her almond-shaped eyes half in dreamland.

Hard to believe now that the two of them had left home with only twelve dollars between them just six years ago, when Eve was fifteen years old. Her father had died, and Chickie's mother took a strap to them one time too many. For a while they stayed with their Aunt Mamie trying to finish up high school, but one night Eve's cousin invited them both to the Leader House, where there was dancing upstairs. When they walked in a hunchback called Toadie was playing "Squeeze Me" on the piano and singing, and Eve got so excited by what she heard that she went back the next afternoon and asked Toadie to teach her what he did.

Toadie wouldn't take any money so instead she brought him sandwiches or her aunt's fried chicken or a schooner of beer. He taught her how to hit her notes and control them without using pedals. He changed her hand position so her fingers would stay flat on the keys to get a clean tone. Toadie was obsessed by rhythm. "Remember the rhythm, remember the rhythm," he told her over and over. "Make each note count."

Later she played at the Leader House herself, or with Toadie at little after-hours places when the Leader House closed. She learned by heart the piano rolls of players he liked—Jelly Roll Morton, especially—and she also played along with records, slowing the phonograph down sometimes, which put the song in a different key so she could try it that way. All this was her education. Her mother had wanted her to go to college, like her, but Eve just wanted to play the piano. She never thought about writing her own songs until the first one came to her almost without her noticing. It was Christmastime, and she was helping a cook at a rich white woman's house for extra money. Eve was moving pots around on the enormous double stove and at the same time trying to cut up a chicken, and she was thinking about her mother's kitchen when her mother was still alive, and at some point she realized she was hearing music in her head. When she got back to her room she wrote it down and then sold it to a publisher in Chicago for twenty dollars plus royalties. Her very first published song. It was about wishing for a place of your own.

She looked out the window. Well now, here she was living her dream, playing the piano professionally and writing songs, but wasn't it just one hard turn after another. Watching her money, watching Chickie, always afraid she was going to end up broke and back in Pittsburgh. The train shook her back and forth moving steadily toward Chicago, the flat dry land outside stretching on without end. They passed an old abandoned house with a long front porch and broken-out windows, the kind of house she had seen many times from different train windows. She rested her head back on the seat cushion and closed her eyes. Dozed a little.

When they crossed the line into Illinois she woke up. An attendant came by to tell the colored passengers they could use the dining car now, his voice like a low train whistle. Maybe it was because they were in Illinois now or maybe she was just foolish and still half-asleep, but when the attendant left, Eve decided to count the money, keeping it low in her lap. As she passed two hundred her throat went dry, but she didn't stop until she got to the end. Three hundred and seventy-five dollars, mostly in fifty-dollar bills.

Her fingers shook. She had never held so much money together at once. Something made her turn her head. And wouldn't you know it, there was that smoker back in the same old seat. How long had he been there? His eyes stared fixedly at the newspaper but he had a look about him like he hadn't been reading.

After a minute Eve made herself move her hands, cursing her foolishness. She put the coin purse back in her handbag like there was nothing in it but pennies. Then she got up and started toward the bathroom with the basket and her handbag, hitting a seat or two as she passed. She didn't look at the smoker when she went by, though her heart was beating fast. She wished she was in some little house right now where she could watch the trains pass and wonder where they were going, then close up the front door and be by herself. She knocked on the bathroom door, waited a moment, and went in.

The space was tinier than a closet and smelled like rust and sweat. There was no washbasin, water, soap, or towels. Eve bolted the door and took the money out of her coin purse. She wrapped the bills in a little rag she carried with her to polish her shoes, and hid the rag in the bottom of the basket. Then she covered the basket with her handkerchief. After a moment she took the money out again and put it back in the coin purse and put the coin purse down the front of her dress, where it bulged. She took the money out of the coin purse and wrapped it again in the rag and put the rag down the front of her dress, where it still bulged.

What mattered, Toadie always told her, was to keep the thing going. He taught her the music of joy, of indignation, of anger, but not—Eve thought now—the music of fear. Her heart was still pounding and the smell of the close room made it worse. Maybe fear and music don't mix, she thought.

She took the money out of the rag and put it back in the coin purse.

After ten minutes someone knocked at the door, and the train lurched heavily to the right. "One moment please," Eve called out as she reached up to straighten her hat.

When she walked back she still didn't have her train legs. The smoker was in his seat smoking, and this time he looked up as she passed. He had gray eyes like the smoke he was blowing, and a beard that needed some treatment. But it was his nose you mostly noticed— starting out thin at the bridge then widening into a firm flower bulb over a raggedy moustache. He seemed like a chained watchdog, patiently waiting for someone to make one wrong move.

She got back to her seat and busied herself organizing her things. They were well into the north now and it was colder. Outside a gray snow was lightly falling— or was that fog mixed with engine cinders? The conductor came into the car and announced that there'd be a slight delay in Cranston.

Eve looked out the window. The countryside was behind them. A block of empty brick factories with shattered windows went by, and after that the newer factories began. It was cold in the car but her face felt hot and flushed. Only two more stops, then the stop just outside Chicago, then Chicago.

Chicago and Chickie.

The conductor picked up a crate of candy from up front to sell back in the white cars, and as he passed Eve asked him how long they'd be at Cranston—she wanted to visit the ladies' room, she said, if they had soap. He told her maybe ten minutes, just long enough to uncouple two cars.

She said, "I'll hear the whistle? 'Cause my husband is meeting me in Evanston."

The conductor assured her they blew it three times.

At Cranston she got out with her basket and her handbag and her suitcase so no one would steal it while she was gone. For a few minutes she just stood on the platform to watch them uncouple the back cars and to breathe in the clear, cold air. The smoker stayed on the train. But what sun there was glittered on the window-panes, so she couldn't see inside.

When the trainmen were almost done she looked around and saw two signs: "For Ladies" and "For Colored People." The bathroom door had no lock. Eve was in there not two minutes when she heard the first whistle. Then the door suddenly opened.

It was the smoker.

He grinned at her meanly, little ragged teeth in a raggedy-beard face. His clothes were good but not clean, and his body blocked the door.

"I seen you with that purse," he said.

Her heart was hitting her from the inside, and even though this was what she expected, she knew that her sudden fear showed.

"Give it here," he told her.

"I don't get to Evanston with that purse, my husband'll slit my throat. Then he'll come after you."

"That don't half scare me," he said, and he put out his hand.

The second whistle blew. After a moment, her fingers shaking, Eve offered him her handbag. She noticed he had his suitcase beside him. So he wasn't going back on the train.

"No," he said. "Your food basket."

Her heart was still racing. "What, you hungry? I ate everything up already except for the pickles."

"Give it to me."

He took the basket from her and threw off the handkerchief. Dug down and came up with the coin purse. Inside was the fold of money, a fifty-dollar bill on top.

He grinned looking down at it. "That's some good food." The third whistle blew. "And this I believe is my stop." He closed the coin purse, stuffed it inside his dirty pants, then gave her back the basket. The train started its come-up-from-the-dead groaning and he moved aside. "Now you best get back on that train before I come after them pickles."

Eve stepped out onto the platform and looked quickly around. The porters all seemed to be deliberately staring somewhere else.

"Not a one to help you," the man said with obvious satisfaction.

She looked back at him, trying to think how she could say what she thought of him while still making the train. The wheels were starting to move now. She hung her basket over her arm and picked up her suitcase and ran for the train car.

Back behind her she heard him laughing. "Nice doing business."

When she got inside she looked out the window and saw him still laughing. She went to the end of the train and watched his figure start toward town. Only when the train turned and picked up speed did she return to her seat.

Eve looked around. No more smokers. Carefully she pulled out her hatpins and placed her hat on her lap, checking with her fingers to make sure that the wad of Gavin's money—less fifty dollars—was still pinned to the inside band.

3

Chicago, Illinois

NATHAN COBB, MANAGER AND half owner of the Oaks Club in Chicago, was a large man with thick brown hair and almond eyes, tall enough to not be called fat, with a slow important way of speaking. When the telephone rang he was sitting in a wide office chair in what used to be the club's box office, calculating his musicians' drink expenses from the previous night and then adjusting their pay.

He always gave an exact account to Henry James, the club bandleader, a fellow who played the trumpet and had a few curious sounds: a white baby's cry, a horse's laugh, and a fly bumping up against the window of a train. Cobb once played trumpet himself, so he knew how difficult that was. But you could really hear that fly when Henry James played it on his horn, and also the train behind it. How Henry managed that he did not know.

"Nathan Cobb here," he answered on the eighth ring.

He prided himself on his white desk telephone and a signed picture of the mayor, Big Bill Thompson, hanging on the wall behind him. Beside it hung an unsigned photograph of President Harding, a handsome man who, it was said, found himself in office only because women could now vote and they voted for a pretty face. Two men—lanky ill-fed fellows who were passable musicians but made most of their money doing errands for Cobb—sat on wooden chairs tilted back against the wall.

"A comet was what hit the earth," the fellow with the banjo was saying. "That's what started the Great Fire. Not no cow."

Their names were Travis and Moaner. Moaner, the banjo player, tuned his instrument to play like a ukulele. Wouldn't surprise Cobb if Moaner had made the gizmo himself—the ragged gray strings looked like they might have once been used to tie cloth flowers to a ladies' hat.

"See, the comet hits Chicago first," Moaner said, demonstrating with the palm of one hand and the fist of the other. He had a whole lot of theories about a whole lot of things, but this one was his current favorite. "It starts the fire, then bounces over to the town of Peshtigo and starts up that fire there."

Cobb covered the mouthpiece. "Hush up." Then he said, "How's that, Mr. Hardy?" His face grew tight. "Tonight, of course, I'll be here," he said in his slow, important way. He listened. "Better make that ten thirty. I like to see the start of the show. By the way, have you given any more thought to my offer?"

Pause. Cobb replaced the receiver. "Damn kraut."

"What's up?" Travis asked.

"He's raising his prices."

"Again?"

"Why not? Practically got the monopoly."

Moaner said, "What's a monopoly?"

Moaner was born on a hog farm in Missouri, one of fourteen children. His father let them all go to school for four months every year, and the rest of the time he hired them out to a grain farmer for the money. Moaner was smarter than he looked, but not by much.

"I wonder where he gets the corn," Cobb said. "Probably has a partner somewhere, some farmer. Or a couple of farmers, even."

"Maybe we could go to some corn farms and mention his name around," Moaner suggested. "Find a farmer who knows him."

"You know how many farmers in a three-hour circuit from here raise corn?" Cobb asked him. It irked him to see the trucks lined up at the railroad siding every other Monday night alongside his own, all those club owners paying to get corn sugar from Rudy Hardy. Club owners like him who needed the sugar to make their own hooch. All it took was fifty pounds of the sugar and some water and a good copper still. One hundred proof, one-ten, you could make it as strong as you wanted. But the corn sugar was key. Even just a small cut of

Hardy's operation would be a good one, Cobb imagined. One thing he hated was to be just like everyone else.

The other man, Travis, tilted his chair forward and then back again. "Rudy Hardy," he scoffed. "Should I let the Walnut know that he's coming?"

Cobb said, "Indeed," without looking up.

"Where do you think he's at?"

"This time of day? Maybe Saul's." Cobb started to write a note. Travis watched him.

After a moment Travis said, "A stupid young pup, that Hardy."

Cobb kept writing. "Mmh."

"Like to get himself whipped one day."

Cobb lifted his pen, looked over what he had written, and blew on the ink.

"Now, that might just scare him into taking up your offer," Travis said, watching him meaningfully. "Say something happened."

At that Cobb looked over.

"Some little accident," Travis went on, giving him a nod. They stared at each other a moment as if both were considering the same plan. Then Cobb looked out the window. On the street two sad-looking, sway-backed horses stood tethered to a hitching post. A college boy in a raccoon coat and a derby blew his horn at them as he turned the corner in his motorcar, causing the horses to shy up in distress. Soon there'd be more motorcars than horses, if it wasn't that way already. Cobb knew he had to change with them.

"*Fort mit schaden*," Travis said. Good riddance. During the war, Travis had landed in a German prisoner camp after his very first battle, and he left the war with an outsized hatred of officers and a smattering of German phrases. Rudy Hardy was German, or half German at least. Enough for Travis to hate him.

But just as he spoke, someone rapped on the door in perfect rhythm with the phrase, *fort mit schaden*: tap tap, tap tap.

A tall colored woman stood in the hallway.

"Mr. Cobb? My name is Eve Riser. I'm Eulalie Riser's stepsister."

"Chickie's sister?" He looked at her sharply.

"Her stepsister, sir."

"I didn't know she had a sister," Cobb said.

"I just got back in town today. I was on the circuit these last six months."

Came out that she was hoping for a job playing piano, a position that, curiously enough, he was just at the moment looking to fill. The little boy playing now was fifteen years old but looked about eight. Small reach, too. Only thing going for him was that he could play certain songs with his elbows, made the audience howl.

Girls on the stage could be trouble but they could also be a draw. There was that one playing at the Dreamland now everyone wanted to see, Lil Hardin. He listened as Chickie's sister listed the places she'd played, the bandleaders she'd played for. Some impressive names.

Miss Eve Riser. Certainly fine to look at, Cobb thought. Striking. He couldn't see a bit of Chickie in her, though Chickie was beautiful, too. They were stepsisters, she said, so not actually related? Eve was much darker than Chickie, with prominent cheekbones. But there seemed to be something wrong with her hat—it looked curiously pushed out on one side. He peered at it more closely.

"You have something in that hat?" he interrupted.

Eve blushed. She said, "My train ticket and a few dollars for dinner. I bought a return ticket but I don't want to return."

"What's wrong with your purse?"

"Got my purse stolen out from under my arm the last time I was in Chicago," she said. She was looking very bold.

Moaner was watching now, his sorry banjo loose on his lap. Travis coughed. He had opened his coat a little so he could show off the gun in his waistband—the kind of fellow who liked to scare women and little unarmed boys. Cobb looked at his watch. Well, what did he care what she carried around on her head.

"Happens I do have a place," he said. "Come here and let me look at you."

He examined her as if the Emancipation Proclamation had never been thought of, and watched her press her lips together in annoyance. On impulse he put out his pinkie and stroked her cheek, then looked down at his finger.

"My mother always told me there were two kinds of women: women who paint themselves, and decent women."

Outside in the hall, someone walked by whistling "The Long, Long Trail."

Cobb held out his rouged finger. "I don't employ whores."

Travis laughed a mean laugh. Eve said, "Only stage makeup, sir."

"Well wait till you're out on a stage then to wear it."

She said, "Yes, sir," in a voice that seemed designed to sound meek.

"Fifteen dollars a week plus dinners," he told her. "I'm told that's fair." It was a good three or four dollars less than the clubs downtown. "I'll be watching you tonight. I don't like what I hear, I'll go back to what I had before."

He turned his back dismissively. Travis closed his coat around the gun as if he too had finished his business with her.

Eve said, "Thank you, sir. I'll just go and see Henry James then."

But Cobb was looking out the window again like his mind was already working on something else.

Eve heard herself say thank you sir in her best white voice and closed the door carefully behind her even though she wanted to slam it on his big fat self. Everywhere she went it was just the same thing. A white man running things and her saying yes sir. The world so wrong it didn't make sense.

She put her hands up to her hat and tried adjusting it without taking it off. What would she have done if

Cobb had asked to see what was in it? Giving up, Eve pulled out her hatpins and took the hat off. Yes, there was an odd lump all right.

Although she'd reached Rudy Hardy at the telephone number Gavin had given her, he wouldn't agree to meet Eve before midnight. You'd think he'd be a little more eager, Eve thought. What was she going to do with the money until then? She had already found a rooming house near a block of clubs, but she couldn't trust leaving the money there. The house was old, still using gaslights, but clean. There was enough room for both her and Chickie, and she thought Chickie would like the tall ceilings. A Mrs. Jenkins ran it. Eve left her suitcase as a deposit.

But she couldn't trust the rooming house just like she couldn't trust her purse. And what would she do when she was up on stage? Couldn't trust the dressing room, that was for sure. A million people going in and out whether you were dressed in a slip or nothing at all, hungry people who weren't thieves as much as opportunists. Well, she knew how that was. There were times playing vaudeville when all she could afford was an onion sandwich for dinner.

She re-pinned the money inside the hat and smoothed the material with her fingers, thinking that if Cobb had seen all this money he'd have taken it. But at least then she'd be done with it, she thought sourly. She wanted to hand over the money and leave the rest alone. Go back to her room, take a hot bath, and wash the smell of train off of her. She needed clean white gloves and something pressed that she could wear for tonight.

The heat came on through the registers. Eve could hear people fooling around on stage, talking and tuning their instruments. A banjo plucked out an old New Orleans tune she knew—

I thought I heard Buddy Bolden say
Funky butt, funky butt, take it away

Eve smiled. Then, more faintly, she heard a woman singing scales.

Chickie.

Quickly Eve walked through the swinging door onto the club floor. A light went off above the stage and then flickered back on again. All the men were wearing white shirts and regular suit pants without jackets. Henry James, the bandleader, a tall lanky man she remembered from the last time she was in Chicago, stood with his back to the empty tables looking over some arrangements. And there was Chickie, looking beautiful in a beaded headdress and a silver cape with slits for her arms. It was the start of their afternoon rehearsal. In an hour or so they'd break for dinner, and then be back for the eight o'clock curtain.

Eve noticed two things at once. They had a little tiny boy playing piano—some nephew of someone or other, or maybe someone's son. No wonder Cobb wanted her to start right away.

And Chickie was pregnant.

4

RUDY HARDY'S SISTER, LENA—tall, twenty years old, but still with the round face of a young girl—walked into the Oaks Club that evening dressed in Rudy's old Army uniform, on a bet. "You see, with her hair up?" Rudy had said back at his apartment, balancing the uniform cap on her head. "Just like a boy." This to his friend Pin, who had arrived at the apartment with a girl, a stranger, something Lena had not expected.

Lena had blushed at Rudy's words. It was true, her features were round and boyish: her broad face, her wide mouth, her downturned nose. Not the sharp coquettish features currently in vogue. People thought she was a farm girl raised on pork and milk, although she was not—she had grown up right there in Chicago. Before they left the apartment, Lena stared at herself in

Rudy's long mirror and thought, I really do look like a soldier. Once she heard you could tell someone's sex by the length of their neck, but Lena didn't see anything particularly long or short about her neck. People tended to call her handsome rather than pretty. Healthy, they said. She tried smiling without opening her lips.

"It's amazing that his uniform fits you as well as it does," Pin's friend—a rich girl called Marjorie—commented. She was a pretty girl with brown hooded eyes and bobbed hair, her skin paler than a baby's. "Lucky you're so tall."

Tall and broad like her German mother, yet willing to bet on nonsense like her Irish father. "I'll stake five dollars you won't wear my uniform to the club tonight," Rudy had said to Lena. "Funny you should say that," she told him, "because I could use five dollars."

But now that they were actually inside the club she felt nervous, wondering how to walk like a man and what to do with her hands. The Oaks was a black-and-tan club on the South Side of Chicago with a mixed audience—white and colored—and colored musicians. The room was wide rather than long, and dozens of round wooden tables filled the space all the way up to the dance floor. It had once been a neighborhood dancing hall and still had old posters from the Juvenile Protective League on its walls. But about six months ago white patrons discovered it, and now they stood around the room in their dark suits or in new, short dresses alongside colored patrons wearing the same, the girls looking into compact mirrors no bigger than aspirin tins and the men holding soft hats.

Rudy turned to her, his cheeks flushed. "Ready to go home yet?" he joked, taking off his hat and smoothing it with the palm of his hand. Rudy was boyish and energetic with snapping brown eyes and thick dark hair that he had recently started to grease back.

"I believe I earned my five dollars," she said.

They threaded their way toward a front table, Lena limping a little like she always did when the weather was changing.

Marjorie took her arm and whispered, "People will think you were wounded in the war."

Gray fans rotated slowly from the low ceiling, and the air smelled of peanuts and sweat and stale hops. After they sat down, Lena tried crossing her legs, pinching up the trouser material as she'd seen Rudy do. That felt strange too. A man came around with glasses of something and put a few down on each table. He waited while people pulled out their coin purses, and then gave out some change and moved on to the next group. Two colored girls sat down at the next table. The girls wore long coats with matching magenta hats—they were twins, Lena realized. For a moment their eyes met. Lena was not sure if she should say good evening to them or not. What did men usually do? She touched her cap. One twin looked embarrassed—so that was not the right thing? Lena looked away.

Well, she had never been to a club before, on the South Side or anywhere else. She was a nurse and lived with six other girls in a rooming house near the hospital, reading, sewing, washing out stockings—these were her usual activities at night. The uniform felt large and heavy and transparently wrong. She wasn't quite sure why Rudy had asked her to go with him tonight. Maybe just to make a round fourth?

"We still have to think of a name for her," Pin said. His blue eyes narrowed and he smiled a little. He had thin lips and a narrow face and a long thin frame— hence his nickname. Lena had known him for years, ever since the war.

"How about Archibald?" she teased. That was Pin's real name.

A curious sensation, trousers. They made her more aware of her two legs, and the place where they met. She glanced again at Pin, but now he was looking at Marjorie.

Marjorie lifted her glass. "To Archie," she said. Her eyes were shining. She was enjoying this.

Pin and Rudy emptied their drinks in one swallow. Lena took a small sip of hers—a heavy, viscous liquid, not good, but not as bad as she expected. Pin said, "You'll have to do better than that, soldier," so she took a breath and drank the whole shot. Her throat burned.

"How can they serve liquor so openly?" she asked Rudy.

"They have their own stills in the cellar."

"What if the police find out?"

"Oh, I think the police know." A little smile. These days he seemed to know everything.

He was the only one left to her: both their mother and father were dead. Lena had nursed her mother in her last illness; this was less than a year ago now, not much more than six months. She adjusted Rudy's uniform cap, which was pinned to hide her long hair. She thought wearing men's clothes would make her feel free, but instead she was just wondering at every turn what she should do with her hands, her feet. "Don't touch your face so much," Rudy had said when they were out on the sidewalk.

A young colored girl brought out some folding chairs and pushed them up to the tables, crowding two or three more places around them. A Saturday night crowd, everyone drinking openly as though it were their legal right. Lena had never before been in a place where they served liquor. She adjusted her trousers again, trying to get more comfortable. At last the bandleader came out, a tall, handsome colored man looking out over the audience with slightly droopy eyes

Rudy's eyes were shining and he was jiggling his foot under the table. He leaned over. "The man with the magic. Henry *James*." As if she should recognize the name. She didn't.

There was a scuffling as all the musicians went to their chairs on the stage and sat down. A few took a moment to sip from beer bottles by their feet.

"All right now, brothers," Henry James said loudly when they were all settled. He raised his arm, held it up a moment, and then lowered it fast like an ax.

The music came roaring out, and the whole room suddenly filled with sound. There was no introduction, no easing into it. People jumped up from their seats. Lena sucked in her breath, astonished. She had never heard music so fast and so determined. At first she wasn't even sure if she liked it. The banjo stopped, the drum stopped, but the brass went on and on as if fighting for breath.

She found herself standing with everyone else. She forgot she was dressed as a man. She forgot about her work at the hospital, her worries about her brother—everything. The stage divided itself into two camps, each goading the other. I can do it, bragged the horns joyfully. No you can't do it, sang the reeds playfully. At last the banjo came back and the brass took a break. Some people were dancing and some people shouted out to the music. Lena wanted to shout too, or do something else back to it. It was like she had never before been able to hear and suddenly now she could—she didn't know how to describe it.

When the piece ended, all the men and women clapped as hard as they could and so did she. She sat down smiling around at the people at other tables. They were all smiling at her too, and at everyone else, colored and white alike. The twins at the next table looked over at her and nodded, and Rudy was still clapping hard enough to hurt. Even Marjorie looked less languid than usual.

"What do you call this music?" Lena asked Rudy.

Almost immediately the band started up again. Rudy stood up and hollered, and then he sat down and said something. The pupils of his eyes, she noticed, were dilated with excitement.

Lena turned her head slightly. "What?"

He cupped his mouth. "Jazz!" he shouted.

"I gained some weight is all," Chickie told Eve.

Eve said, "Let me see you outside of that cape."

"You leave me alone now!"

"Anyone know?"

Chickie sat erectly in her dressing-room chair. They were alone. It was just before curtain, almost eight o'clock. Eve hadn't seen a bed in two days.

"They all fools," Chickie said.

Eve shook her head slowly. "No, Lovie, you did a good job with your costumes."

But what she was thinking was that the band members had almost certainly noticed—Chickie was normally so willowy—but they were protecting her. Everyone loved Chickie. If Mr. Cobb knew, however, she'd be out, so he must not know.

Chickie smiled a little—her faraway smile. "It's a nice cape, isn't it?"

"Very nice. Pretty work here." Eve fingered it.

"The braid I just put on at the last minute."

"Reminds me a little of Daddy's band—remember that gold braid they tried on their hats?"

Chickie laughed. "Should have just thrown those hats away."

"I like it in silver, though," Eve said. The room was small and warm with cracked yellow walls but a good mirror. Eve stared at one of the cracks, which ran all the way up to the ceiling. She could hear someone going up the little wooden staircase down the hall. Any minute the boy would come fetch her. Henry told Eve he wanted to introduce her special, two songs in. Strategic. Didn't give the folks time to gawk at a woman musician. Chickie would come on to sing halfway through the first set, and then she'd sing all of the second.

Eve turned and looked into the mirror at Chickie. "All right now. What are we going to do?"

"What are we going to do," Chickie repeated. It wasn't a question, it was her way of keeping up the discussion. "We're gonna have this baby."

"And when is that?"

"Little over a month."

"And then what?"

"And then what. We find a nice orphanage."

"You want to give this baby away?"

"Oh, Evie," Chickie said. Her face crumpled and then tightened again. She said, "You see something I don't?"

Eve thought, if Chickie keeps the baby, she'll be out of the band. They could set up house together and maybe Chickie could get a day job somewhere—but not at a store or anywhere nice like that since now she's a woman with a baby and no husband. And who would watch the baby while both of them worked? The baby would grow up on the streets like her brother Kid did after her mother died. Kid turned out all right, but he'd had Eve and Chickie watching out for him.

Eve sighed. Somewhere along the line, Chickie for sure would be back in Pittsburgh with her baby—the end of her dreams. Eve, too.

"I suppose the father cut out," Eve said.

Chickie shut her mouth tight.

"All right, don't tell me." Eve frowned. "You have any money saved?"

"A few dollars."

The stage boy knocked on their door. "Five minutes, Miss Eve."

"All right," Eve said, and she checked her dress one last time. Her brassiere felt lumpy, but that was because of the two wads of money she'd pinned to the inside. In the mirror it didn't seem noticeable. She hoped the mirror was right.

Let me just get through this night, she prayed.

Chickie smiled her faraway smile and hugged Eve a little sideways, because of her stomach. Hugged her tight.

"I wanted you to come, Evie," she said. "I wished you here. Did you know that?"

"Then you cost a bootlegger his life and a white man fifty dollars," Eve told her, hugging her back.

After the second number, Lena was astonished to see a woman walk onto the stage. She wore a long white dress with creamy white sequins dipping at the neckline like the curve of a shell, and for a moment she just stood still facing the audience. Then she made a small bow and sat down on the piano stool.

"Let me please introduce to you all Miss Eve Riser on the piano, just back from her tour of the South!"

Henry James announced, smiling. He made the woman stand again and he held up her hand in his. The sequins on her dress caught the gaslight like something winking.

Henry James held his trumpet upside down and something dripped out of the horn—saliva? He said, "We had a little bitty child in here playing last night— let's see if she can do better than he did!"

The woman allowed herself to laugh at that and then sat back down.

Miss Eve Riser. Lena had sometimes seen women in vaudeville acts, singers or dancers, their cheeks a large red circle of stage paint like they wanted to look silly. This woman looked like she was the honored guest at a gala event. Watching Henry James calmly, her back as straight as a nun's.

He raised his hand and pointed to her. Immediately she bent over the piano and began pounding out the rhythm, both arms moving furiously, one-two-three-four, one-two-three-four, chords like a drumbeat. Henry pointed to the drums, and then to the banjo, and finally to the brass, who picked out a melody and ran away arguing.

The piece was fast, but not as fast as the one before. The musicians had scores in front of them but mostly they just watched each other. They wore loose white shirts, suspenders, and caps—Lena could picture how they must have looked in their school marching bands with little white epaulets and scratchy collars. Already they were dripping with sweat.

A few couples skimmed out to the dance floor, holding hands, and a boy came up to the table with a note for Rudy. He unfolded it, read it, and looked around. Later, Lena wished she had looked, too—was Rudy searching for someone?—but she was staring at the piano player, wishing she could see her fingers. Lena played piano herself. Once did, she corrected herself.

Rudy stood. "I'll be back in a moment."

On the piano the woman was threading her way up and down the keys, arguing with the saxophone and packing more notes into one bar than Lena thought possible.

"Pick it up!" the bandleader, Henry James, shouted to the band.

The music became furious. Lena leaned forward. The sax asked a question, the piano answered, but apparently not to the sax's liking because it asked the same question again. The two battled it out. A heavyset couple danced along the edge of the room—the woman smiling, the man like it was the most serious thing in the world.

Henry James turned to the audience. "Are you gonna take it?" he shouted. On the piano Eve Riser was smiling. People all over the room shouted back.

"Oh yeah," he yelled, "you gonna take it and you gonna ask for some more!"

The audience was caught and everyone knew it. People hollered again, this time louder. The music was a force gathering up all the air in the room, and Lena felt as thought she'd been gathered up with it. Her clothing, her uniform, everything was gone except for her ears and her heart. On the dance floor, colored couples danced side by side with white ones. It took no leap of imagination to see them suddenly mix, a colored man dancing with a white woman or a white man with a dark-skinned girl. Her heart surged with excitement. Henry James blew a steady loud sweet note over the crowd. Anything was possible, the note said.

Then all at once the musicians stopped all together on a heartbeat. As they lowered their instruments sweating and grinning, Henry James turned around to gesture triumphantly, holding his trumpet up. Above the noise of the crowd he made a joke that Lena didn't understand.

Everyone laughed. Up on the stage Eve Riser took a moment to smooth her dress. Lena shook a cigarette from Rudy's pack, offered one to Marjorie, then felt her pocket for a match. Her hand was still shaking from the excitement. She looked around for Rudy but he wasn't on the club floor. The note he'd been given lay next to his napkin on the table. His glass was empty. Lena picked up the note. It said, *Midnight. N.C.*

"Thanks," Marjorie said to Lena, blowing out smoke.

Pin said, "Excuse me," and he went off, too. Women walked across the dance floor showing off their short dresses. Marjorie smoothed the fabric of her own short dress and then crossed her legs.

"How did you get your limp?" she asked Lena.

Lena had forgotten about her limp.

"An accident. When I was fourteen."

"What happened?"

Lena looked around up on the stage, but Henry James was giving instructions to the horn section and seemed in no hurry to start the next set.

"I used to go to my aunt's house on Fridays for a music lesson on the day the street cleaner sprinkled the streets. Mr. Davos. He used to give me a ride. One day, I don't know why, I jumped off a little early and Mr. Davos didn't know—he didn't see me. He turned the truck and part of the water tank rolled over my foot. But I don't always limp, just sometimes. Like when it's going to snow."

Marjorie tapped off her cigarette ash and looked toward the door. "I knew I should have worn my other coat," she said. She looked at Lena and smiled. After a moment, Lena smiled back. She was used to getting comments tinged with pity, which she hated.

"So how does it feel now?" Marjorie asked.

"A little ache."

"I meant the uniform."

"Oh." Lena touched the front of her jacket. "All right. At first the cut felt, I don't know. Stiff."

"I know a girl who bought some harem trousers. They're wearing them in Paris."

"Really?"

"Well, not everyone. But my friend Sylvie, she won't wear them outside. I would wear them outside. Have you ever wanted to be a man?"

"I never thought about it."

"Go about wherever you want on your own. Drive. Travel if you wanted."

She was thinking of a man with money.

"I don't know," Lena said.

"It's good that you have that deep voice," Marjorie told her.

On the stage Henry James raised both hands. "Now we're gonna play an old church tune I know y'all know," he said, "so come on and sing along. Miss Chickie Riser is going to lead us."

The singer came onto the stage, a tall woman wearing a cape with silver braid. The band took a minute while people settled a bit, and then began a slow tune. After the first few notes, some of the women began smiling but Lena didn't recognize it. Pin came back and touched Marjorie on the silky back of her dress. The names of the musicians were posted on a long piece of cardboard near the stage, and after a moment Lena pushed her chair back and walked over to look at it. She wanted to know the name of the woman playing piano.

Baby Diggs on Drums. Teddy Bailey on Saxophone. Miss Eve Riser on Piano—that was penciled in at the bottom. Up on stage the musicians were improvising now, and a group of high school students, white boys, sat at a front table watching them with soft open mouths like baby birds. Some of them had instruments in their laps, and Lena watched one boy try out a sequence of keys on his clarinet without blowing into it. The singer, striking with her long white gloves and her dark hair, swayed as she went from note to note.

Lena moved a little closer to the stage. If she were dressed like a woman, they would assume she was a whore, walking about as she was on her own. As a man they ignored her. That was thrilling. Her whole body felt alive, like sparks were flying from her skin.

She saw Rudy making his way across the floor toward their table. Behind him, at the far end of the room, a large white man wearing a fitted gray waistcoat stood looking over the crowd. Was he the one Rudy had gone to meet? She limped a little as she went back to the table, and remembered what Marjorie said about a war wound. Sure enough, as she passed one group, a man saluted. Lena touched her cap like she'd done it a thousand times.

Still standing, Rudy took a cigarette from his pack. "I have to go off and talk to someone, just a little business," he said to Pin. "Would you see Lena home?"

"Sure," Pin said easily. "We were thinking of going over to the Lakeside when this set's over. Carol Tanner is singing."

"Ever hear her?" Marjorie asked Lena.

People were still singing along to the music. One by one all the instruments fell off. Now it was only the piano and the singer. Lena wanted to watch the band all night. She wanted to get closer to see how the pianist, Eve Riser, made her fingers fly over the keys without stumbling. It was warm in the room and she unbuttoned the top button of her uniform jacket. As a man, she could do anything. Well, Lena thought, not anything. But enough.

"I think I'll stay here," she said.

5

BY MIDNIGHT THE SHOW AT the Oaks was over, but the city showed no signs of slowing down. The sidewalk in front was crowded with people calling out to each other and laughing, or crossing the street at an angle to say hello to someone they recognized. Eve had changed out of her dress, washed her face, lied to Chickie; and then with the money and the letter in her purse she went outside the club to wait for Rudy Hardy. But the excitement of the night's show was still with her even out here in the cold air—she felt exhausted and exhilarated and in love with her music all over again. Maybe it was a good thing, coming back to Chicago.

A light snow began falling like someone was knocking out the last bit of flour from a sifter, and groups of people walked up and down the street, the men arm-in-arm and smiling. One old man was offering bonded bourbon for six dollars a bottle, and a woman came around selling slices of some kind of bread or cake. Eve could hear different kinds of music playing on different corners. In the summer there'd be homemade stands selling chitterlings or fried chicken and fish on big tin platters. Now it was too cold to linger, but still people did.

She waited in front of the club like she'd been told, wondering what Mr. Rudy Hardy looked like. A few minutes more and she'd be done with this business.

At last a man came up to her, a young soldier with a round, good-natured face. Eve hadn't expected a soldier. Just as she opened her mouth the soldier spoke first.

"Excuse me, ma'am, I just have to say—are you Miss Eve Riser? I saw you play over there." A gesture back at the Oaks. "You were wonderful."

So, only an alligator. Eve smiled cautiously. "Yes." He seemed too young to be a soldier, with an awkwardness about him as if he were just out of short pants. Amazing what they'll take into the army, Eve thought. Didn't look like he could fight off anything stronger than a cold.

Meanwhile the soldier was gushing about the show. This happened sometimes—people got hepped up on the music, felt a connection. Told you about their life because there was a barrier down. They didn't realize it only went one way.

"And the third number, the blues number. All the way down low on the register. The song was in C, am I right? But you did your tremolo on F?"

Eve glanced at him, surprised. "You play?"

"I used to. I took lessons. Then I had an accident . . ."

"Well, you sure do know a lot." Politely, wondering how to cut him off.

"I still read scores, I don't know, for fun. Sometimes I think about getting an instrument. Tell me something—that last song you played, it was so beautiful. Who wrote it?"

"I wrote it," Eve said.

The soldier couldn't hide his astonishment. "You compose, too?"

"Time to time." She pulled her cape closer around her, her purse with the envelope hidden beneath it.

"What did it mean? That is . . ." The soldier hesitated. "The song had a feel to it, a certain feel, and I just wondered, well, what you were trying to say."

"I was just trying to write a good song." Now she was truly cold and she wanted to sleep. The after-hours shows were starting up, and she wondered if the street noise would keep her awake. How far was Mrs. Jenkins's place from the nearest club? She needed to get away from this man, make it clear she was waiting for someone.

She said, "Now I'm sorry, but you'll have to excuse me, Captain . . . ?"

The soldier hesitated. "Hardy," he said.

Eve looked at him sharply. "Rudy Hardy?"

This time it was the soldier's turn to look surprised. But before either one could say anything more, a young man in a trilby hat strode up the sidewalk toward her, saying "Hiyup!" like she was a horse. "Miss Riser?" he said loudly from a few yards away. "I'm Rudy Hardy."

She looked back at the soldier, a long full look. The soldier looked at the man in the trilby hat and said in a softer voice, "Rudy."

Then Eve said, "Why, you a girl."

The soldier blushed.

"Are you Miss Eve Riser?" the man called out again.

"Yes sir," Eve said, still looking at the girl. Her mind spun out into darkness like she just couldn't take this last one in. Why was this girl dressed like a soldier? Why would she say her name was Hardy, when this fellow said his name was Hardy?

A Kokomo Coffee truck pulled into her line of vision, and Eve watched it a moment as if it would have some sort of answer. Unusual for a truck to be driving around this time of night, and a few other people looked at it, too. The kind of truck with no doors. A man leaned out from the driver's seat looking at the sidewalk, steering with one hand. In his free hand he carried a rifle.

As Eve watched in frozen shock, he lifted the rifle and took aim. Hardy was saying something to the soldier, his back to the street; he couldn't see the truck or the man. Eve looked at the gun and heard herself say, "No." At that, Hardy half-turned to her and suddenly there was a loud bang, and then another and another.

Eve felt a sharp hit to her leg, and a deep, pulling pain started up. She looked down to see what it was and something buzzed by her head like a bee that could fly through her hat. She was still wearing the hat she carried the money in. Was the money still affixed? She tried to feel it; it seemed important to find out. No, that's all right, it's in my handbag now, she remembered.

For some reason she felt like laughing. Maybe she did laugh a little, only it was blood coming out of her mouth. She could taste it. She thought of Gavin's sour breath when he was pulling that body in Hoxie. Fear turned to something you could smell or taste, that really was true. People were making noise now, running away, hard to tell what.

She fell against the building and then down into the snow, hitting her head against something hard and unforgiving. But this time, although she waited for the pain, she felt nothing. Stars seemed to be shooting down on her, and she had a nice clear view of two brown branches against a white sky, the white like a piece of fabric bunched up over her mother's lap while she sewed. She remembered her mother sewing.

She closed her eyes.

Her body seemed to lighten and break up into sections, each one complete but light. She could hear a song somewhere. Joy and pain, she thought, the same ache. This was what she had tried to write into that last song. Who was it that asked her about that? Not two sides of a coin, but the same side together.

Ghosts seemed to hover overhead, her mother's among them. She heard a voice. Someone knelt down beside her. The noise of the world took a step back and that felt right, too. Music is a fight against silence. She waited for whatever came next.

For a moment, nothing. Then above her head a man's voice said, "Dead."

6

COBB SAID TO HENRY JAMES, "Always give what the audience expects."

"Yes, sir."

"I don't want any hotdoggers."

"Yes, sir."

"But there must be some innovation, too, a little surprise."

"Mm-hmm."

"But not too much surprise," Cobb said.

He was in a bad mood, and it felt good to give instructions to a man who could outplay him on every instrument, including and especially his own beloved trumpet, a man furthermore who knew more about music than Cobb knew about any other subject, maybe even all other subjects put together.

They were at the club, the Oaks; it was Monday morning. Cobb liked to hold auditions on Mondays just to see if anyone amazing swam up from New Orleans or Kansas City over the weekend, someone who could be the making of the club. How he'd love to garner the fame of, say, the Dreamland or the Sunset or even Lincoln Gardens, where Joe "King" Oliver reigned with his Creole Jazz Band. Of course, anyone that good would probably be already known, but this was Cobb's vanity. He knew that Henry was just playing along.

Cobb liked to think he knew something about music and maybe he did. After he left his home in Mississippi, he had spent some time in New Orleans working on the river while watching the riverboats go up and down for pleasure, and often he could hear the band on board playing some tune loud enough to carry prow to stern.

That was when he fell in love with the music. The sound coming over the water made him think of a faraway land, someplace you could see but never quite reach. One June evening he found a way to stow away on one of those boats. He wandered around until he found a poker game going on in one of the public rooms. A large, yellow-haired oaf dressed in torn coveralls who couldn't be more than twenty had a pile of money beside him that he'd won off of the dapper men around him, while nearby an old blind man played on a trumpet drunkenly, a jug of whiskey by his feet.

Later he came to find out they were a team, father and son, the father eyeing the men's cards and then playing signals on his trumpet so the boy could win the hand. Cobb stayed with the pair for six months and learned how to play poker from the boy and how to play the trumpet from the old man, who of course wasn't actually blind, and his whiskey jug was full of weak tea. This was how Nathan Cobb learned the trumpet and also how he paid his way to Chicago.

At least that's the story he told.

He looked back at the bar at the end of the club floor where Moaner and Travis were waiting with the Daily Racing Form between them and a pencil not much bigger than a thumb to its knuckle, Travis as always with a cigarette going, Moaner with that damn banjo on his lap. For economy's sake, Cobb didn't stoke the furnace until noon and it was cold in the room. He glanced irritably at Henry, who had just sneaked a look at his watch.

"All right then, let's take a look at what the cat dragged in," Cobb told him.

Henry opened the side door to the club. He was chain smoking and drinking cup after cup of black coffee, and he looked like he hadn't washed or slept in two days. Cobb thought, I'll have to talk to him about that.

"Come on in, now," Henry called to the group of men waiting outside, who at once began filing in with their instruments.

It was still snowing out. Cobb yelled, "Watch you don't wet up my stage."

He could smell the smothered steak and gravy the cook was making for the club supper that night, only the musicians would get it with ham. Travis was eating a hard-boiled egg as he smoked.

Moaner said, "I'm telling you, it wasn't no cow kicking over a lantern. The earth struck a comet, is what."

Travis swallowed. "Here we go again."

"Or maybe part of a comet," Moaner said.

Up on the stage a young boy stood facing Henry James with black hair so slicked it looked painted. He opened his instrument case and pulled out a tarnished cornet, fitted the mouthpiece to the horn, and pressed a few keys. Then he took an empty water glass from his other pocket and placed it on the floor.

"'Hotter Than That,'" he said, naming the song.

He opened lightly like a happy dog sniffing around. Henry James accompanied him on the piano—rumor had it he could play any instrument made. After a few bars Henry let the boy solo, and the boy took the beat with a quick succession of eighth notes as if beating a drum.

When the music was loud enough, Cobb walked around the counter and poured himself a glass of seltzer.

"What the hell happened Saturday night?" he asked in a low voice.

Moaner didn't speak for a moment. Then he shrugged. "Guess my aim's better than I figured."

"Did I *say* to kill him?"

Moaner wet his lips, considering the question.

"I did not say kill him," Cobb went on in the same low, disgusted voice. "I said hurt him up or scare him some, that's it. The Walnut's gonna get pretty riled up when he finds out." Although Cobb was not really sure about that. Moaner put his hat on his head and then took it off.

"That right?" he asked sullenly.

"That's right. I'm meeting him this afternoon to talk it over. I'm thinking you better guess pretty good with those horses today 'cause you might be out of a job."

Though he didn't actually think so. Something had just occurred to him. Although he hadn't wanted Rudy Hardy dead, well, now he was dead. And being dead there was an opening, he realized. He didn't have to persuade Hardy to be his partner. He didn't have to persuade him he needed protection and Cobb was the man for it.

Because now Cobb could *be* Rudy Hardy. Take his place. Be the South Side man in this corn sugar operation. The man was dead.

After the boy up on stage got a chance to use his water glass as a mute, Henry cut him off. "All right, son, that's fine," he said, and the boy laid his cornet across his lap and wiped his mouth with the back of his wrist.

"Union or nonunion?" Henry asked.

"I could go either way," the boy told him. "I'm waiting for my card."

"You read music?"

"Read or follow along, either way."

"All right then." A round metal ashtray lay across the bottom black keys with a cigarette smoking among the crushed-out stubs, which Henry picked up. He took a drag from it. "That sounded just fine."

But the boy stayed on the stage a moment. "You ever heard Vic Williams?"

"Who?"

Cobb shouted, "Vic Williams! The piano player! You played with him once!"

"Oh sure," Henry said. "That's right. Vic Williams. Had a great reach."

"He was my uncle," the boy said.

"Is that so? Well!"

Cobb called out, "All right!" Meaning, enough.

Henry patted the boy on the shoulder while the next musician, a clarinet player, warmed up his instrument. A few men sat at the front tables with their legs stretched out. As they waited, they passed around a vial of yellow oil and oiled their instruments with bits of chamois cloth. You could tell the New Orleans men because they walked in with their instrument cases on their shoulders. Everyone else, even the bass players, carried their case in their arms like a baby.

The clarinet player was tall and skinny, and when Henry asked, "Whatcha play, hot or sweet?" he replied, "Whatever you need." He started a blues number in B flat.

Cobb said softly, "All I wanted, all that was *required*, was to scare Hardy into thinking he needed some protection. Make him go whine a little to his field partner. Be receptive to a deal."

"You want me gone?" Moaner asked Cobb, his hat halfway to his head.

Cobb looked at Moaner like he was deciding.

There was a moment. Then Travis said, "But you know, boss, all we need to do now is find the partner. Offer to step into Rudy Hardy's shoes." Just what Cobb had been thinking. Travis took a bite of his egg and then, still chewing, dragged on his cigarette. "He was a dumb pup," he went on. His fingertips were yellow with nicotine. "Raised prices too often. Coulda been any of a dozen club owners that shot him."

"True," Cobb agreed.

"Maybe that's what we should tell the Walnut," Travis said.

Moaner seized on this. "That's right, that's what we should say. Why should he know any different?"

"Because he's part owner of this club," Cobb told him. And he'd agreed to put up the money so that Cobb could get into Hardy's corn sugar operation in the first place, if Hardy let him. But he didn't need to tell the boys all of his business. Let them think he got the seed money on his own.

"It was an accident anyhow," Moaner said. Now he put down his hat and picked up his banjo like it had all been decided. On the stage, the clarinet player soloed the ending and then paused, letting the last notes speak for themselves before he put down his horn. Henry stared at the piano keys and absently scratched his head. The clarinet player waited. Cobb looked up at the stage.

"Well?" he called out to Henry.

Henry looked up at Cobb, and then he looked over at the lean man across from him, who was holding his clarinet in his lap.

"All right, yes, that's just fine," he said as if he'd been listening. "That will do nicely."

"What's eating him today?" Travis said, nodding his head in the direction of Henry. "He looks like hell and he can't follow what anyone says."

Cobb said irritably, "Christ, don't worry about him, he's fine."

7

BECAUSE OF A SCAR DOWN the center of his face, everyone called Victor Rausch the Walnut. It had happened
like this: One Saturday afternoon when he was about
ten, he rode a sled down some icy steps—he and his
friends had thrown water on them the night before to
make them icier—that led down to the high school
gymnasium. He went too fast and too far, splitting his
face open on the building's brick corner. Everyone
thought he was dead. But the doctor came and stitched
him up and set him on his feet. It wasn't a great stitch-
ing, to be sure, it didn't heal all that smoothly, but here
he was anyhow, alive.

At twenty he started to go bald. By thirty he was
completely bald, but with barely a mark or wrinkle on
his face besides the thick central scar that ran from

hairline to nose. He had small black eyes and olive-toned skin. The nickname fit.

It had finally stopped snowing and the square of sidewalk outside the restaurant was covered with long wet pine needles like a broom had been cut and its straw scattered. Inside, the Walnut chose the last booth in the back and sat on the side facing the door. Something his father taught him always to do.

The waitress bustled about though he was the only customer there—it was late, after two. She was fair-haired and as thin as a wire with a wide, bony face. Just as she started over with a menu, she noticed someone loitering in the doorway—a colored woman looking in.

"Hold on a minute." She went back to the door and flipped a sign on the glass that said "Members Only."

Coming back she muttered, "Keepin' out the riff-raff." With a little puff she handed the Walnut a menu and poured coffee into the thick white china cup set before him.

He looked out his window but the colored woman was already gone. Outside a group of children were playing "Oats peas beans and barley grows," singing and stamping their feet. They pretended to plant a seed in the cold snowy sidewalk, some of them wearing only thin spring jackets with sleeves barely down to their elbows.

This was a mixed neighborhood near the clubs, not far from Hyde Park with its architects and doctors. But the children outside weren't the children of architects and doctors. Back-of-the-yards children, some of them fifteen to a house. He knew how it was, though he wasn't colored himself. When his father died, he became one of them.

Didn't make him like them more, however, and all he wanted now was to stay out of that life. By the time he was twelve he was peddling bottles of a remedy that he claimed cured tuberculosis—Coca-Cola laced with salt—and he made himself nearly one hundred dollars that way. This was before the war, when a schooner of beer cost a nickel.

"I'll have the special," he told the waitress, folding his menu closed. "And a slice of your cream pie."

Cobb came in shaking snow off his hat, and he made his way to the booth, turning sideways a moment to let the waitress pass.

"Snowing again," he said.

The Walnut looked outside. "That didn't take long."

"I wonder if the lake might not freeze. What did you order? I'll just have the same."

"Do I look like a waitress," said the Walnut.

They'd met five years ago at a famous poker game where the ownership of the Oaks Club changed hands— a long, late game with the mayor and his alderman in the basement of the same hotel where Irene Castle liked to stay when she was in town. Some said the whole game was a cheat. At a crucial moment the Walnut fronted Cobb a few chips, asking a thirty percent return if he won. Six minutes and a handshake later, the part- nership of the Oaks was formed. The local neighborhood council was furious when they found out; the Oaks had been a neighborhood club and now white patrons were showing up at every show. But the money was good, and Cobb gave the council a little—a very little—extra to compensate.

Man had a poker face on him at all times, the Walnut found himself thinking now, looking at him. While they ate, he considered how much to tell him. Figured Cobb was doing the same. Partners! Something else his father warned him away from.

After Cobb laid down his fork, the waitress took away their plates and brought them coffee. They spoke about that week's take and then about Hardy. Gingerly, but with that slow confident speech—you had to feel the weight of the man—Cobb put forth his idea about becoming the new point man and supplying corn sugar for the South Side stills. Not just taking a cut, like they had discussed last week, but becoming a full partner. Taking Hardy's place.

"Yes, but who do we approach about it?" the Walnut said.

"I feel sure I can find out who the partner is."

"Do you now."

"I heard a rumor he's a musician."

"A musician?" The Walnut thought about that. "Well, that would make some sense. Someone on the circuit, maybe. Has access to the farms, the farmers. Going from town to town. And if he's on the circuit, he's played here. Unless he went straight out from New Orleans."

"Not many who'd skip Chicago," Cobb said in his kingly way. "They all want to try their luck here. See how good they really are. Make real money." Everyone was leaving New Orleans: Joe Oliver, Freddie Keppard,

Sidney Bechet; he might name a dozen more. And who could blame them, Cobb went on. There were more clubs in Chicago, more bands, more people to listen. A colored man could earn more up here than he could down south. Even Jelly Roll Morton, he'd heard, was on his way back from Los Angeles.

The Walnut picked up his hat from the seat beside him. Fingered the brim. "When you find him, send him over to me," he said.

"You want to talk to him yourself?" Cobb asked, surprised. The Walnut always left the day-to-day details of the club to him.

"I arranged for a small shipment for myself."

"Corn sugar?"

The Walnut snorted. "I'm not a bootlegger. No, it's not sugar."

Cobb looked at him.

"Nose around. Ask at the clubs," the Walnut told him. "I mean the white clubs."

Now it was Cobb's turn to snort. He reached for his hat. "Where else do you think I'd go?"

8

FIRST SHE SAW BRIGHT WAVING lines like light in a pool of clear water, and then she heard music. Piano. Ragtime. Scott Joplin.

She remembered playing this music. Behind that memory there was something else, a curtain of dark white like unbleached muslin that she couldn't draw back, and the feeling of something heavy, like a rock, in her arms.

Scott Joplin in D major. What was it? She knew this song. She saw a man courting a woman. The music was jaunty but at the same time sad. A stolen break from the workaday world.

Her face was wet and she realized someone had just been mopping it—that was what woke her. A cool wet cloth on her forehead. Gone now. But if she opened her eyes she might see the person. She struggled, and opened her eyes.

She was in a darkened room she didn't recognize with high ceilings and chipped green paint and two long windows facing the street. There was a slight smell of medicinal alcohol somewhere nearby. An open doorway led to a second room with a piano. Profile of a girl sitting on the piano stool, playing ragtime. A white girl. I'm in some kind of white girl dream, Eve thought.

Did she make a noise? The girl stopped playing and looked over.

"You're awake again," she said, standing up from the piano bench.

Again?

"Henry had to go to the club. Do you know who I am?"

Eve looked at the girl's face. "No." Her voice came out as a whisper. She looked around for Chickie.

The girl seemed to know what she wanted. She said, coming over to the bed, "Your sister was here last night. Do you remember? You woke up and spoke to her."

Eve didn't remember.

"You've been sleeping on and off for almost two days, the first stretch for close to fifteen hours. We were worried—you have a head wound, which bled a lot but it turns out the bullet just shaved you. On top of that you hit your temple hard when you fell. Knocked you out. I'm a nurse," the girl explained. Eve looked at her carefully. There was something about her.

"I thought the music might help you wake up," she went on. "I hope it wasn't—" she left off, as if actually she didn't know what she hoped it wasn't.

Eve said, "I do know you, though, don't I?" She couldn't tell for sure. The girl was tall and broad-shouldered, with light brown hair pinned back loosely into a bun. Her face was round and pleasant looking, with wide cheekbones and dark blue eyes.

"We've met," the girl said.

Her eyes were red-rimmed, Eve noticed. From crying?

"What time is it?" Eve asked.

"I don't know."

Eve closed her eyes. She felt cool hands on her head. "I'm just going to change your bandage while you're awake. My name is Lena. How do you feel?"

"My leg hurts."

"You caught a bullet there. Don't worry, it didn't get far, I got it out easily." Her hands were very gentle. "You were lucky. Lift your head just a little for me. There, that's good."

Eve concentrated on keeping her head as still as she could. At last she said, "Why didn't you take me to a hospital?"

A noise at the door. "We weren't sure maybe you were mixed up in something," said a low voice. Eve tried to turn her eyes without moving her head. Henry James stood framed in the tall doorway.

"Henry," she said weakly.

"Glad you could join us," he told her, coming around to the wooden kitchen chair by the bed. He sat and took hold of her hand on top of the blanket. There were two kinds of people, Eve felt suddenly, gripping his fingers—friends and foes. Henry was a friend. The girl she wasn't sure about.

Something was bothering her, she didn't know what.

Henry said, "You sure had us worried. Could hardly listen today at the club auditions, kept wondering about how you were getting along."

"Where are we?" Eve asked.

Henry put his hat down on a chair. "My rooms. We brought you here because we didn't know where you were staying. You remember where your rooms are? You remember where you put your case on Saturday when you got in?"

Eve thought. "A Mrs. Jenkins on Dearborn."

"Good girl," Henry said. He turned to Lena. "How's that coming along?"

"There." Lena stood back, her hands full of soiled bandages. She stuffed them into a linen bag to be washed. Then she rinsed her hands in the small bowl on the dresser, pouring in fresh water from a pitcher. When she walked more than two steps she limped.

Eve watched her, still not sure why this white woman was doing all this or even who she was. She could smell old blood and something else, perspiration maybe. She looked across the room at the two side-by-side windows trying to remember what had happened. The windows were tall and narrow with olive green shades and long white curtains that could use a good soak. Henry's rooms, Eve thought, trying to fit that together. She couldn't feel the bed beneath her; it was as though she were suspended, as light as a three-note melody. Where was her mother? For a moment it seemed she would see her.

"You're all right now," the white girl, the nurse—Lena—said. But Eve was still looking at the windows, waiting for something to fly in and take her away.

Lena handed her a cup, "Drink this. Do you feel any nausea?"

"What is it?"

"Clove tea. It will help if your stomach feels sick. Also stimulate your appetite. You need to eat to get well." She helped Eve to sit up so she could drink it.

"Where's Chickie?"

"She should be back soon," Lena said.

"I sent a note over to her this morning," Henry told her. He stood up and went to the windows, pulling one of the stiff shades aside. After a moment he said, "I think I see the boy now, but what's he doing? Let me just go see."

He closed the door gently behind him just as Eve took a sip of the lukewarm tea. When he was gone, Lena sat down on the wooden chair by the bed. First she tucked in the sheet more firmly. Then she folded her hands in her lap. "I have to ask you something."

"All right," Eve said, turning her head.

Her eyes searched Eve's face. Eve thought, a handsome girl.

"How did you know my brother?"

Eve looked at her. "I don't think I did."

"You were waiting for him. Why? Why did someone shoot him?"

"Your brother got shot at? Oh, you mean at the rail-way station?" She was thinking back to Hoxie. But the Black Hand Society did that, she thought confusedly.

"Not at a railway station, on the street. In front of the Oaks Club. Do you know who did it?"

"Who's your brother?" Eve asked.

"Rudy Hardy. Klaus-Rudolph Hardy."

Rudy Hardy.

"Do you remember?" Lena asked.

Eve said, "You mean that white man dressed in an army uniform?"

"No, that was me." Lena turned the chair impatient-ly. "You were waiting for him outside the club. He came walking up the sidewalk and he said—oh I don't know, hey there or something. Miss Riser."

Eve frowned, then winced. "No, that's right, he said hiyup, like I was his horse."

"And you—"

"I remember now. I looked down the street—"

"You said—"

"I saw the Kokomo truck. Man in it with a gun."

She'd been wearing her new green shoes with a rhinestone at the strap. Where were they? She was afraid to wriggle her feet lest she should feel nothing. Her hip hurt. The tea scratched at her throat.

"A Kokomo Coffee truck?" Lena asked.

"Didn't recognize the man. Couldn't see in the dark."

"But there were lights from the club, and the street-lamp—"

"What did you say your brother's name is?"

"Rudy Hardy."

Eve closed her eyes. Touched the blanket with her hands. All at once it felt heavy on her legs. She was hot, that was what was the matter. She remembered being scared.

"Where's your brother now?" she asked.

Lena's mouth twitched. "He's dead. He was shot, like you. I was standing there, too."

Rudy Hardy.

Henry knocked softly and came in with a frown on his face. "Well, that's strange."

He carried a note in his hand. From Chickie?

"Boy said Chickie wasn't there. Said he waited around for an hour."

"But she left Eve a note?" Lena asked him.

"No, this is my note that the boy brought back to me."

Eve tried to put that together with the other things.

"We have rehearsal in an hour," Henry went on. "I'll just tell her then. She'll want to see you." He was still frowning.

Eve looked around the room again. Rudy Hardy. She looked at Lena. Now she remembered the soldier who'd been gushing to her outside the club about her music. But she wasn't gushing now. She looked like all the air and blood had been sucked right out of her.

"Is that my handbag there," Eve asked, "on the dresser?"

Lena fetched it. Eve put her hands on the mattress and tried to sit up. The movement made her tired, and then nauseous. Lena took hold of her arms, gently guiding her up and back, and took a moment to angle the pillow better behind her.

Eve breathed for just a minute. Then she opened her handbag.

The money was gone.

9

CHICKIE DIDN'T SHOW UP AT rehearsal that afternoon, and although Henry asked around, no one knew where she was. Another girl came up to sing with them that night, so that was all right—he could always find singers—but Henry hated to tell Eve.

What Chickie was especially good at was slow blues. Even pregnant—which Henry could certainly see—Chickie always took care of her throat and warmed up properly. When she sang she really stayed with the song, just stayed right with it every beat, which is what you have to do and what is hard to do when you sing a slow song.

Where could a pregnant girl get to? The next morning he took it upon himself to find her, but after a few hours of nothing he began to wonder if he was just going to wander from club to club laughing and having a smoke with whatever group of musicians and owners and hangers-on he found at each one, casually bringing up Chickie's name just to find no one knew a thing. She'd been gone, what, two days? It was only Tuesday; she was probably fine. Still, it was unlike her to miss a rehearsal, let alone a show. Anyone else, he'd be looking for a permanent replacement. But the crowds all loved Chickie.

Now it was almost noon and Henry was still walking the sidewalks. He crossed the street and walked toward one of the larger Chicago hotels, famous for its ground-floor barbershop that was lined, on the ceiling, with silver half-dollars serving as tiles. A hotel for whites. He headed to the service entrance, where a scissors sharpener was just leaving, stepping out onto the street and beginning to ring his bell with his long machine strapped to his back.

"Miss Geneva Woods here today?" he asked the fellow at the door, whose only job seemed to be reading the newspaper.

"Back there with the shoes. Behind the kitchen."

Henry thanked him and made his way down the narrow corridor, glad at least to be out of the wind. The walls were high and painted white, and it was rumored there were underground passageways tunneling out to the street with water pumps and electric lifts and storage areas. Probably useful now that you couldn't keep liquor openly.

He had grown up in New Orleans, and although he didn't mind the cold, he hated the wind. He was a summer child, born in July. As a boy his favorite thing to do was to go around looking to latch onto some parade or another and play a little bugle that his uncle had given him. His aunt had a piano and she let him play it whenever he wanted. She taught him how to read music, too, and brought him little sour apples from a sour apple tree in her backyard. Sometimes when he got really hungry he'd go fishing for crawfish in the gutter that ran along her house. Then he'd go back to the piano.

Most of his learning came from just picking up an instrument and playing around with it, and people said he could play anything with strings or a mouthpiece. In Chicago he got a reputation for teaching, too—he had a soft spot for any boy that got caught by this music. That was something he understood. The boys paid him in pork pies, cigarettes, and once a silver hat crushed a little on one side found God knows where. In exchange he put their fingers right and talked to them about how to get some weight behind a chord.

All told, he knew a lot of people, but so far none of them had helped him find Chickie. What he needed was someone else who knew a lot of people, and who heard a lot. That was when he thought of Geneva Woods.

As he was coming up to the hotel kitchen—behind which was the mending, pressing, and shoe room, where Geneva worked—he heard a door open and shut quickly, then open and shut again. Footsteps running fast. Before he could turn his head, a white man went running by him heading for the kitchen door.

Another man was chasing him. Henry tried to move aside, but the man doing the chasing stopped short behind

Henry, took hold of his arm, and said with a soft Irish brogue, "Hold still there for me." Then he rested a pistol squarely on Henry's shoulder for balance and aimed at the man running away.

He took two shots. Henry inhaled sharply. The noise was earsplitting and left a sort of vacuum in his right ear. The first man disappeared into the kitchen, and the man behind Henry pushed him heavily toward the door. The walls seemed to shrink around them, and Henry could feel his suspender strap slipping. Now he wasn't sure if he was being used to steady the gun or as the Irishman's shield.

Either way he couldn't move. Just inside the kitchen the man pulled the trigger again. *Pop. Pop.* Again Henry went deaf for a moment. The cook walked quickly to the back of the kitchen and watched from behind the heavy range. The kid washing dishes did nothing.

The first man was struggling with a door at one end of the room.

Pop.

As Henry watched, the man's shoulders gave a sudden tug as if he were being pulled by two strings. A large dark stain appeared on the back of his coat and started spreading. He fell face forward against the door.

"Are ya thinkin' things over now, Soddy," the man behind Henry said. As he spoke, he released Henry and went over to Soddy with his gun still out but his voice almost gentle. "Ya know ya done wrong."

Soddy opened his mouth. Nothing came out.

"What's that?"

Nothing came out.

Now the gunman got impatient. He said, "Well, I ain't gonna waste another bullet. Let me know when he's done." This to the cook.

"Next time go to the bathroom for your business," the cook told him peevishly, still holding his carving knife. "They got drains for that."

Henry walked over to the man called Soddy, stretched out and alone now on the kitchen tiles. Soddy opened his mouth again and Henry took his hand. His grandfather had been a minister, and all the men in the family were the kind of men people took their troubles to. Soddy looked up at him, his blue eyes watery and scared. He opened his mouth again.

Henry bent down. "What is it?"

Finally Soddy said, "Stings."

He was talking about his wound. "That's all right," Henry told him. "That's what it does."

Soddy nodded. A few seconds later his eyes fixed and Henry touched his neck but found no pulse. He wiped his palm down over Soddy's eyes to close them, his own heart still beating like a racehorse's.

The gunman was watching him, holding a bowl of soup in two hands. He took a sip of soup straight from the rim. "You a musicianer?" he asked. They had a room upstairs famous for its orchestra, but as a colored man Henry had never played there. The gunman didn't look like the kind of man who would listen to long explanations, though, so Henry just said yes and let him think what he liked.

"What instrument?" the man asked.

"Trumpet."

"Trumpet! I heard you! You're good."

Now the cook was looking at Henry with a half-smile on his face. Of course the man had never heard him.

"Thank you, sir," Henry said anyway. He looked back at Soddy. "I believe this gentleman has passed."

The gunman shrugged. "Well, I'll just finish my soup."

As Henry straightened up, he saw through the upper glass portion of the door—the same door that poor Soddy had been trying to open—someone standing in the little room behind the kitchen. Mrs. Geneva Woods. She motioned to Henry and then unlocked the door.

"Excuse me," Henry said to the gunman as politely as he could while at the same time trying not to look him in the eye. You never know what a man who's recently fired a gun might do. Geneva opened the door and then shut it behind him. For a moment she looked down through the door's half-window at Soddy's body, or what she could see of it.

Turning around slowly—she had to be seventy if she was a day—Henry saw that she held a gun partway under her apron. She went to the long shelf of unpolished shoes along the wall and dropped it into an empty coffee can that served as a bookend.

She said, "Well, now. You still think you want to find Chickie Riser?"

Henry could not immediately answer her, or say anything. He could tell by her face that she was enjoying his surprise. But it didn't take him long to figure out how she knew his errand: her son Teddy at the Granger Club, that must have been it. He'd been sitting at the bar when Henry went round there that morning. At the time Teddy didn't appear to be listening. But that was the way with all the Woods children.

Geneva offered to make him coffee, knowing he was from New Orleans and therefore unable to find a bought cup to his liking.

"Down there they make it strong enough to stain the rim," she said.

"How do you know about that?"

"Oh, I lived there for a summer some years back."

She claimed to have lived or visited every place worth seeing, though she never was seen to leave Chicago. Her face was heavily wrinkled in lines moving over her cheeks like the deep, regular pleats of a skirt. Just now she was wearing her hotel uniform: a blue-checked dress under a bleached white apron with white stockings and polished white shoes. She smelled like lemons: the polish she was using on the shoes. Geneva had a little device on which she could make coffee, and near it stood a half loaf of sugar bread in white paper wrapping.

"You telling me that man out there had something to do with Chickie Riser?" Henry asked, accepting a white cup and saucer with the hotel's crest on it.

"I don't think that man is part of your trouble," Geneva said. "Directly," she added. She sat back down in her chair and picked up the shoe she was working on. "No, I don't think it will come to that."

Henry sat on a wooden chair in the corner, his head even with the lowest shelf. Geneva and her husband, Mack, kept a little house south of here, and every Sunday she served a big afternoon meal to any child, grandchild, or great-grandchild who happened to come, and they all tried to come. It was a great time to gossip and visit and quarrel and get some relief watching babies—always someone there who would hold a baby while drinking a cup of Mack's hot corn liquor doctored with Coca-Cola. Geneva and Mack's children were musicians, two of them, or worked at the packinghouses or at the Pullman plant. One was a laundress for nightclubs, three worked in restaurants on the South Side, and two worked for the newspapers in various capacities. Mack used to help rich men with their horses but now he was studying motorcars.

Between all of them they had Chicago pretty well covered. They knew everything worth knowing in the city and they shared it all with Geneva; besides seeing her on Sunday, they often dropped into the hotel for a visit, cake, and coffee.

"Sicilians don't forget being crossed," Geneva said.

"What Sicilians?"

She put down the one shoe and picked up its mate. "Like that gentleman out there did," she said, indicating the kitchen.

"What are you telling me—Chickie got mixed up with Sicilians?"

She didn't answer right away. A noise sounded against the door, and Henry realized someone was finally moving Soddy's body. Was there another back door to the hotel? Probably there were many back doors.

He was beginning to feel impatient. "Miss Geneva, would you please tell me what you know?"

"I'll tell you. But first you tell me this: ever wonder how Nathan Cobb got ownership of his club?"

Henry never had wondered. "Bought it, I guess."

"On a trumpeter's salary?"

"There's that old rumor of a poker game . . ."

Geneva nodded. "That's right. But he didn't win the club outright. What he won at that game was a partner."

Henry's eyes rested on some ladies' shoes with white square heels that still needed polishing. He worked his jaw, thinking.

"And the *partner* has ties . . ." he said.

Geneva looked up with bright eyes. "Good boy."

"What's the partner's name?"

"Victor Rausch."

"Man with a scar?"

"That's right. Called the Walnut or some nonsense like that. Times he helps out the Sicilians. Rumor there's a deal going on he's in charge of."

"But how is Chickie mixed up with him?"

"Chickie is mixed up with Nathan Cobb."

"What?" Now Henry stared at her. She kept on rubbing her shoe. He put his cup and saucer on the floor by his feet. "That the father of her baby?"

Geneva stopped rubbing to scratch out some mud with her fingernail. She made a motion confirming.

"Cobb know about the baby?"

"Is she still singing for him?"

"Yes she is."

"Then he don't know." She moved the chamois cloth over her fingers, looking for a fresher spot. When she found one, she began rubbing the shoe again.

Henry shook his head. "A person close to you would notice your changes, seems to me."

"Some people can only see from a distance."

Was Nathan Cobb the sort of man who would do something to a woman? Henry wondered. Say he found out she was having his baby and he didn't like that? He felt more than impatient now. He felt scared. "Miss Geneva, do you know where Chickie is right now? I need to know—her sister is worried."

Geneva stopped rubbing the shoe and rested it a moment in her lap. She looked at him like he was her own little boy and she was sorry but he'd have to hear the bad news. "I do not know where Chickie is right at the moment," she told him. "All I know is what April told me—" April was her daughter, the laundress "—and that is that Chickie was waiting around Monday afternoon for Nathan Cobb in his office. When April went in hoping to get her bill settled, she spoke a few words to her."

"Chickie was waiting to see Nathan Cobb?"

"Along about two o'clock."

"Give any reason?"

Geneva made a soft grunt with her mouth closed and shook her head.

Henry sighed. He picked up his hat, put it on his head, and then took up his dirty cup and saucer to bring to the kitchen. "None of this looks good," he said.

10

FOR THE REST OF MONDAY Eve slept—waking every so often to take beef broth and, around midnight, a few swallows of some salty pea soup—but on Tuesday she felt well enough to sit up so that Lena could shave the area around the bullet wound. It was cold in the room, and Eve wore her gray sweater under three blankets. Lena made up a cup of shaving lather out of castile soap with honey and nutmeg oil. The wound was just above Eve's ear, and Lena told her she needed to keep it clean.

Eve said, "I'm really feeling much better."

"Hold still," Lena told her, moving the razor carefully above her ear and then wiping it on a wet cloth. She was wearing the same brown voile dress she'd worn the last three days, her hair braided into a single light brown braid down her back with strands coming loose. For the past few nights she had slept on a cot in the room with the piano, and paid Henry's landlady, Mrs. Tribble, four dollars for the privilege. Mrs. Tribble said, "I ain't never had a white girl before in my house but all right," with a look that seemed to say everything led to more trouble anyway. She showed Lena an old nail in her pocket that she kept there to ward off the evil eye, said it came from a coffin.

"It's Tuesday?" Eve asked. "That means I slept off three days."

"Pretty much."

"Think you can help me into a dress?"

"Henry looked for Chickie last night and he's out looking for her now," Lena said. "Your job is to get well."

"But he can't know where to look."

"Then why don't you tell him?" She was leaning over Eve closer than close, her breath on Eve's cheek. Eve tried to keep very still. The razor blade felt like a tiny, sharp tooth.

"I'm the one should be looking. I'm her sister."

Lena's hand stopped for a moment. Eve glanced up and saw that the skin under Lena's eyes was dark gray, as if bruised. That's when she remembered about Rudy Hardy, Lena's brother. Here is this woman tending to my head, Eve thought, and her brother barely cold. That was a puzzle.

Lena wiped the blade on a wet washcloth and began shaving Eve's scalp again.

"Whatever happened to that suit you were wearing?" Eve asked her.

"What?"

"The army uniform."

"Oh. That's right," Lena said. This time her hand didn't stop moving. "Well, I changed out of it. I went back to my brother's room to change out of it."

"Then you came back here?"

"It was right after—I wanted to make sure you were all right. And I thought you could tell me something about Rudy. About what happened."

"Mmh," Eve said.

"But maybe you can't."

Eve said nothing. She closed her eyes. She could hear Lena rinse the washcloth, the drips falling into the basin as she squeezed it.

"To be honest, I thought I would leave this morning," Lena told her.

Eve opened her eyes, waited for her to say more. Finally she asked, "What happened?"

Lena shrugged. "Then I stayed."

"You have family around here, parents?"

Lena rinsed the washcloth. "No, my parents are both dead."

"No one at all that can comfort you on?"

"I have an aunt . . . I just . . . I'm fine. They gave me some time off from the hospital, but I . . . it's good to have something to do. Being useful."

Eve wasn't sure she believed her. "You're in shock."

"Maybe." Lena wiped Eve's head, and then she tilted it a little with her fingers, gently, to get a better look in the light. "Your wound is healing up nicely. Maybe to-morrow we can move you to your own room." She picked up a cloth and began to pat dry the shaved area before bandaging it. Outside on the street a hurdy-gurdy started rolling out a song. Eve closed her eyes again.

It felt good to have her scalp cleaned, even just this one little area. She touched her head gingerly with her fingertips. It was true that she really did feel much better as long as she didn't turn her head too quick. She opened her eyes to look at Lena, but her face was hard to read.

"I have to find her. Just fetch me my dress and button me up the back—I'll be fine."

Lena said calmly, "You're still ill."

"I'm going one way or another," Eve told her fiercely. "She's my sister. My *sister*."

They looked at one another.

"You know how it is," Eve said, taking a chance. "You and me, we're the reliable ones. That's why you're here, why you didn't leave this morning."

At that Lena frowned. "How is that?"

"Your brother. You want to find out why they killed him. And I'm a tie to that night."

"Who did kill him?"

"I don't know. Man in a Kokomo truck."

"But who was he?"

"Like I said, I don't know. Maybe we find Chickie we'll find out a few things." She didn't know if that was true. But she had to find Chickie, and she needed Lena to help her.

"You think Chickie's involved?"

Now Eve hesitated. "No," she said. Then she said, "I don't know. But maybe she can help answer some of your questions."

"The letter you were going to deliver to my brother." Eve had told her about the letter this morning. Maybe that was a mistake. "Where is it now?" Lena asked.

Gone with the money. But Eve hadn't mentioned money. "I don't know," she said, turning her head.

It wasn't Chickie, she kept telling herself. Chickie did not take that money. Hadn't she always had spells where she went off by herself? Up that old maple tree for half a day, or in the back of their yard where they kept a couple of pigs, that fearsome smell. She'd always gone off to be by herself now and again. Didn't mean she took the money. Anybody could have come up to Eve when she was lying on the ground looking up at the stars.

"Any idea what the letter said?" Lena asked.

"Not a blessed word."

"Who sent it?"

"Just a man who knew I was going to Chicago."

"Surprised he didn't just telegram." Lena adjusted Eve's bandage and then straightened up the bed pillows. "I feel like you're not telling me everything."

"Do you want to know everything?" Eve asked. "If you do, help me into my dress."

For a moment Lena looked away. The room darkened as clouds blew in from the lake, and Eve could no longer hear children in the street. It was early, still morning, and it wasn't snowing at the moment.

"It's hanging just there in that closet," Eve said.

Lena pulled a watch from her dress pocket and looked at it.

"One hour," she said. "And I'll go with you."

Lena thought about what Eve said as they left the house, stepping into the cold, clear air and making their way carefully over the inch of unshoveled snow on the sidewalk. Do I want to know everything? She told herself that she did. She remembered Rudy that last night jiggling his knee under the table, so excited about the music or maybe about whatever scheme he was up to. Then the stillness when he was dead, his head thrown back onto the snow-bank, blood like a spatter of mud. What she wanted was to go back six days. What she wanted was for it never to have happened. It was hard to get past that.

At times the sidewalk was so icy that they had to walk on the street, and not a few people looked at them twice, a white woman in this neighborhood walking with a colored woman. Lena limped as they walked and then took Eve's arm.

"Now they'll think you're my nurse," Lena said. "Instead of the opposite."

The neighborhood had changed during the war; it used to be Irish and Polish, and then Mexican. Now it was filled with colored families who had come up from the South following the stream of Mexicans for war jobs, and even with the war over, more still came up by train every day. The Great Migration, the newspapers were calling it. Lena felt odd, out of place, but it was better than grief. She set her face against the wind and matched her pace with Eve's.

"I need to visit Chickie's room first so I can see for myself she's gone. We can take the streetcar."

"And she might be back now," Lena said. After all, it had only been two days.

They passed a barbershop with a line of shaving mugs on a shelf; through the window she could see the barber taking one down for a customer. Two days, Lena thought. When her father died—he had caught a mild strain of influenza during the war, and she still couldn't believe it killed him—she found herself mourning him by counting time. It was three days, four days, fourteen days since he died. Later, with her mother, she did the same thing.

Now, she thought, it's Rudy.

On the tram Eve and Lena sat next to each other, and the car rattled back and forth as it moved over clumps of snow on the track. A white man stared at them from across the aisle. She saw two colored women looking, too.

Lena addressed the white man. "She's my nurse. I need her to help me get up."

The man said, "She should stand in the aisle."

Eve's face hardened, but she started up from her seat. Lena said, "No, please . . . I get spells." She put a hand on Eve's sleeve. Eve wasn't strong enough. She needed to sit.

"Shouldn't be out then," the man said, not pleased.

Eve didn't look at Lena, but Lena could tell she was uneasy. One by one the passengers glared at them and then looked away. I don't care what they think, Lena thought. I need her to find out what happened to Rudy. Lena was younger than Rudy, but she had always been healthier. Her very first memory was her mother coming into the bedroom and bending over Rudy's bed because he was sick. The walls of the room had been wallpapered with green and brown paper, but when her father stripped it away one summer they found a charcoal drawing that he said one of the builders must have drawn—a caricature, perhaps of the boss. He had a thin nose and smoked a pipe; the drawing was in profile. Her father hadn't painted over it but instead let Lena help him color it in with mixed colors. Because the profile happened to face Rudy's bed, Lena had the impression that the man watched over him.

She had always been stronger. She was supposed to take care of him. By the age of eight she was able to tell at a glance if Rudy had a fever. She never thought the army would take him but it did.

The wind howled through the thin glass windows like a question with no answer. I should never have let down my guard, Lena thought. When she told Eve it was better when she was doing something, being useful, that was only half-true. The other part was that she didn't want to begin the next chapter, where Rudy like everyone else now was dead. She didn't want to go back to where she lived, her job, her regular life, because she knew what was coming, the grief and the loneliness. If I stay and take care of Eve, she thought and almost believed, all that can't start.

"Coupla more stops," Eve told her.

"How's your head?"

"Holding up. Can you see my bandages under my hat?"

"Only if you really look closely."

Eve pulled her hat down a little more.

"Try not to fuss with it," Lena said.

The train was filling up. "Pretty soon there'll be no more seats for white folk," the man across the aisle said. "She'll have to stand then." He leaned away from them and spoke loudly, as if both Lena and Eve were infected with something.

The tram stopped for a light, and the conductor set the brake and then made his way back through the car. Lena didn't notice him until he was standing next to her seat.

"You with this woman?" he asked Lena.

Lena looked up. Then she looked over at Eve. Eve held herself taut, her hands in her lap holding her purse. "Yes," Lena said.

"You shouldn't be sitting with a colored woman. You tell her to move. Plenty a seats without having to sit with the white folk."

The man had a long moustache with waxed ends that were beginning to unfurl. Small, mean gray eyes. Lena guessed he had looked back and seen them chatting.

"She's my nurse," Lena said again.

"Don't matter," he told her. The light had changed but he made no move to go back to the front. All the other passengers were watching.

"It's all right," Eve said. "I can stand."

Lena felt indignant. "No. She has—she was recently injured. Her leg."

But the conductor didn't care. "Not much use as a nurse, then, I'd say. Get along there," he said to Eve with a shoo like she was a dog or a cow.

Lena stood, too. Eve shook her head at her, one quick shake.

"Actually, I believe this is our stop," Lena said.

As they waited outside for the next tram, Eve scolded her. "You didn't have to do that. I could've just stood." A tone like all this was nothing she wasn't used to, but Lena heard the bitterness underneath. A wave of anger and embarrassment came over her.

"I'm sorry," she said.

Eve looked away. "Now we're out here in the cold."

The next tram was only a few minutes back, and this time they sat in seats across from each other and didn't talk.

"There's a seat up here, ma'am," a young man with wildly curly hair said to Lena, but she shook her head and pretended she did not understand English.

When they got off, Lena could hear a horn playing somewhere, a trumpet or cornet. As she and Eve made their way up the block, she thought about that night at Eve's club, how it felt like it was the first time she'd ever heard music. White customers and colored customers together in the same room, at the same time, at the same tables even, some of them. And no one cared.

Then the snow, then the shot, and now this.

Eve stopped in front of a brick rooming house, and Lena followed her up the steps, one step behind her with her hand on Eve's elbow in case she slipped.

"Looks nice," Lena said about the house.

Chickie's landlady was the tallest, largest woman Lena had ever seen. She had fleshy cheeks and a lower lip so heavy it seemed to sag from its own weight. Mrs. Salt, she called herself. Said she hadn't seen Chickie since Sunday. On the bottom floor, in the parlor, she held séances on Friday nights and practiced automatic writing—a new method, she told them, for speaking with the dead. "Only thirty cents. Every Saturday night is when we do it."

She led them up three flights of stairs to Chickie's room, breathing heavily. Her keys hung on a chain around her neck next to an old tarnished cross, and she unlocked Chickie's door without taking the chain from her neck. After she pushed the door open, she held out her hand. Eve gave her two quarters, and Mrs. Salt started wheezing back down the stairs.

The room had one square window and a sink next to an iron bedstead painted white. There was also a wooden chair, a metal music stand with sheet music on it, and a dresser with old issues of the Chicago *Defender* shoring up one leg.

Chickie had arranged pictures on the dresser top, photographs of singers and actresses cut out from newspapers and stuck into six-cent frames. The largest one, in the middle, was of Bessie Smith with a fur stole around her neck.

Eve opened the dresser drawers. They were filled with clothes. A rack with some dresses hanging down neatly stood in one corner. Under the bed she found a straw suitcase and a collection of hatboxes with hats in them. One box contained several handbags instead of hats; Eve opened these, but they were all empty save for a few folded handkerchiefs and an empty lipstick tube.

Lena picked up a newspaper clipping left on the music stand. "Here's an article about the Oaks Club."

Eve said, "Must be something nice in there about Chickie."

Lena scanned it. "No. It's all about Nathan Cobb."

"Nathan Cobb?" Eve looked over Lena's shoulder. There was a slightly out-of-focus photograph of him standing in front of the club.

"Why would she cut that out?" Lena asked.

Eve didn't know. She looked around. The bed was made, the curtains were drawn. Chickie always liked order. On the table by the bed was a slightly larger, more expensive frame than the ones on the dresser. Eve picked it up. It was their brother, Kid. Tucked into the back of the frame was a letter addressed to Chickie in his writing.

"Who's that?"

"Our brother. He was like our baby, Chickie's and mine. We helped raise him." Eve held the photograph in her two hands. "I don't think she'd leave without this."

"Not to mention her suitcase and her clothes." Lena waved her hand toward them.

But there was a musty smell, like there'd been no new air in for some days.

"I have one more idea," Eve said, getting ready to leave.

"Do you want to leave her a note?"

"If she needs a note to come see me, then she better not come."

Back on the street, the wind had shifted slightly and a fresh lake smell blew down the sidewalk. Eve and Lena rode the streetcar for two stops and then changed cars. When they got off the last one, there was a little girl on the street speaking English to an old woman, who answered in Italian. The girl reminded Lena of herself as a child—two long braids coming undone, a thin frame. Turning to translate for her mother, although with them it was German, not Italian. Lena looked at her watch.

"How do you feel?" she asked Eve.

"I'll do," Eve said. Her eyes were watery from the wind.

"I can see a lending library on the corner if you want to rest."

"We're almost there."

They passed a man selling chicken eggs ten cents a dozen from a box hanging around his neck, and then turned in to an alley where a blue metal sign beat back and forth in the wind. "The Blue Room," it said.

"I got a job here not too long after Chickie and I moved to Chicago," Eve explained. "Chickie still sings for them time to time."

A few steps led down to a heavy black door with a square brass peephole. Eve rang the bell. After a minute the peephole door slid open.

"Hi, Porely," she said. "It's me, Eve Riser."

Nothing happened. "This is a friend of mine," Eve said. "She's all right, she a nurse. Is Lester up there? I need to see him."

The little peephole door slid closed and the big door opened. A tall, broad man with slicked hair and arms like two thick clubs stood back to let them in. He glanced at Lena quickly as though he'd just as soon bite her as see her. But to Eve, he tilted his head and smiled.

"Eve Riser," he said.

"You're looking fine, Porely, how you doing?" Eve said, smiling back.

"Heard you had some trouble." He had a large gap between his two front teeth and a surprisingly soft voice for such a big man.

"I'm all right," Eve said. "Just caught in some cross-fire meant for somebody else."

"Ain't that the way."

The club was windowless, lit only by a smattering of dusty overhead lights hanging down from the ceiling. Eve and Lena followed Porely to the back of the club, where there was a wooden bar painted like bamboo and a back door beside it. The stage, if you could call it that, was a small area on the other side of the back door, where two lines of chairs—the musicians' chairs— sat facing the tables. A line of beer bottles arranged in a semicircle separated the stage from the club floor.

"Don't tell me it's our beautiful Eve Riser come back for a visit?"

A tall, thin, light-colored man wearing a porkpie hat came out carrying a glass of something that looked like bourbon. When he looked at Lena, his expression changed slightly.

"I'm Lena," Lena said, consciously not using her last name because of Rudy. She put out her hand. "Eve's nurse."

"Lester Glide," he said shortly, and then to Eve, "You have your own nurse now?"

"Didn't you hear? I hit the big time."

Lester laughed at that and took a sip of his drink. He gestured Eve to sit down with him at the bar and Lena followed, feeling somehow invisible.

"The boys'll be in shortly. You looking for work?"

"I might be," Eve said. Lena looked at her quickly but Eve was smiling at Lester. "Unless you still dress everyone up in those striped pants and white top hats," she went on.

"Nah, nah," Lester laughed. He waved his glass around and some of the bourbon slid up close to the rim. "We're through with the hats—folks starting to seriously listen to the music now, we don't need all that anymore. And all these young lions, too, playing like it's their ticket to heaven. Serious about their business."

"Heard you took out your clarinet."

"That's right. We're up to three saxes now, any given night."

"Well, I can see you're doing all right. You look good. Eating well?"

"Fanny Ann's, three times a day."

"She still keep a room for you upstairs?"

"Can't complain. Every once in a while Tom slinks back around trying to get him some of Fanny Ann's money, and I just lit out for a couple of days. But that's hardly once or twice a year." He took another sip of his bourbon. Lena watched his face, smooth and unperturbed, a businessman's face, happy to chat, but also on the alert for anything that might make him money. He never glanced at Lena. A white nurse had nothing to offer him.

"How's Chickie?" he asked.

"She's good, she's very good," Eve said.

"Haven't seen her since you came to town."

"Oh, she's been eating with me."

"That explains it."

Eve picked up her gloves. "Well, I won't take up any more of your time. You find you need someone on piano, you come look for me, won't you?"

"I sure will."

Eve stood up. "Still making your own hooch?"

"Chicago's finest."

"Hope that business with Rudy Hardy doesn't affect you."

Lester's eyes narrowed. "That's right, that was you out there, wasn't it?"

"Teach me to stand outside my own club. Next time I put on my gloves *before* I go out the door."

Lester shook his head matter-of-factly. "I just thank goodness he wasn't my supplier. Bad business. They say he was raising the prices north and south—that's why he snuffed it. Guess he got his wagon fixed."

"Any idea who it was?" Eve asked mildly.

"One of the club owners, they say, though it don't make much sense to cut off your supplier before you get you another. Thinking with your fist, I call it. Belfiore, now that's my man. With Rudy gone he's gonna make out like strawberries in July."

Lena tried to keep her face as still as possible, although her heart was pounding hard as she followed Eve to the door. One of the club owners, Lester said. *He got his wagon fixed.* Neither Lester nor Porely said good-bye to her, only to Eve. Lena buttoned the top button of her coat and pulled on her gloves. She was only a visitor here in other people's lives. These men didn't particularly want to see her. Resented her presence, even, like the white passengers resented Eve in the streetcar, though without the same obvious malice.

Outside Eve and Lena stood in the alley for a moment with their backs to the wind.

"Why didn't you ask him about Chickie?" Lena asked.

"Didn't need to. He told me. He hasn't seen her."

Lena didn't understand.

"Chickie always eats at Fanny Ann's," Eve explained. "Every morning she has her breakfast there. So does Lester." She paused, and then she said, "If Lester hasn't seen her, then where's she been eating at all this while?"

Lena saw tears come up in Eve's eyes, and without thinking she took hold of her hand. "Oh, Eve." She tried to think of something consoling to say. Eve looked down at Lena's hand in her own like it was something strange she didn't know what to do with, but she didn't pull away.

"Now I'm worried," Eve said.

11

THREE O'CLOCK IN THE afternoon: breakfast time for musicians. Cobb had plenty of time to ask around about Rudy's partner, eat a meal, and get back to his office at the club by nine. Most of these musicians boozed all night and slept all day. They slicked their hair wet just enough to say it was combed before making their way to whatever club they happened to be associated with at the time, an instrument tucked like a baby under one arm.

He missed playing music but he dressed better now. A nice suit, a good hat, and not one of those rat-catching hats but a soft gray fedora with a respectable brim. Sometimes he felt a little guilty—music was once his best love—but the money sat well. Bills in his pocket, a gold watch on a chain. "Where's my watch and chain?" he remembered one musician calling out once, meaning the bandleader. It was around that time he realized he wouldn't ever be the bandleader.

Now what was he, a bootlegger? Straight after his meeting with the Walnut the day before, he went with Moaner in the truck to the train station to pick up that week's supply of corn sugar. With Rudy dead, there had been some confusion—it took several hours just to find the right siding and train car. Might even be the last shipment, considering Rudy was the one who coordinated everything and now he wasn't there to do it. When it was finally sorted out, he sent Moaner off with the sugar and a note for Travis, and then went on home and slept until noon like he used to, back when he was a horn player and full of dreams.

Not good. Not good for what he aspired to be.

He passed a Catholic church and tipped his hat, although he hadn't been inside a church in years. His mother was Catholic; she'd died at fourteen giving birth to him. His father was fifteen and ran off even before her body was cold. Cobb had been raised by his mother's father, an imposingly large man who worked at the dry goods store and spoke in a slow, lordly way. He kept the store stocked, paid the bills, tallied the books, did everything, in fact, but own it—that honor was held by the half-drunk great-nephew of one of the town's founders.

When his grandfather died, that's when Cobb decided to leave. He made his way to New Orleans carrying only a loaf of bread and an extra pair of socks, and got a job working on the river. Later he reflected that his grandfather was born in Shreveport, not too far from New Orleans, so maybe that's why he headed that way. And now here he was in the greatest city in the country, according to the people who lived here, at least.

On South Dearborn Street some boys had set up an old mahogany sideboard they'd gotten from somewhere and were sitting behind it selling tobacco, apples, and cider. Cobb bought an apple and gave them an extra penny for a tip. He wanted to be like his grandfather, but with more money. And the owner, not someone who worked for the owner.

A block and a half later he came to a red brick club with a low marquee in the process of being changed. Inside, the Garden Club was grander than it would seem from its squat façade: two tiers of round tables were arranged in a semicircle around the stage, and the white walls had curling vines, flowers, and birds painted up to the ceiling. The club owner, a man named Lloyd Oren, saw Cobb from across the floor.

"Dixie!" he called out. He called everyone Dixie who was from the South; he was from Georgia himself. "Come on and listen to this! Why don't you start that again, fellas," he said to his musicians. "Sounds just fine."

His band was ridiculous, eight old men in starched collars sitting in cane-backed chairs, but they were a Chicago tradition. Their ricky-tick beat made Cobb think of a heart that was just about to give out. One man, the bass player, dropped something into the open piano, and they had to stop to rummage around for it among the piano strings and hammers.

"My lord, these fellows . . ." Oren said to Cobb under his breath. "If one of them isn't going blind, then the other one's lost his false teeth. Some nights I have to check they're still breathing before I take them off the stage." He looked around. "Hey, Jake, there! Get this gentleman and myself a little taste, would you?"

Hard to believe any of these musicians could be partnered with Rudy Hardy, and Cobb didn't believe it. But Oren Lloyd ran the oldest music club in the city, and if there was anything to know about the goings-on in the other clubs, he would know it. Cobb accepted the glass brought over to him. What was Oren now, a hundred and eighty years old? Cobb tasted the drink. Whiskey.

"Last of my crop," Oren said. He had a full head of white hair that resisted a part, and a dog, a toy schnauzer, on his lap. "Soon I'm going to have to call up your fellow and start making my own." He winked.

"Haven't you heard?" Cobb said calmly. "He was shot dead Saturday night."

"Well, come to think of it, I did hear that. My, my." He stroked the dog with a gnarled hand, but his eyes were as sharp as a rat's. "What will the good people do?"

"I heard he might have a partner in one of the clubs," Cobb said.

"A partner, is that right?"

"Someone said a musician."

As the sax player tried out a flutter-tongue, Oren looked over at the stage. "Boys!" he interrupted. "Hold on a minute, boys!" The music dwindled to a stop. "Listen up!" Oren said. "Any one of you partnering with a man named Rudy Hardy? Who is now by way of one of the deceased?"

Cobb drank his whiskey, letting the old man have his joke. All the musicians dumbly shook their old gray heads, and Oren turned back to Cobb, smiling. Raised his shoulders. Well?

But Cobb was still thinking of his grandfather. How he questioned a person like he already knew the answer and the asking was done just as a courtesy. He said slowly, "You know more than anyone else in this town; that's why I came to you. I know you would help if you could. This is good whiskey—I thank you for sharing it with me." He put down his glass. "Your supply keeping up?"

"Well, I got a few boxes somewhere still, I suppose."

"Wonder how long they'll last," Cobb mused.

How long would any of these pre-Prohibition supplies last? In the newspapers there were photographs of politicians pouring barrels of beer into the gutter—staged photographs, that was true, but what if they took it in mind to really investigate what was stored away in all these club cellars? And even if they didn't, one way or another at some point the stock would be finished, and all the club owners would be looking to buy corn sugar to make their own whiskey.

A good business to be in on. Others must be thinking the same thing.

"Could be useful to know who to call on," Cobb went on, "when it comes to that."

Oren tilted his head, non-committal.

"No telling how long the nonsense will last."

"Nonsense, indeed."

"And a man like you likes to know what there is to know."

Oren stroked his dog without speaking. After a moment he lifted the dog up off his lap and laid him gently on a sewn-up burlap sack at the foot of the table.

"Just had that made this morning," he said about the dog bed. "Had the girl fill it with pine wood shavings on account of the smell of pine keeps fleas away. Know who told me that? Dusty Snider, over at the Common Club. A man who's also looking for Rudy Hardy's partner, as it turns out."

"Is that right?"

"Told me so last night. Wants to get in on the act himself," Oren said.

Cobb said, "It's a pretty good act." So he was right: there were others looking to get in on the corn sugar trade. All a matter of who could find the partner first. "I guess it comes down to choosing who you trust," Cobb told him coolly. "Who you want to do business with in the future. Dusty, he's got a pretty hot temper, I'm told."

Oren said nothing to that, and Cobb sat back patiently. Thought, we'll just let that sink in. After a while he said, "You keep this place nice."

"Yes I do," Oren told him. "Yes I do." Finally he leaned forward and put his gnarled, silvery hand on Cobb's shoulder. He was reputed to like young, clean-shaven men. "You know that gal they got up there at the Elite Club? Kind you don't know maybe she might be a man? Tack Annie they call her."

Everyone knew Tack Annie.

"You might talk to her," Oren suggested. "I'm told she hears quite a bit."

Cobb was annoyed with himself for not thinking of Tack Annie in the first place. The Elite Club was an after-hours club not four blocks away, frequented by musicians and entertainers after the other clubs closed. It wouldn't open for several more hours, but Cobb found Tack Annie outside, directing a young girl who was sweeping the walk.

People called her Tack Annie because when she was drinking she tacked across the room like a sailboat. She was a tough woman, the toughest he'd seen, the kind who took the whores from mobsters after they were through with them, and paraded them around town like they were her own. There were two prostitutes standing beside her now, beautiful white girls, one in a green dress and one in a gold. Tack Annie wore dark satin-like pants and a high-collared white shirt, a man's shirt, but somehow prettied up a little.

"Miss Annie," Cobb said respectfully. She didn't like being called by her nickname.

The prostitutes looked at him, summing him up professionally, while Tack Annie took her time turning around. She had a face like a bulldog ready to bite:

large jaw, large mouth, wide forehead, and close eyes. A skin shade between cocoa butter and ivory. Nobody knew if she was colored or Mexican or what.

"That would be Mr. Nathan Cobb," she said, her voice rising at the end. She had a sweet high voice but you couldn't let that fool you.

He said, "The lady I'm looking for. Can I buy you a cup of coffee?"

She said, "Or make that a beer."

The two white girls followed her inside. The club was ill-lit and technically closed, but Cobb could make out groups of men and women scattered about at the tables talking and drinking, and off in one corner a tonk game was going on. The place had once been a music hall, and there was a small, enclosed space for dancing set off by a brass railing. Cobb smelled a familiar scent of old hops seeped into wood, and something like cabbage.

"Irish trash in the flat upstairs," Tack Annie said. "Always cooking meat, the teeniest square of meat you ever saw, and they cook it and cook it and the smell wafts down here. I tell them, 'Close up yer windows!' They look at me like they don't speak any English. But they speak English in Ireland, don't they?" Again the voice going high. "As well as Irish?"

A middle-aged colored man named Tynan Williams owned the club. Williams dressed better than anyone Cobb knew, his black shoes always shined to a mirror finish, and had first owned a club in Hyde Park before the area became all-white residential. Made more money on this place anyway, he liked to say now. It was rumored he answered to the Sicilians, who had set up a

gambling room in the back. Tack Annie managed everything, even the gambling. These days, people were saying that the Sicilians were the ones to watch even more
than the Irish, although no one knew yet what they
were watching for.

Tack Annie showed Cobb to a table with a window
looking out to the street. Pulled two chairs out for the
girls, then raised the green shade so she could keep a
lookout on anyone walking under the outside lights of
the club. She called over to a fellow for some beers
while her ladies lit up cigarettes in long white holders.
The girl in green passed a thin, brown cigarillo to Tack
Annie.

Tack Annie put her arm around the girl in gold.
"Emmeline Belle," she told Cobb. "Ain't she pretty?"
Emmeline turned her head and Tack Annie kissed her
on the lips.

"Now." Tack Annie took a drag off her cigarillo.
"What's this about?"

He told her what he'd told Oren, that he was looking
for Rudy Hardy's partner, that he'd heard the partner
was a musician. Her eyes, dark brown and ringed with
kohl, were dull and expressionless as if she were high.
Cobb didn't believe for one second that she was. When
she moved her hand, there was a tinkling in the air
from all her thin gold bracelets.

Some music started up on the stage, beginning with
a powerful, rhythmic piano riff played by a man wearing an undershirt and brown suspenders. Another man
placed a new reed in his clarinet, adjusted it with the

tip of his thumb, and then twisted it in while the saxophone player watched.

"Where's that skin beater, now?" the piano player asked, still playing, looking around for his drummer. Rehearsal had begun.

"And why do you want to find this man?" Tack Annie asked Cobb.

Cobb looked back at her and smiled. With Tack Annie it was best to be honest. "I want in on the business," he said.

She laughed. "Who wouldn't! They had a nice little operation going up there, didn't they. Mr. Rudy Hardy. Only met him once. He didn't know what to do with me. But Mr. Tynan, you know," she waved a hand vaguely north, "he's worried, too. Wondering if his source'll dry up. Everyone wants to find this partner."

She took a drag from her cigarillo and looked at Cobb and then exhaled just to the right of his face. "You, though. You want more than supplies." She kept her eyes on him as if considering his character. "You have ambition," she decided.

"As do you," Cobb countered.

The piano player started syncopating the melody while the bass player, not yet playing, draped himself over his instrument with his head bent as if looking to tie his shoe. Suddenly the two horns started up together and the piano player shouted, "There you go!" The bass player cut in quick, not to be left behind.

"Rudy Hardy was just the same," Tack Annie went on. "Ambitious. And look where it got him. Strange fact, I heard that *your* man went to see Mr. Hardy just that afternoon. Saturday."

My man? Must be thinking of Travis. Cobb picked up his beer mug and swirled it. "Travis Pitts? I don't think so."

"I meant your man with the scar."

"Victor Rausch?"

"That's right, the Walnut. Some say he was seen talking to Rudy Hardy at Saul's that Saturday."

Cobb took a sip of beer. He didn't like the sound of that. "Must be a mistake."

"Man with a face like that is hard to mistake."

"Then they must have made a mistake about Hardy."

Tack Annie shrugged, non-committal. She chewed on the end of her cigarillo like a man. Cobb watched her, waiting for more. Her white shirt was open at the neck. If she were pretty, you'd say she had style.

"Have a girlfriend these days?" Tack Annie asked Cobb.

That was a fast switch. "Why, are you on the market?" Cobb asked.

Tack Annie laughed. "He's *quick!*" she said to Emmeline. Emmeline smiled, dumb and beautiful and out of reach, like an angel. The other girl laughed quietly. They were both, the prostitutes, very high on something. It was hard to read Tack Annie.

She said, "So your singer off then?"

Another incomprehensible switch. "Which singer?" he asked.

"Chickie Riser. She off then, having her baby?"

Cobb stared at her. His eyes narrowed. All at once he felt cold, and he wished the music would stop for one second. But the piano player was laughing and banging away trying to outpace the drummer, while outside a streetcar began ringing and ringing its bell, telling something to move.

A baby? Chickie?

What did Tack Annie know? Cobb stared at her. He was having trouble forming a question. Tack Annie smiled.

"You should talk to Chickie's sister," she told him. "Miss Eve Riser. Plays the piano, don't she, for your club now? Word has it she used to play with Rudy's partner."

12

BACK IN HENRY'S ROOMS, Eve took off her shoes and let Lena unbutton the back of her dress. Her head ached. She wanted to sleep for a week.

"I let you do too much," Lena said. She helped Eve sit on the bed. Pulled her feet up. "Don't fall asleep yet. I'll be right back."

She left the room and came back a few minutes later with a basin of steaming water and a bar of mustard-colored soap. Without jostling the basin she shut the door with her foot. "Mrs. Tribble makes her soap from egg yolk, she says."

"Expensive soap," Eve commented. Her eyes were closed.

"Only she called it egg yelk."

Eve smiled, too weary to even lift her eyelids and look. She could hear Lena setting something down, fetching this or that. The rushy sound of fabric.

After a moment she sensed a body near. Now she opened her eyes. Lena was gently pulling her blanket back.

"You smell a bit ripe," Lena said.

"You think this is bad," Eve told her.

A warm soapy cloth on her shoulders, then her forearm. Lena lifted Eve's right arm gently and washed her armpit and around to her back. Then she patted her with a dry towel.

"I don't want you wet for too long, so I'm going to dry you off as we go along."

"Once I was at a place for three days," Eve said, "where the only soap they had was dried ash. Didn't even have a drugstore. Only meant to play one night but we got snowed in." She paused, remembering waking up cold and looking at a foot of snow on the window ledge. "That's when Gavin and I . . ." She drifted off, almost falling asleep.

"Gavin, is that your boyfriend?"

Eve inhaled. "We almost started up. Didn't work out."

"Where is he now?"

"Still out on the circuit."

"Can you bend forward?" Lena asked.

Eve thought: I shouldn't talk about Gavin. She opened her eyes to see Lena unfolding a clean nightdress that smelled faintly of bleaching powder.

"I'm going to make you some tea." Lena helped Eve into the nightdress. "Try to stay awake for just a tiny bit more."

The next thing Eve knew, there was the smell of ham in the room. She must have fallen asleep anyway. The quilt was up over her but she was still sitting up.

"Eat this," Lena said.

She had a few bites and then lay back against the pillows again. "Mm."

"Can you drink some tea?"

Eve sniffed. "What is it?"

"Just a sip. It will help you. It's made from pot marigold leaves."

Eve looked at her sharply. Lena was smiling, the afternoon sun making lines down the walls behind her. "I'm not drinking flower parts!"

"It's delicious."

Eve took a sip. It tasted of somebody's dirt garden, if you could call that delicious.

"When it cools, I'll put a little on your head. It's good for wounds. Helps seal the edges."

"This what they teach you in nursing school?"

"My mother. She brought some seeds over from Germany, these and lots of others. She always had a kitchen garden with different herbs—I don't know everything she knew. I wish I did. It was her dream to be a nurse. When I was born, it became her dream for me."

Eve wanted to ask if that was Lena's dream for herself, but her mouth felt done talking. Lena put the cup up to her lips every few minutes. In between times, Eve felt herself drift along in the place before sleep.

"Be glad I didn't make you her tea for fevers. Made from sheep's dung." Lena helped Eve ease down on the bed and bunched the pillows under her head. "There. You rest now. When I come back, I'll soak a cloth in the rest of the tea and wash your head again."

"Come back from where?" Now Eve opened her eyes and turned her head. Lena had her back to her; she was fetching her coat.

"My brother's funeral," Lena said.

According to Lena's pocket watch it was just after two o'clock. The funeral was at three. Should she have worn more black? She was still wearing her old brown dress—it was the only thing she had with her—but at least she'd washed out the lace collar last night. She supposed she might have gone home and changed first, but now there wasn't time.

To make up for it, she stopped at a drugstore to buy a black ribbon for her hat. Then she walked for several blocks just trying to get warm. At last a streetcar came along and she waved it down, choosing a seat in the back. Nobody looked at her. The color of the sky made her think that night was coming early, and she hoped Eve would have a good, long sleep.

She didn't want to think about Rudy.

She stared out the streetcar window, the snow only partially scraped off of it. Outside the tree branches were like stiff brown ropes, and she thought of how her father kept a piece of string tied around his wrist to re-mind himself to breathe deeply. It's not uncommon, she told herself, to lose three people in your family in such a short space. Not uncommon at all. But the thought did not help her. Her throat constricted, and she pushed her fingers into the cloth of her purse, trying not to cry. Now that she wasn't paying such close attention to Eve, she had all the time to think about her parents and her brother. And herself now, alone.

At the church a few people were gathered in the front pews: her Aunt Clem and Uncle Mortie, a couple of neighbors, Rudy's friend Pin. Aunt Clem took her arm as she stepped into the pew beside her and looked like she might say something, then apparently changed her mind and just kissed Lena on the cheek. The minis-ter was already speaking. Lena hadn't gone to see her aunt in days; that was wrong of her, but she couldn't help it.

Outside the high windows the sky lightened and darkened as though it couldn't make up its mind which way to go, and the feeling of church settled around her like a shawl. After the minister finished, the organ started up with slow heavy tones and everyone stood. A man across from her drew her attention, a short thin man she didn't recognize, maybe someone who worked at the station with Rudy? When it was time to view the body, the man stood up with the rest, his hat in his two hands respectfully.

Afterward Lena couldn't remember standing or walk-ing down the aisle to the casket. She looked at Rudy's soft, waxen face framed by a yellow pillow. His hair was parted on the left, that was wrong, but she saw it was done to try to hide the bullet wound along his right temple. And he was dressed in his horrible uniform— that was one thing Lena was glad she'd never see again. When she wore the uniform that night, she'd been thinking maybe this was the start of a new life for her— a new Lena, forward-thinking, modern. All that was over.

Three days now. The last time she'd been in this church Rudy had been with her. A week ago he'd sent her a note asking what was she doing on Saturday.

Her heart felt heavy and full, like it was made from wet paper. Well, here she was. She hadn't been able to keep it from coming. Slowly she walked out of the dark church back into the wind thinking it didn't matter if she'd been in her own rooming house or with her aunt or with Eve—she hadn't been able to stop it from coming. This heavy feeling, not of loneliness, but of being alone.

It wasn't fair. No matter what Rudy did, what price he tried to set, even if he'd tried to cheat someone, this wasn't fair. He didn't deserve this, and neither did she.

Her aunt had some food laid out back home in her parlor, but on the sidewalk Lena took hold of Pin's arm as he started to walk off. "Drive me home?"

"I was thinking of stopping somewhere for supper," he told her.

It was only just after four o'clock.

"That's fine," she said. "I'm starving."

He was wearing a black armband on his gray suit and seemed paler and thinner, if that was possible. He looked at her as if he wanted to shake all this off him as fast as he could, and his long thin lips tightened. But how could he say no? Briefly, she spoke to her aunt and uncle, made up some lie.

He led her to his car, a Morris, parked around the block. In front of it a bunch of kids were playing like they were a band with homemade instruments—a cigar box guitar strung with wire, a straw suitcase serving as a drum, and an inverted butter tub with a broom handle nailed to it and some waxed wire stretched taut for plucking. A few children without instruments stood behind the others and clapped out the beat. Pin put a nickel in their overturned hat. Music was everywhere in this town. Lena didn't know if she had noticed this before or was just noticing it now.

"I know a place with great pie," he said, "but terrible coffee."

"I'm a tea drinker anyway," she told him.

For a moment she looked at the biscuity clouds through the window, and then Pin started up the car and pulled away. She glanced at his profile. It wasn't as though she still had ideas about him; those had died long ago. She'd met Pin during the war, when her friend Violet Nilles and Violet's mother hosted a servicemen's club, which meant that two Sundays a month they entertained the servicemen who were stationed in the area. Lena helped on most Sundays, and one Sunday she met Pin. Violet she'd met in nursing school. They had an instructor who used to go to the school cafeteria each day and say to the girls, "Let's see how much sugar we can save today for the children in Belgium."

Pin wasn't a parlor snake, like a lot of the other servicemen they met; he had a polite smile and Lena always felt he really listened to her when she spoke. But it was Violet he wrote letters to after he was shipped overseas. Well, Lena could imagine how he saw her: a tall, broad girl with a pleasant smile and a limp. Violet had a sweet heart-shaped face and a quick sense of humor.

When Pin came back to Chicago, he was thinner but otherwise seemed just the same. One day he came to visit Violet and Lena at the nursing school—their last year—and they went out on the green with him to hear him play his ukulele. By now Violet wore an engagement ring given to her by Robbie Thomas, who was out in Oregon surveying for the railroad. Pin played "My Mother's an Apple Baker," Lena remembered. This was after the influenza started to appear in the city; Pin would contract it but live. Afterward he formed a dancing club in town that he called the Fortnightly, and Lena got Rudy to join it, thinking it would do him good.

And that was how Pin and Rudy became friends. They shared the same feelings about many things—especially the war. They complained about President Wilson, and when Harding became president they complained about him. There was an attitude they shared—Lena tried to put her finger on it. An air of rebellion that was sometimes forced. Whenever anyone asked Pin what he had been during the war, he would just say mockingly, "Something for someone to shoot." But today Pin didn't look rebellious; he looked grim.

He parked in front of a corner restaurant, and inside he motioned Lena to one of the tables by the front windows while he went to make a phone call. From where she sat, Lena could see a heavy ironwork bridge holding up the elevated train tracks. She hated walking under those—they always made her nervous, maybe because of her leg. Usually she crossed the street to avoid them. Pin was still talking on the phone at the counter with his back to her. She moved to the other side of the table where she couldn't see the bridge.

"All right?" he asked, coming back.

She wasn't sure if he meant about Rudy or the table. After the waitress took their order, Pin started talking about the singer he and Marjorie had gone to see Saturday night, Carol Tanner.

"A real sapphire," he said, fiddling with his napkin. "A hard woman. Have to be, I guess, to make it in the club scene. But her voice . . . I don't believe she breathed for a whole stanza. Even Marjorie stopped talking to listen. The bandleader, he was amazing, too." He named someone famous, a trumpet player from New Orleans. "Before each number he'd beat his foot against a brass cuspidor to set the tempo. Every once in a while he'd spit into it right on the beat. Everyone was dancing. The way some couples clung to each other . . . well!"

A train rattled by noisily over the bridge.

"It's all changing," he said. "It's the war that did it. Everyone is mixing together."

Lena hesitated, and then she said, "Do you know who Rudy was going to meet that night after you left?"

Pin shook his head. "No. Someone about some business, he just said."

"What *was* Rudy's business?"

"You know, his job at the train station."

"What was his other business?" She stated it as a fact, as though she knew something about it.

"Oh that, well, that was just a little thing he had on the side. Most of the fellows at the station do that now and again."

"He received a note when we were all at the Oaks together. From someone named N.C."

Pin turned his head and gave her a long, steady look. It was that same look from before the war, as though he was really listening to her, thinking about what she said, turning it over in his mind.

"N.C.? That would probably be Nathan Cobb. The owner of the Oaks."

Lena looked at him and waited. Pin turned as if checking on their food, which was nowhere in sight. "Well, he had a little business with some of the club owners, like Nathan Cobb. He sold them corn sugar, which they used to make liquor."

Lena thought back. "I remember he said the club kept their own stills."

"That's right, down in the basement. Guess they have some sort of deal—some arrangement—with the police about it."

"But how did he get it? The corn sugar."

"Has a partner outside of Chicago. Partner buys it from the farmers. Ships it up to Rudy at the station."

"Do you know who the partner is?"

For a moment Pin didn't answer. Then he said, as though it were nothing, "Colored fellow named Saint.

That's what Rudy called him, at least. Dressed nice, I take it, like every day was Sunday."

"Rudy had a colored fellow as his partner?"

"They met up during the war. Like I said, everyone is mixing together."

Lena thought about riding the streetcar with Eve, how the conductor made her stand up, and about the way Lester Glide and Porely wouldn't look at her, at Lena, at their club. Not everyone is mixing, she thought. Pin examined his fork and rubbed it with his napkin. Maybe he was trying to make up his mind about something. To Lena he seemed frail, like her brother. Their food came, and for a while they ate silently, staring down at their plates.

"I don't know if you knew this," Pin said after a while, "but Rudy had a hard time in the war because his mother—your mother—was German. He told me that the officers didn't really trust him, though sometimes if some captured German came in they would ask Rudy to translate. The regular soldiers were worse, always playing tricks on him, sewing his pant legs together, that sort of thing. He didn't see too much actual combat—they kept him busy doing little useless chores around camp. Not trusting him to go out with a gun. I think it was humiliating for him, though a guy like me can only envy someone who missed out on the trenches."

He told her how Rudy met this man Saint when Saint's brass jazz band came playing for the soldiers. Rudy—lonely, isolated, bitter because of all the tricks and distrust—fell in love with the music. He used to visit Saint in the entertainers' tent sometimes after a show, and they'd play together. Saint even showed him a few tricks on the horn.

"They formed a friendship, I guess," Pin said. "Both feeling left out. Both wanting to fight instead of pussy-footing around. Got to talking to each other like friends. At some point they hatched this plan about what they'd do after the war. Saw the advantage of how they were placed—Rudy working at the train station, Saint being a traveling musician."

"My mother and I were so glad he had that railway job to go back to," Lena said.

"Of course, they didn't know then what they'd be transporting. Maybe they didn't even really mean it— maybe they were just passing the time thinking up schemes. But then when Prohibition started up, I guess Rudy contacted Saint. Corn sugar itself is perfectly legal, you know. Just what folks do with it isn't."

They had finished their food, and now Pin was smoking. "A good scheme," he commented, exhaling a thin stream of smoke.

For a while they said nothing. Pin looked out the window. Lena didn't know what to think of all this.

"Ever smell mustard gas?" Pin asked after a while, stubbing out his cigarette. "Smells like rotten hay. If they throw it at you when it's raining, even just a little sprinkling rain, and you're wet, it burns all over your skin. Of course, whenever it rained they'd throw as much as they could."

He took a sip of coffee and then replaced it carefully on the saucer. Lena thought: he should be married. He needs someone to talk to. Violet had married her surveyor and moved out to Oregon, but Lena knew plenty of other girls who would like to look after someone as handsome as Pin.

"Ironic that your brother and his partner both felt left out. What brought them together probably saved both their hides."

"You're all right, though," Lena told him, not sure if he was.

Pin looked at her. He smiled faintly, revealing a line of small, even teeth, one of them chipped. "Just barely," he said.

13

WHEN EVE WOKE, THE SUN was just setting, and she found herself alone for the first time since her accident. She didn't mind. But then a knock sounded on the door, and Mrs. Tribble came in carrying a tray with a cup of beef broth and a ham sandwich on bread with the crusts cut off. Folded up next to the plate was yesterday's Chicago *Defender*.

"Bless you," Eve said, with feeling. As soon as she saw the tray, she realized she was famished.

"Don't want you having an attack when I'm out," Mrs. Tribble said, "and I noticed your nurse friend is gone. I'm off to the pictures."

She brought with her a slightly scorched smell, like she'd just been ironing. She took some time arranging things: pulling the piano bench into Eve's room, setting the tray down on the bench, and moving the one straight-backed chair up next to it. After Eve got settled on the chair, Mrs. Tribble arranged a knitted blanket across Eve's lap.

"There's four dollars for you over on the dresser," Eve told her.

"You're looking all right," Mrs. Tribble said, "you're healing up all right, aren't you. Just leave the tray on the bench there when you're done with it."

It was pleasant eating supper and looking out onto the street. People were beginning to gather for that night's entertainment, some girl shouting out to someone else to wait up. While she ate, Eve read a piece in the paper about more strike threats. The ham sandwich tasted good, a little chow-chow spread on the bread as relish. Off in the distance a train whistle sounded and she looked at her watch. The train from Pittsburgh should be just about in—the train she and Chickie rode on when they had first arrived. About this time of day, too. She thought: maybe I can write a song about that? Her notebook was on the dresser and she found a stub of a pencil in her handbag. When she sat back down and turned to a clean page, she stared at it, willing something to come. She was trying not to think about Chickie.

Starting out, let's have a two-bar walking bass, she decided.

Outside more girls shouted, and she could hear a car honking in A-flat. She wrote down the first two bars and waited. Nothing more came. She thought about some new songs that Henry's band played, got up and looked at a score hoping for inspiration, then sat back down and thought about rhythm. Still nothing. She tried to push thoughts about Chickie away, but in her heart she was feeling cold and fearful again, and fear never inspired music, not for her. She looked at the notebook in her lap. After a minute or two she erased a note, changed an A to a D, then made a notation in the margin. Technical stuff. She couldn't find her way into the song.

For a moment the street was quiet. Then a door slammed and Eve heard a window open followed by the scratchy sound of a phonograph in the middle of playing out—what was it?—it sounded like James P. Johnson. Yes, that was it, "Harlem Strut." Eve closed her notebook and listened. She liked how wandering the tune was, how it followed its own surprising logic. The father of stride, that's what they called Johnson, bridging the gap between ragtime and jazz. She used to play this very song when she worked for that cook back in Pittsburgh when she was a girl. Chickie had a job helping a wigmaker for two dollars a week. They were saving their money to come here.

After the record was over, Eve drank the last of her beef broth, now cold. If she were back at the club, she'd be getting the meal they kept for musicians, not quite as good as the supper they served to the guests but still good. Part of her pay.

That's when Eve realized how Chickie might be feeding herself: she was eating at the club. It was the only place where, if she timed it right, no one she knew would see her eat. No one would think to ask the cook.

And the cook fed so many musicians he couldn't remember who was singing or playing when, who was off, who was gone. That's where Chickie was, Eve told herself. At the club.

She heard footsteps in the hallway, a soft knock, and then Lena stepped in still wearing her coat, wet snow on her shoulders.

"You're awake," Lena said with a smile.

Either Chickie's at the club, Eve thought, or she's dead.

14

THE WIND HAD TAKEN SOME man's old felt hat and was playing with it out in back of the Oaks Club. Chickie watched it from the club's basement window, her eyes just above ground level. The hat skittered over the snowy ground, got caught by a branch sticking out of the snow or some grass, and then the wind blew harder and pushed the hat off the branch, moving it along.

She sat back down on the bed and counted the money again, over three hundred dollars. She was in the room next to the boiler room in the club basement, the bed pushed up against the wall where it was as warm as a heater. This room used to be an extra dressing room back when the theater did vaudeville and there were more people going on and off the stage. Now it smelled like wet dog. Probably I do, too, Chickie thought. She hadn't had a bath of any kind in four days.

It was after two now and she was about to miss another rehearsal. Wasn't singing. Wasn't making money. When would Nathan come? This was the room where they used to meet, and even back then she wondered if he put the bed in for her or for someone else before her. Once she thought she heard his voice, but when she peeked out, no one was there. She had a deck of cards and a half-pound bag of boiled-sugar candy, and she waited for a knock on the door. Her back was beginning to hurt a little; there was only one hard chair and the bed. An old mirror ran against the opposite wall with a slanted, unpainted shelf underneath it for makeup, brushes, those good-luck cards actors gave one another. Pipes coming out of the ceiling.

Didn't make sense to be stuck here. Evie would be worried. One thing: Chickie made sure Eve was all right before she left; the nurse said so. That was one thing. But Henry would have known Chickie was gone when she didn't turn up yesterday at rehearsal or the show. She should have at least gone to rehearsal.

When would Travis get back with Cobb? All yesterday, Monday, she had waited for Cobb in his office with the letter she'd found in Eve's purse in her hand. He hated being interrupted during his Monday auditions so she just waited, but he left the club without going back to his office. It was Travis who found her sitting by the door. He looked frightened when he read the letter, and then something else, maybe sly? He pocketed the letter, saying he would "pass it on to Mr. Cobb," and told her to wait down here in this room. Maybe she shouldn't have trusted him. Eighteen hours ago that was. She was bored.

Travis said, "You wait down there and don't come out." He said it like she was in danger, which scared her at first into staying. She brought her meal down here and then slept the longest sleep she'd had for weeks. That felt good. A little vacation. When she woke up, she didn't feel the urgency of last night, Travis's urgency, but she played cards for a while thinking why not. Now she was too bored to be scared.

The furnace knocked into action again on the other side of the wall. Chickie slipped on her coat, the seal-gray one lined with fake fur that Cobb had given her before they parted. Took a moment to stand in front of the mirror putting on lipstick, and then she examined the half of herself she could see. Her dress, especially with the coat over it, concealed the ball of her belly. If you knew how slim she'd been as a girl, you might guess she was pregnant; otherwise she just looked like any other large nightclub singer, a woman who liked her fried chicken and pie maybe a little too often.

Upstairs the first thing she did was stop at Nathan's office. Either Travis told Nathan and Nathan wouldn't come, or Travis hadn't told Nathan at all, and that would be because—because why? Even before she tried the door, Chickie could tell the office was empty, and the door was locked anyway. Well, at least there's no Travis there either, Chickie thought.

The money was folded up in her handbag, and her handbag was dangling from her wrist by a thin metal chain. She saved out two twenty-dollar bills and tucked them into the bra of her dress girdle. She felt fine. Out on the sidewalk she adjusted her hat. How good to smell the fresh, cold air again.

She was thinking, why not get Evie a dress for when she's better, a little surprise? And while she was at it she'd get herself one, too. A slim, slithery dress, short like they were wearing them now, for when she got her figure back.

Just a dress or two; then she would go back to Evie's place and give her the rest. She'd taken the money along with the note because she couldn't resist, but she always planned to give it back unless Nathan said something, needed something. At the time she didn't have a definite plan, only the thought: here's an opportunity. Well, that opportunity came to nothing. Nathan wasn't coming and Travis had abandoned her, too.

Chickie walked carefully down the street, avoiding patches of ice. Her feet were cold, and she was wearing high heels. People glanced at her face as she passed them. She was a good-looking woman. Back in Pittsburgh there was a family Chickie was friendly with, the Dixon family, fourteen children and as poor as hand-me-down shoes. Billie Ann and Clay, they were the ones her age. Billie Ann was about as beautiful as they came. She and Clay used to follow the train tracks picking up dropped nuggets of coal to use in their stove. Sometimes Chickie would go along with them and help. Just the tiniest little nuggets scattered down the track. Billie Ann picked up every one.

Chickie grew up poor, too, but not as poor as Billie Ann and Clay. She and Evie put beef tallow on their dry hands instead of hand cream, and if their throats were sore, they just got hot tea and a dirty stocking to wrap around their necks. Her brother Kid used to smoke rolled-up corn silk with the other boys, pretending they were cigars, and their best toy was an old piano box they kept in the side yard until the rain finally melted the cardboard away.

She didn't want to go back to that. She wanted to stay here, get herself famous, have her store-bought dresses delivered. After she bought a few things, she would go to Evie's room and see how she was doing, and then give her the presents and the money. Enough of Nathan. She'd had enough. Even as she had the thought, she knew she was lying to herself.

At Ingie's, Chickie looked at quite a few dresses before she came upon a nice yellow chiffon taffeta, which would look beautiful against Evie's dark skin. A pale moiré ribbon running through the neckline. Next door, she found some tiny-heeled shoes that would go nicely with the dress, only fifteen dollars. She squeezed them on, but her feet had widened in the last few months. Usually she and Eve wore the same size shoe, though Chickie was taller. A man with an old-fashioned waxed moustache wrapped the shoes up in tissue and then drew her attention to a line of hats.

One had a long feather, like an aigrette but cheaper. "Neargrette," he called it. He told her monkey fur was quickly replacing ostrich, and Chickie said, "Is that so?" and took the hat with the feather.

Outside the sun began to shine, making the street snow sparkle. She went into a department store next and bought some buttons and braid, the girl at the counter wrapping them up for her while Chickie examined their necklaces. She played a game: she would choose one without even checking the price, whatever one she most fancied. Turned out to be a long stage necklace with green paste beads and it cost her two dollars, which she thought wasn't so bad.

Back on the sidewalk Chickie had to stop a moment to rearrange all her packages. Nearby a man stood behind an overturned crate shouting, "Repairs, any repairs?" and two trucks waited for another man to lead a horse by its halter off the street. As she turned to go, Chickie noticed a tall stick of a man wearing a low fisherman's cap who was leaning against a greengrocer's window. He seemed to be watching her. He was under a heavy brown awning, in shadow, so it was hard to see his eyes.

Chickie's heart started to beat faster. She walked quickly in the opposite direction, and she didn't think he followed. Now I've done too much, she thought. But as she passed a store advertising caps and furs and hats, she thought: wouldn't I just like a fur stole!

As she turned, she looked down the street from the corner of her eye. No sign of the man in the fisherman's cap. Just to be sure, though, she stayed in the store an extra long time, trying on this fur and that. The clerk, who kindly kept her packages for her behind the counter, was a small white man with long sideburns. He showed her his most expensive line and called her ma'am.

But the man in the fisherman's cap was there again when she left the fur shop, this time with a friend in a mustard-and-brown checkered suit. The first man was leaning against the fireplug when she came out, and he nodded to his friend. Chickie's heart beat harder and she turned to go back into the store, but in a minute they were on either side of her, one on each arm, and they steered her into the alley.

Before she could shout, one of them covered her mouth with a gloved hand. Chickie tried to bite him, tasting the tang of leather on her tongue.

"My glory," he said, pulling his hand away. Laughed meanly. "What do you think you can do?" He smelled strongly of applejack whiskey and looked like he hadn't shaved or bathed in a week.

The other one pulled out a knife. "We saw you doin' some shopping," he said with the blade held up right to her eyes.

"Don't you hurt me. I have a powerful boyfriend," she said.

"Is that so."

"A white man, one with money."

"Oh really, a white man," the one with the knife laughed. "And how do you propose he find us?" He pulled the purse from her wrist, breaking the chain. Pulled out the envelope with the money.

"Stop! That's mine!"

"Now don't throw your bonnet over the moon, you know it's not yours. And the man wants it back."

"Stop!" Chickie screamed and tried to pull the purse back.

"She's a tiger, Lenny," the knife man said.

"I like tigers," said Lenny. He pulled back his arm and hit her in the eye.

Chickie gasped, then started to sob. Her eye felt like it had burst into flame. She reached blindly for the purse. "Give it here!"

Lenny hit her some more while his friend counted the bills. A couple of trash bins blocked the view from the street, and an old cuspidor was pushed up against the alley wall, its bottom stained yellow and brown. The man with the knife tucked the money into his pants.

Chickie's head throbbed and she thought of Eve. "Don't! Give it back!"

"You're making too much noise—now don't make me cut you," he said, coming up close.

"Stop!" she screamed again, hoping someone would come into the alley. But who would help her against two white men, one of them with a knife?

The man brought the blade up to her face. "Shut it up," he said. "Where's the letter?"

"I don't have a letter." That was true, but still he moved the knife closer. "You can look in my purse—I don't have anything like that!" Chickie said.

"But you know what I'm talking about, dontcha?"

Chickie smothered her cry, but the man brought the knife down on her anyway, a thin scrape along her jaw line but enough to draw blood. Chickie clapped her hand to her face.

"Wouldn't touch it with that dirty hand," Lenny said without looking up. "Liable to get an infection of the blood."

His friend still held the knife to her face. His breath was bad. She could see her own red blood on the knife-point.

"We're gonna take your packages now," he said. "And you don't say a word."

Chickie whimpered. Her jaw stung. The knife was still touching her cheek.

"Go on back to your powerful boyfriend," Lenny said with a smirk. He hitched up his pants. It was late, after five, the sunlight hitting low on the bricks of the building. "Here," he said suddenly and threw her the package from the department store, the buttons and the braid. She was wearing the necklace. "Whaddya say. Something to remember me by."

He turned to leave, but the one with the knife stayed to look her over. Chickie's nose was running and her face streamed with tears. She tried to quiet herself; she didn't like the look in his eyes. No one could see him. He could do anything. No one came into the alley.

Lenny slipped past the trash bins and disappeared while his friend stood deciding what to do. Now Chickie held her breath. The man took a few steps toward her until he was close enough to kiss. He held the knife up dramatically so she could get a good look at it. Then he turned it sideways and wiped the blade clean on the front of her dress. Chickie put a hand over her belly. He smiled again and she thought he was done. But suddenly he plunged the knife quickly into the flesh of her forearm then out again, like he was a post office official quickly stamping some document.

Chickie gasped and reached out to cover the wound, and then she changed her mind and covered her belly again with both hands.

"Don't you say a word to no one," the man told her. "You don't want anything to happen to yourself or to that little bitty baby you got cookin' in there."

Her legs were shaking; she couldn't control them. When he was gone she just sat right down in the alley where she was. Her right shoulder rested against the old cuspidor, and after a moment or two Chickie gingerly felt her left arm, the one he had cut. She parted the wet, torn sleeve of her dress to get a better look. It wasn't as deep as she had thought. For a second she thought she might spit up. Then she put her two hands on the cuspidor and pulled herself up.

Her arm ached. Her purse with its broken chain was lying open on the ground. Breathing hard, she found her handkerchief and wrapped it around the wound. After that she held her arm close to her body to keep the handkerchief in place.

Gathering all that they hadn't taken—her purse, the department store package, the hat she'd been wearing but which fell at that first hard punch—she walked carefully out of the alley. She had the thought that someone might see she was pregnant and hurt, but no one did, or at least no one came up to her. Her face was bloody and swelling up; she could feel it rise like a bee sting.

No one looked at her.

Chickie thought of her mother drinking and falling down, always a cut on her somewhere. She was not one to hold back when it came to slapping a child, but at least she was tender when you got hurt on your own. Rubbing wood ash on Chickie's blisters, or if she got stung. In her mind's eye Chickie could see her mother's hands so clearly. She'd like to feel them on her now. After a block and a half she spied a scrawny little man with an old milk cart making deliveries—a rag man, it looked like, carrying his supper in a tin tobacco box. She said, "Please." She had to clear her throat.

"Please," she said again.

He looked at her, taking his time. She was glad she couldn't see her face herself.

"Your man caught you out?" he asked. He had three or four teeth missing, and the rest appeared only loosely held.

Chickie nodded. It was as good an excuse as another. "Can I have a ride?"

"Two dimes," he said.

She looked in her purse. One of her eyes was swollen almost shut.

"Or your hat."

She gave him her hat.

The horse moved slowly and unevenly like maybe it had one leg shorter than the rest. Every bounce seemed to go straight to her head. It took forever. The sun was gone now and the snow looked gray and old. Some of the store owners were wiping down shingles with rags. About a block from the Oaks Club, Chickie tapped on the man's shoulder and he slowed the horse not quite to a stop. When she realized this was the best he would do, she made herself jump. Her one foot slipped on the ice and she put out her left arm to catch herself against the snow bank. The sudden pain was intense.

Now someone will help me, Chickie thought, but no one did.

She went around to the back entrance of the club, where the kitchen was. The cook had his back to her, but the boy drying glasses stared at her face without stopping the circular motion of his dishrag. She thought, if I can just wash myself. She went down the back stairs into the basement, where—besides the boiler room and the room for the stills and the old dressing room where she used to meet Cobb—there was a storage closet with a toilet and sink.

The hall lights were out; Chickie felt along with her fingers until she found the round wall switch and she twisted it. Then she made a noise and jumped back, forgetting her face, her arm, the pain in her back, everything.

There, in the hall, slumped against the boiler room door, was a dead body.

15

W<small>HEN</small> E<small>VE</small> <small>AND</small> L<small>ENA</small> <small>GOT</small> to the Oaks Club that evening, they found Chickie sitting on the basement stairs
with her head against the wall and one hand on her belly. Eve felt a rush of tears come into her eyes when she
saw her. Only as she shook Chickie awake did Eve take
in the state of her face. Then she turned and saw the
dead body on the floor of the hallway.

Lena put her hand to her mouth.

"What?" Chickie said, trying to open her eyes.
"What?"

It took them a while to wake her up fully.

"What happened to you?" Eve asked. "Who is that?"

The light was dim and the body's face was turned
the other away. Blood had pooled beneath the man's

head, Eve could see that much. On the floor beside him lay a stiff gray hat upside down, as if set there for tips.

Chickie looked bad, her face beat up and dirt all down one side of it. Eve felt something sour and hard in her throat. "Who did this to you?"

"I don't know. Two men. I never saw them before." She kept her hand on her belly.

Lena went into the storeroom closet, where there was a sink and some rags, trying to find something clean with which to wash Chickie's face. Upstairs Eve could hear music going. *Tuttela tuttela tuttela pow,* the trumpet blew out. "Twelfth Street Rag."

She held Chickie's two hands while Lena wiped her face. Rehearsal was running late tonight and the music drifted down through the floorboards. A horn started off with some back phrasing, a jerky mess of notes that somehow worked, like a man pushing a cart with uneven wheels. Then the trombone came in, trying to tell the man how to do it.

The stairs were uncarpeted and hard, and even though Eve kept her face turned away from the body, it was still there at the edge of her sight line. When the song finished playing, she went upstairs and came back down a few minutes later with Henry.

Without a word Henry went over to the corpse and looked at it. Chickie was more awake now, and Eve spoke to her in a low voice while watching Henry. He didn't touch anything. The body lay on its side in front of the boiler room door and rivulets of blood had run along in the dark floor cracks. The dead man's hair was caked with blood, and his cheap, celluloid collar had come undone and stood raised on one end like a tiny tombstone.

"Travis Pitts," Henry said, coming back to them. "Shot in the neck."

"The Travis who does errands for Cobb?" Eve asked. "Plays cornet?"

"That's the one."

Lena was wiping Chickie's face with the wet cloth. At each touch, Chickie winced. Henry watched, his face guarded, maybe scared. There was a smell of chicken and gravy coming from upstairs.

"My back hurts something bad," Chickie said.

"Your back?" Lena drew the washcloth away. She and Eve glanced at each other.

"When did that start?" Eve asked.

"I didn't notice it with everything else. Maybe I hurt it in the alley. I sat down but sort of fell when I did it."

Her eyes were wide and vacant as though they looked and looked but still could understand nothing. She was in shock and maybe, Eve thought now, in the beginnings of labor. "The alley? What alley?"

"I'm sorry, Evie—I took your money, I only meant to keep it safe. I thought I'd buy you a present with it. But some men saw me shopping and took me into an alley and beat me up and took all the money back."

"What do you mean, took it *back*?"

"No, I mean—" She put her hands on her belly. "I just meant they took the money."

Eve looked at her. "You still have the note that went with that money?"

"Well . . ." Chickie looked away and closed her mouth.

"You need to tell me now," Eve said.

"I gave it to him." Her head jerked toward the boiler room door. "To Travis."

"Why?"

"So he could give it to Nathan Cobb."

"Nathan Cobb? Why give it to him?" Henry asked.

When she read the note, Chickie told them, the idea came to her that Nathan would want to see it. Nathan had business with Rudy. He liked to know what Rudy was up to. She thought she might just get on Nathan's good side if, on her own, she delivered this note to him. Nathan might be grateful.

"Why you calling him *Nathan?*" Eve asked her suspiciously.

It all came out. Nathan Cobb was the father of her child, though he had broken it off with Chickie almost six months earlier and didn't know about the baby. Chickie wanted—well, she didn't know what she wanted exactly, but she recognized the note and the money as some kind of opportunity. She was close to Cobb once; why couldn't they be close again? She thought he would feel grateful, maybe remember the other feelings he'd once had. She found herself having fantasies about the two of them back together, setting up house with a baby.

"I just wanted him to love me again," Chickie said.

Eve sighed. "Oh, Lovie."

Chickie explained that she had waited and waited but Nathan didn't come, so finally she gave Travis the letter. Travis promised he would see that Nathan read it.

"And now look at him," Chickie said, though she didn't look over herself.

"We need to get you away," Henry told her.

"You think that boy got killed because of the note?" Eve asked.

"The only people I can tell read that note was Chickie and Travis Pitts," Henry said. "And Travis Pitts is dead. I say let's not take our chances."

"Wait just a minute," Lena told him. She stood up, walked over to the boiler room door, and looked at the dead man. The sound of a saxophone drifted down through the ceiling—a big, full-throated sound like a hungry man diving into a meal.

"I've seen this man before," Lena said. "He was at my brother's funeral."

"When was that?" Henry asked.

"This afternoon." She turned to Chickie. "What did the note say?"

"I don't remember just exactly," Chickie told her in a tight voice. "Said someone's dead. Said there'll be no shipment on Saturday, or was it Sunday. And . . ."

"What?" Eve prompted.

"Well, it said something about loading up guns."

"Guns!"

Lena said, "But Rudy sells corn sugar, not guns. Sold," she corrected herself.

Chickie shrugged. "I don't know."

"Guns would be . . ." Lena stopped. "Well, it's not legal to sell guns, is it? You need permits and things. A license?" How did it work? "Rudy didn't have any of that."

Eve said, "Lena, honey."

"The corn sugar was legal," she insisted. "Pin told me. Rudy wouldn't do anything that wasn't legal. I know he wouldn't."

"Sometimes people get mixed up in things," Eve said gently. "One thing leads to another, you find yourself in a place you didn't expect. Kinda like where we are now."

"But guns!"

Henry turned to Chickie. "Do you remember anything else in that letter?"

"Just that at the end it said something about Shugs. Go see Shugs, or something."

Eve looked at her sharply. "Shugs Burroughs?"

Chickie shrugged. "I guess."

"Who's Shugs Burroughs?" Lena asked.

"A man who works around the clubs," Henry told her.

"Lord," Eve said, "I hope Shugs Burroughs doesn't take it in his mind to come after us. I just hope he does not."

Henry frowned. "I can talk to him."

The music finished with a flourish. Now they could hear some voices in the kitchen; it sounded like questions and answers. The floorboard above them creaked.

"Let's go up through the stage door," Henry said in a low voice. That was on the other side of the passage.

"But Evie—" Chickie began, and together Henry and Eve both said "Shh!"

"I want to see Nathan," Chickie complained in a lower voice.

"Well, I don't want him to see you," Eve told her.

16

MOST MIDWIVES LEARNED THEIR trade from relatives or apprenticed themselves to older midwives, but Miss Angeline Fletcher had received three months of training at the Northwestern Academy of Chicago and had a framed certificate hanging in her kitchen to prove it. It was said she birthed over two hundred babies a year and was the first person in her neighborhood to install a telephone.

All of Chicago south of the Midway knew Miss Angeline, which was unfortunate because by the time Eve and the others got there, Miss Angeline was already engaged with another laboring mother in her special rooms in the back of the house. The woman who answered the door gave Eve directions to Miss Viola Bay, another midwife but one without a certificate or a telephone.

"She said go through the side alley next to the butcher?" Henry asked at the corner. He looked up and down the dark street. "Which butcher do you suspect she meant?"

"We're not that far off from Mrs. Jenkins," Eve pointed out. "We can go right over to my room and have the baby there." She looked at Chickie, who was resting on the low brick wall in front of a house. "Chickie, you're getting grit on the back of your skirt."

"Are you having a birth pain?" Lena asked her.

Chickie said, "Or maybe it's indigestion."

It was crowded and windy on the sidewalk. People kept brushing by them in groups. A city at night with its dark, cold, quickening heart getting ready for anything. Motorcars honking just for the fun of it.

"We can't go to your room. Nathan Cobb—" Henry protested.

"How's he gonna know where I live? If he's even looking." Eve pulled Chickie up from the wall. "We don't need a midwife, we've got a real nurse right here. Now let's make a decision," she said.

"I've done it before," Lena told them. "I used to go out with a midwife during the war when I was in training, some of the back-of-the-yard houses north of here."

"Well, then," Eve said.

Mrs. Jenkins's house was tall and narrow with unpainted wooden shutters. Inside there was a strong smell of soap and, from the kitchen, horse fat for cooking. Eve owed Mrs. Jenkins for another week, although she had yet to sleep there one night.

"I did wonder where you went to," Mrs. Jenkins said to Eve in the hallway, looking her up and down. Then she eyed Chickie with her swollen face, her big belly. She shook her head back and forth. "Now who would do something like that to a pregnant lady? Who would do that?" she asked.

Chickie said nothing. She looked back at Lena as if she might know the answer, and that made Mrs. Jenkins look at Lena, too. Then she kept on looking.

A slight pause. "I don't want any trouble in my house," Mrs. Jenkins said.

"I'm a nurse," Lena explained. "A midwife. I'm here to help Chickie."

"Don't want the police knocking on my door looking to see why there's a white girl here."

"No one will knock on your door, Mrs. Jenkins," Eve said. "I promise."

Mrs. Jenkins cocked her head suspiciously. "Lucky the room's at the back of the house. But I might need a little extra this week." She looked at Chickie again. "I'm gonna get you something to put on your head, you poor thing, and also a nice glass of fresh milk."

"Thank you, Mrs. Jenkins," Chickie said.

Eve turned to Henry. "I think you ought to go on back to the club. Thank you, Henry. We can take it from here."

"I don't know," Henry said.

"Well, I do," Eve told him.

He frowned, rotating his hat in his hands with small, circular motions. His neat white shirt was streaked with a cobweb. He's a nice man, Eve thought. Man who cares about his people. Gavin would not have stayed with us one hot minute.

"They need you back at the club," she reminded him.

"They're covered. I already asked Marvin would he step in for me tonight."

She touched his arm. "We'll be just fine."

"Well . . ." Henry looked around again. He pulled out a handkerchief to touch his brow. "All right, I guess. Just send a boy if you need me. I'll be at the club until I hear from you, there or Leo's if it gets to be time for breakfast." He put his handkerchief back in his pocket and turned to Chickie. "Now you do what you're told, hear me? I need you back on stage as soon as you're able. You know everyone comes to my club just to hear you."

Chickie said, "That's nice of you, Henry."

"Let me walk out with you," Eve said.

She followed him to the door while Lena and Chickie went upstairs. In the hallway stood a tin bucket with rags soaking in borax and water, Eve could smell it. Mrs. Jenkins kept a clean house—that was good. And none of the other boarders seemed to be around—another good thing. Eve wanted to keep Chickie's birth as quiet as possible.

"She tell you why she got beat up?" Henry asked at the front door.

"I only know what you know—two men saw she was shopping, pulled her into an alley, took her money. Maybe Shugs would know what it's all about. Will you talk to him?"

He made a movement with his head: he was planning on it.

"Chickie was staying right there in the basement these last two days," she told him. "If she hadn't decided to go shopping, she might've been there when that boy was killed. Might have been killed herself."

Henry turned his hat around again in his hands. He nodded like that was in his mind, too.

"I'm worried someone's out looking for her. For her and for that note and the money."

"Seems like someone already got the money," Henry said. "Men who mugged her—maybe they were sent by someone."

"I thought of that myself." Eve frowned. "Chickie won't say much. Makes me think there's more to the story."

Henry paused, and then he said, "I don't know if this will help, but I heard something today about Nathan Cobb's partner, man with a scar down his face. Victor Rausch. You know him?"

Eve cocked her head. "Nathan Cobb has a partner?"

"With ties to the Sicilians, they say."

"Name Rausch sounds more German."

"I don't know exactly what's his connection." Now he put his hat on, angling it just a little. "But I know this: Cobb wants to take over Rudy Hardy's job. Wants to get in on selling that corn sugar off the train. Couple of other men looking to do the same."

Eve shook her head. "I don't want anything to do with it."

"Good," Henry said. "Listen, Evie. Stay away from Nathan Cobb. My advice if you'll take it."

Eve looked up at him. He was a handsome man, different than Gavin's kind of handsome, though, not so showy. His long shadowed eyes made him look sad but he spoke cheerfully, a combination she never realized could be so attractive.

"All I wanted was to find my sister," she said. "And I found her."

"Good," he said again.

"Believe me, this business has nothing to do with me."

"That's it."

"But something is going on here," Eve told him. She heard Mrs. Jenkins come out of the kitchen, her flat worn slippers slapping the floorboards. She lowered her voice. "And every time I try to get away from it, I find that I can't."

Before she did anything else, Lena washed her hands twice with brown soap, using water as hot as it would come. She was glad there was a sink right in the room instead of the new modern way, in the bathroom. After she washed up she bandaged Chickie's arm, and then she knelt on the floor and began unbuckling Chickie's shoes. Chickie was sitting on a straight-backed chair with uneven legs. Gently Lena lifted one foot out and then the other.

Chickie closed her eyes. "Oh, that does feel good."

Eve brought in some clean rags and towels that Mrs. Jenkins found for her, and the glass of milk. It was late now. Outside the window the moon was high and small against the black sky. The room was warm, Lena noticed, that was good. Also well lit. Although she sometimes helped deliver babies in the hospital where she worked, most women like Chickie still had them at home. But she knew that was changing for rich white women and even the middle class—the number she heard was one out of two now went into the hospital. But Lena had received most of her training during the war when women walked around their own bedroom instead of being confined to a high, narrow hospital cot. She felt comfortable being in a little room overseeing her patient, in this case Chickie, as long as it was warm and clean.

The real danger was childbed fever—puerperal fever, as they called it in the hospital. It was absolutely vital to keep everything clean. One doctor she knew used to wash his hands with a mixture of chlorine and water before he went into a lying-in room.

Lena took out a tube of lotion from her purse and looked over at Chickie. "You having a pain?"

".Just finished."

"Next one, take my hand and squeeze it."

She rolled down Chickie's left stocking and then squirted out a dollop of lotion and began rubbing it onto Chickie's foot. She was glad Eve suggested that she, Lena, might help with the birth. She didn't want to impose, but even at the midwife's house she thought to herself that she would stay as long as they let her. So much better to be doing something hard and good, like helping a baby come into the world. Rudy was far away but the idea of him could suddenly overwhelm her, and that's when the pain was the worst.

"I heard you sing, you know," she told Chickie. "Last Saturday night. To say you have a beautiful voice . . ."

She squeezed more lotion from the tube and started on Chickie's other foot. "There was one song where I kept thinking you'd never reach the next note, or the note after that, but you did. You reached every single one." She paused. "You have more power than you look."

"And you remember that," Eve said, coming over to them, "when that hard little baby skull starts pushing to come out." She and Chickie laughed.

Lena massaged Chickie's toes. "How do you do it? Sing like that."

Chickie put her hands on the hard sides of her belly. Then she said, "If you feel something, you sing it. And if you sing it truly, other people can feel it, too." She smiled a beautiful smile, even bruised and swollen as she was. She has the kind of face, Lena thought, that makes you want what she wants. Maybe that was part of her magic.

She leaned back on her heels. "There. In a couple of days you won't have the swelling."

"Oh, I don't mind," Chickie said, "long as I can still fit them into some nice-looking shoes." She opened her eyes. "Evie, I don't feel too good." She stood up unevenly, lurched forward, and vomited into the sink.

Lena exchanged a look with Eve as she took hold of Chickie's arm. "Sick is quick," she said, an old nursing adage, meaning if a woman is sick at the start she'll have a fast labor. She gave Chickie a cloth to wipe her mouth. "I'll rinse the sink. Eve, could you ask Mrs. Jenkins for some cleaning powder?" To Chickie she said, "Why don't you turn the chair around, sit on it backwards. Then you can lean forward on the back part."

"Like this?" Chickie tried it.

"That way you take the weight of the baby off your back."

Chickie tried to settle herself more comfortably. "You know what I want when this is over? Some Happiness Candy."

"What's that?" Lena asked, gathering rags to stuff around the window frame.

"Chocolate creams. Dutch. Sixty cents for the pound."

Eve came back with the cleaning powder and sprinkled some in the sink. Chickie said, "Here we go," and reached out for Lena's hand.

"Can you talk through it?" Lena asked her.

"Mm. But this one pinches."

An hour later the pains were so bad that Chickie had to stand up, then she had to squat against the wall, then she had to stand up again. Lena taught Eve how to squeeze Chickie's hips during a contraction. They were coming faster now, two minutes apart. One after another after another.

Chickie said, "I don't like this. I really don't like this."

She wasn't a screamer, but she moaned almost as loud. Lena spread out sheets and towels, and she turned on the electric fire as high as it would go. Was the sky getting lighter? The sounds of city life never seemed to stop—just as one group came home from the late shift, others left for the early one.

"When the baby comes out," Lena said, "we'll need a couple of dry warm towels. Then we'll put him right on Chickie's chest, to keep him warm. Or her."

"Oh, it's a him all right," Eve said. "All this trouble."

By now Chickie was streaming with sweat. Between pains her face was set, closed, like she was scrubbing down a table or squeezing out sheets. Working hard at her job. "I'm sorry I spent up all your money," she told Eve, coming down from a pain.

Eve stroked Chickie's neck with the wet rag. "That's right, you're always sorry later."

"I just wanted to buy you something nice."

"Oh, was that it?" Eve said. But she smiled.

Chickie put her hands on her knees and bowed her head. Then she asked Eve to help her stand up. Lena said, "You're doing so well."

"When's it gonna come out?"

"Do you feel like you want to push?"

"I want it out."

"Pay attention to Lena, now," Eve told her. "She asked you a question."

"I don't need to push. I want it out." All at once Chickie's face changed. "I need to push!" she gasped.

"All right, all right, that's fine," Lena said. "Let's get this baby out."

It seemed like five minutes but it was probably more like forty—Chickie not groaning so much as working hard and resting in the minute or two between pains. "Oh! Oh!" she kept saying, while Lena told her how good she was doing, how close they were.

"I see the head!" Eve said, and the next second Lena was able to get hold of the wet, slippery baby under the shoulders, and she pulled her out.

"You did it! A girl!" She quickly wrapped up the soaking baby in the clean towels. She was crying. "We have a baby girl!"

Eve fell back against the wall and Chickie fell back against Eve. Eve hugged her and didn't let go. "You did it," she kept saying. "You did it."

Lena put the baby on Chickie's chest.

"A little baby girl," she announced, laughing and crying too.

17

BESIDES BEING A PARTIAL OWNER of the Oaks Club, the Walnut owned two steam laundries staffed mostly by women and a small apartment building on the Near North Side. Nathan Cobb dropped into both laundries Wednesday morning looking for him without success, and afterward he sat in a diner opposite the Walnut's apartment building, where he had a good view of the door from his table window.

A woman came around offering fortunes. It was crowded in the diner; at first glance she seemed like a customer. The owner was also the cook and he tried to keep an eye on things through his rectangular cut-through window in the kitchen, but that wasn't always possible during the breakfast rush.

She stopped at Cobb's table and showed him a deck of cards, fanning them out. The waitress had already cleared his plate and he was down to a lukewarm cup of coffee. The cards were orange-colored, soft with use.

He picked one and gave it to her.

Her eyes barely glanced over it. "Your appearance is of great concern to you now," she said without preamble. "Your status in the world. Don't sacrifice your beliefs or your freedom for that. Keep alert to what is outside."

He waited but that appeared to be all. She was younger than he first thought; they always were. A gaunt, slit-eyed woman with high cheekbones and pale frizzy hair escaping its pins, flakes of white dandruff showing at the part. Cobb had never seen such high cheekbones on a woman. They looked like two thin ribs.

"Two bits," she said.

Three tables later the cook finally caught up with her and came into the dining room to wave her out with his spatula. His apron was spattered with grease and he wore a white cap pinned to his hair, and even from a distance Cobb thought he could smell the man's sour breath. For a moment everyone watched, and then it was over. Outside, the clouds cleared momentarily and a shaft of light hit the table like a pane of glass. Cobb pulled out a newspaper thinking to check the day's races.

Another fifteen minutes, he decided, and then he'd go to Saul's and ask around there. But instead of reading, Cobb found himself thinking about the first girl he'd ever loved, or thought he loved: a little colored girl named Mary Ann. Mary Ann had fine, high cheekbones, too, though not as sharp as the fortune teller's. Cobb had been six years old—old enough, his grandfather said, to know the difference between colored and white. When he caught his grandson giving a licorice whip to Mary Ann behind the courthouse, he gave him a beating Cobb never forgot. Only beating he ever gave him. Only time Cobb ever saw his grandfather lose control.

Later, when Cobb first got to Chicago, he liked to go to a certain club owned by a woman down near the stockyards. More of a basement room than a club, really, but the beer was cheap—this was before Prohibition— and the music was good. A few horns, a drum, a piano. Sometimes a singer. The owner, Mrs. Boyd, was plump with doughy hands, smaller than her own twelve-year-old son. She used to do her sewing right there in the front of the place, and when someone came in she'd get up and serve him beer and then go back to her sewing.

Chickie Riser came in there one night to sing, and Cobb fell for her in spite of himself—that voice, quavering and afraid like a young fine bird needing protection. But listen to it enough and you start to hear something strong underneath. A year or so later, when Henry James mentioned he was thinking of hiring Chickie as a regular singer, Cobb encouraged him. He still vividly remembered her first night. He went to welcome her in her dressing room; she was wearing a blue sateen robe. Regal looking. Never before had he welcomed anyone personally, but he didn't think to ask himself why. Probably should have.

Cobb looked at his watch, then pulled some money from his wallet and got up from the table. He was with

Chickie three months before he was able to pull himself off. Foolishness. Plain foolishness. He thought about her neck, her delicate collarbone. Her beautiful, smooth skin. He'd been a fool.

Outside he was just looking around for a taxicab when he saw the Walnut on the other side of the street, but it was too noisy to hail him. Cobb began threading his way across traffic as the Walnut went up the walk to his building.

"Mr. Rausch!" No one called him the Walnut to his face. Cobb noticed how straight he held himself, even when fitting a key into a lock. "Victor!"

At that, the Walnut looked around and saw Cobb. Hesitated, and then with a gloved hand he unlocked the door and held it open.

Cobb jogged up the stone walkway to the building. "Thank you," he said. Inside he exhaled and took off his hat. "I need to talk to you, Victor."

No expression on the Walnut's face. "I'm here to see that my third-floor tenants are all moved out."

"I'll come with you."

The Walnut made no comment but started up the staircase. Cobb followed him, resting his hand lightly on the polished handrail.

"Nice place."

The Walnut didn't answer.

"How long have you had it?"

The Walnut turned to go up the next flight. In profile his scar stood out like a jagged arrow pointing down to his nose. "This what you wanted to see me about?"

"Just making talk until we're someplace private."

"Don't bother," the Walnut said.

The tenants had indeed vacated the apartment, leaving it with an acrid smell not unlike that smell the cook had about him. First thing the Walnut did was wrestle open a window. Then he went to the kitchen to check on things there.

Cobb stood in the kitchen doorway. The Walnut was opening all the cupboard doors, looking inside, and keeping them open.

"I'm told you had a meeting with Rudy Hardy the day he died," Cobb began.

"That so?"

"You tell me."

"I mean, is that what someone said?"

Cobb ignored the sarcasm. "Is it true?"

The Walnut straightened up. He still wore his hat. "We're partners at the club," he said, "not anywhere else. I don't know that it's your business." He brushed past Cobb and went back into the apartment's main room.

"You had a shipment due in on Sunday, you told me that Monday," Cobb persisted. "It never came. What was it?"

The Walnut went over to the radiator. From somewhere—his coat pocket?—he had gotten hold of a wrench. "Didn't tell you about it Monday. Why should I tell you now?"

"It will help me find Rudy's partner."

"Oh? How is that?"

"I have connections at the train station." Not true.

"Still don't know how that helps."

"And things have changed."

"I don't see why."

Cobb was frustrated. "Mr. Rausch. Victor. I found a boy dead in the basement of my club last night. Shot through the neck. Travis Pitts."

That got the Walnut's attention; he turned and looked Cobb straight in the eye. "*My* club?"

Christ. "Our club, then." Cobb thought of the body stretched out by the door, dirt under his fingernails just like every other day of his life. "Cops there late at night asking questions; they came even before the ambulance."

"Which cops?"

"Sergeant Mike Komp was the one who spoke to me."

"I know Komp. You don't have to worry about Komp."

"Did you have Travis killed?"

It looked as if the Walnut wasn't going to answer. He bent over with a snort and started twisting the knob of the radiator again. Cobb waited.

"Do you know what folks are saying?" the Walnut asked finally, changing his hold on the wrench. "They're saying one of the club owners killed Rudy Hardy, annoyed at his high prices. There's some that say it was you." Now he smiled. "But we both know what happened to Hardy. Your man was a little too excited. Forgot to aim at the snow."

Cobb didn't know what to say.

"I did not kill Travis Pitts," the Walnut went on. He put his weight into the last turn of the wrench. "But I have to tell you, the man had a big mouth—he got paid by all sorts of people to tell them all sorts of things. Did you know that?"

Now Cobb was shocked. "My man Travis?"

"That's right, your man Travis. He even told me some things from time to time. Just yesterday he let me know where I might find some money that was owed me. Very useful, but as I say he had a big mouth. Too big. And now he's not here to back you up over Saturday night. I hope you have an alibi."

"I was—" Where had he been? Alone in his office checking the books. What he always did after a show. The Walnut knew this. At the time Cobb didn't think he'd need an alibi because Moaner was never supposed to kill Rudy, just scare him.

Suddenly he felt nervous. He tried to keep his voice stately. "You know people."

The Walnut said, "What do you mean?"

"Who could help with that." He lowered his voice. "You know who to pay."

The Walnut looked up sharply, and Cobb saw that he was still holding the wrench. "Who told you that?"

Cobb didn't mention Tack Annie. "Like Sergeant Komp," he said. "Listen, I'm your partner. I run a good business." He heard a pitiful tone in his words and tried to correct that. "And the profits will only get better."

The Walnut said nothing. Cobb thought of something his grandfather used to say: even your best friend will do you dirt. The Walnut was not his best friend, nor even, really, a friend. "I want to be more than the owner of a club," he said.

The Walnut took a last look at the apartment and then put the wrench back in his overcoat pocket. "Partial owner," he corrected.

Cobb put his hat back on. He was getting nowhere. But he would say what he came here to say anyway. It was his card and he would play it. "I'm on my way to see someone who knows Rudy's partner. Someone who can give me his name."

"About time."

"If I tell you that name, will you cut me in on your deal? The shipment you were waiting for Sunday night?"

The Walnut held the front door open so that Cobb could walk out before him.

"As I said, I got my money back on that one," the Walnut told him. Then he said, "Most of it."

But he seemed to be thinking as he descended the stairs. On the second floor a door opened. A heavy-faced woman looked out, saw the Walnut, and then closed the door again quickly. Cobb followed him down the staircase, noting his clean collar, his buffed shoes. A man who thought about details. Not well liked, maybe, but careful.

In the lobby the Walnut finally turned. "Tell you what," he said. "Get me the name and I'll see."

18

IT TOOK COBB ALL OF ten minutes to find out where
Eve Riser had rented a room.

Not a bad house, though like every other house on
this street it could use a coat of paint. There was a faint
smell of waste rising from the gutter and slushy snow
along the street. Some kids were playing Margy Margy
Marmalade on the sidewalk in front.

Cobb lifted his hat to them but they did nothing,
knowing they were being mocked. One—a little boy in
short pants, his brown knees thin and scuffed up—said,
"You got a motorcar, mister?" He held a cigar box in
one hand and an empty coffee can in the other, Cobb
didn't know what for. The boy's eyes reminded him of
Mannie Noble, his old trumpet teacher. Something
about their color or shape. The story Cobb told every-

one about learning how to play trumpet from two white swindlers on the boat was a lie—although he knew the swindlers and it was true that they taught him the basics. But his real learning came from an old colored man, Mannie Noble, who found him almost starving to death when he first got to Chicago and couldn't find a job. Living on pork-neck bones and potatoes in a room with no windows.

Mannie Noble. Now that was someone Cobb hadn't thought about in a while. At the front door he twisted the bell handle, and after a few minutes the door was opened by a short, stout woman in a checked housedress. She found out his business and then led him into the parlor. Her breath smelled of Sen-Sen. The parlor had panel doors that she pulled together to shut, and a sofa and some upright chairs and a table with a clean oilcloth cover and a hurricane lamp in the middle. Tall windows, wainscoting, a built-in cupboard with leaded glass doors on the far end of the room. A nice house. Once.

He himself rented two rooms in a house that advertised Hungarian home cooking—that meant boiled meat with sour cream most nights for supper—run by a dour Seventh-day Adventist named Mrs. Bazso. Cobb generally ate at the club with Travis, more often than not. Well, not anymore with Travis, he thought bitterly.

The house seemed unnaturally quiet. Cobb looked out the window, where a spindly tree on the front lawn was outlined in snow. So Travis had been feeding other people information; why should that surprise him? Blood always shows, and Travis came from piss-poor blood. Probably he told the Walnut about all of Cobb's plans on the sly. And who else? As he gazed out at the yard, a white balloon floated by, gradually making its way upward. He stood up to watch its progress, wondering about it—this wasn't the kind of neighborhood where balloons generally floated by. For a moment it hung in stark contrast against the blue sky, and then a current caught it and it blew out of sight.

He thought about the fortune he'd had that morning from the woman in the diner. If I was that sort, he thought, I might even think that balloon meant something. Though he couldn't imagine what.

A knock sounded, and then Eve Riser pulled the doors open and stood in their frame. Just her alone, standing there with a gritty expression.

"Mr. Cobb?" she said with a false surprise. She looked like maybe she'd been up all night, her dark hair hastily combed and pinned. Eyes a little bit glazed.

"I told that woman both of you."

"I'm sorry?" Same false voice.

"Tell Chickie I want to see her too," Cobb said.

"Well, Mr. Cobb, Chickie has her own room near the station," Eve told him.

"Tell her to come down. And bring the baby down, too."

Now real surprise showed on her face. "I don't—"

"Go on, tell her, I know she's up there." Though he did not. "You want a job, don't you? When you're through being *sick?*" Sarcastically. That was what Henry James had told him last night. "Now go on up and get Chickie," he told her.

While he waited, he pulled on his collar uncomfortably and found himself staring at the dovetailed corners of a wooden gramophone in the corner, which he hadn't noticed before. His stomach felt tight and strange. Too much of that coffee, he thought. But it's important to be decisive in a situation like this.

He could hear them coming down the stairs, so slow it was as if Chickie had just had the baby a minute ago. Eve had left the parlor doors open, and when the women came in, Eve holding Chickie's left arm, he was surprised to see a white woman holding Chickie's other arm.

"Who are you?" he demanded.

"Chickie's nurse," she said.

"Chickie's *nurse?*" These women clearly didn't know when to stop lying.

"Yes," the woman said evenly. She was tall with a broad, healthy face and looked like maybe she'd been up all night, too.

"What's your name?" Cobb asked.

"Excuse me?" she said, pointedly not answering.

But what did she expect, a polite how-d'ya-do for a woman who tends to the colored? If that was even true.

"Nathan!" Chickie cried warmly, her eyes shining. He took a step back. She'd come down in a loose yellow bathrobe and slippers, a small bundle in her arms that was much too small to be anything like a baby. What did she think he was here for?

"Let me see the child," he said.

Her face looked soft, forgiving. "Nathan—"

He came over and looked down at the bundle without touching it. "Christ, what are you feeding that thing? It looks malnourished."

"She's only a couple of hours old," Chickie said softly.

"A couple of hours?" He had never seen a baby so young. He was expecting the sort that sat on a woman's hip, all white flounces and fat little toes.

"A girl?"

Chickie nodded, looking down at the infant.

His stomach felt very uncomfortable. "Let me see her ears."

"What?"

"Her ears! Let me see them."

The baby was wearing a little white cap with long strings. Chickie moved toward Eve so that Eve could pull the cap away. The landlady was now standing beyond them in the hall, a little whisk broom in her hand like it could be used as a weapon.

He got a good look at the baby. Took in the shape of her ears, her head, everything wrinkled and waterlogged. Sparse light brown hair.

He said, "Not mine."

"What?" Chickie asked. The white girl, the nurse, cocked her head and fixed him with a look. Had he seen her somewhere before?

"Not mine," he said again. "That baby of yours. She's got a colored person's ears. You can always tell colored people by the shape of their ears." Something his grandfather told him.

"But Nathan—"

"Don't you try saying anything different or you'll find yourself in a world of trouble. I mean that."

"I have three white grandparents," Chickie said, her voice shaking a little. "She has the same."

"Not a white child. Not mine," Cobb said firmly. He wouldn't look at her. "And now that that's settled, you can go on back upstairs. Eve, you stay here."

"Nathan—" Chickie began.

"It's Mr. Cobb, remember that if you still want to sing in my club. Go on, you're a mess, go clean yourself up. Your face looks all banged up. And listen to me, I don't ever want to hear of this business again." He turned away, his stomach acting up fiercely. A man of business, he reminded himself. Just a man of business like his grandfather wanted him to be.

"You there," he called out to the landlady. "Get me a glass of water."

Behind him Chickie made a small sad noise, but what did she expect? He didn't turn around. When he heard the doors close, he saw Eve standing there look-ing at him, her lips pressed together in that way women had when they want you to know they are not speaking their mind. The landlady brought him the water, and he drank it and then sat down on the sofa.

A door closed somewhere. The white nurse, or who-ever she really was, had left with Chickie. Cobb didn't invite Eve to sit down.

"Now, Miss Eve Riser, you are going to help me out."

Eve crossed the room and sat on the chair near the gramophone. "Why is that, I wonder."

"Watch now how you talk to me," he said sharply.

Eve didn't flinch. "What is it you want, Mr. Cobb?"

Cobb stared at her. He lifted his chin. "I need the name of your boyfriend out on the circuit."

"You want to know who I was seeing on the circuit?"

"I don't care who you were seeing, I need the name of that man, and I happen to know you were seeing him. I can find out another way if you don't tell me. But if you tell me, you can keep your job playing piano at my club."

"You're gonna fire me if I don't give you a man's name?"

"You and your sister Chickie, both of you out of a job."

"You'd fire Chickie? After—" Eve let the sentence dangle.

"After what?" Cobb challenged.

Another knock at the parlor door. "You all right, Miss Eve?" Mrs. Jenkins called out. Eve started to answer but Cobb just shouted, "Go away, d'ya hear? I'll call if I need you."

Eve shut her mouth and Cobb saw her clench her hands together in her lap.

He said, "You take some time and think about it." Then he said, "All right, that's enough time."

"But—"

"Tell me his name."

The clock ticked. Eve didn't look at him. She closed her eyes, thinking, when will this day end? And they still had to find a home for the baby.

"Gavin," she said without opening her eyes. "Gavin Johnson." God help me, she thought, but I didn't ask for this trouble.

"Gavin Johnson? Man they call the Saint?"

"Yes, sir."

"Well, well," he said. Took off his hat, brushed it with the back of his hand, put it back on. "All right then," he said, turning back to her. His eyes were cold. "Now you listen. As of today you're fired. You're out of a job."

"What?"

"You and your sister, both. And if either of you come anywhere near me or my club, I'll see to it you never have a job in *any* club *any*where."

Eve could find nothing to say.

Cobb went to the panel doors and pulled them open.

A man of business.

19

"WHAT DID COBB WANT?" Lena asked Eve when she came back to the room. She had been gathering up the stained sheets and towels with one eye on Chickie, who was on the bed partly sitting and partly lying with a muslin quilt up over her legs.

Chickie looked carefully away. "I know. He wanted to make sure we never come near him no more."

Eve took her hand and said, "He just wanted to know the name of the man I was seeing when I was on the circuit. You remember Gavin Johnson?"

"You were seeing Gavin Johnson?" Chickie asked.

"That was the man who sent the note?" Lena asked.

"That's right, and the money. People around here call him the Saint."

At that, Lena looked around sharply. "The Saint? But that's the man Pin told me about. That was Rudy's partner."

"Who's Pin?" Chickie asked.

Lena told them the story: how Rudy and this man Saint met in the war, and how they started working together to sell corn sugar to Chicago club owners so they could make their own bootleg whiskey. This man Saint bought the sugar from the farms, Lena explained, and told Rudy what train it was coming in on. Rudy then unloaded it and sold it up here.

"He had a job at the station so it worked out pretty well," Lena told them.

"Partners." Eve nodded. "All right. I wouldn't have guessed it, but it makes some sense. So Gavin was buying up corn sugar while he played around on the circuit. Good way to get to the farms."

"But Pin only mentioned sugar; he said nothing about guns," Lena said, thinking back to Gavin's note, which Chickie had read. "You sure it said guns?" she asked Chickie.

"They had the transportation for sugar figured out," Eve said, "So . . ."

"You're thinking they could do the same with guns? But Rudy was . . . he was . . ." She wanted to say, he's not like that. She looked down at the baby, who was wrapped in a blanket and sleeping in a padded dresser drawer on the floor. One of her little hands was clutching the blanket with pale wrinkled fingers. When her mother was dying, Lena used to cut her fingernails for her—they were extra hard due to the medicine she was taking—and she noticed her fingers had become little wizened fingers like the baby's, and now the baby's fingers seemed like an old woman's, like her mother's.

"He's still the brother you remember," Eve told her gently.

The baby had such a tiny little nose, the nostril no bigger than a pinhead blowing out air. Her mother's breath—well, Lena had to check with her hand to make sure it had stopped, the actual dying took so long. With Rudy, of course, it was different. That was all in a moment. For some reason she thought about how Rudy used to play bobjacks with her behind their building with a small rock instead of a ball.

"I don't know," she said.

He had been kind to her but with a streak of mischief that could sometimes turn mean. She thought about the old stone viaduct Rudy liked to go to sometimes when they were children. It was at the end of their street and the train ran over it, and its dark, heavy façade placed it, for her, in the realm of a fairy tale. She always expected to find something awful there. But Rudy was drawn to it. Why? Once, when she went with him, he found a dead baby squirrel in the tunnel. He picked it up by the tail and whirled it around.

Chickie shifted on the bed and closed her eyes. "That bootlegging business of Rudy's," she said. "Cobb wanted to get in on it. He told me once. Hated the fact that he had to line up his truck with everyone else's."

"Do you think Cobb could have killed Rudy?" Lena asked her. "Or had him killed?"

Chickie shook her head. "I don't see what that would have gained him."

"Wait a minute," Eve said. "Hold on. I heard Cobb that afternoon saying something about scaring a man. Didn't give it a second thought at the time, but . . ."

"You think he meant Rudy?" Lena asked. "You think he wanted to scare Rudy into telling him who his partner was?"

"Or just scare him enough so he would take Cobb on for protection," Chickie put in. "Cobb has a few big old thugs who will do what he wants. Somebody crosses him or one of his people, he gets one of these thugs to get in the fellow's way. I've seen it."

"Like Shugs Burroughs?" Lena asked, remembering the note.

Chickie shrugged. "Maybe like him."

They were all three silent for a moment trying to think that through. Eve and Chickie sat next to each other on the bed. The blankets were pulled back and crumpled, though no one had slept there that night. Eve was holding Chickie's hand.

Lena said, "Chickie, lie down just a minute. I need to check to make sure you're not bleeding too much." She had made up a kind of pad for Chickie out of boiled clean rags, which Chickie was lying on now. Chickie turned onto her side. Lena looked at the pad. It looked fine, not enough blood there to worry about. She massaged Chickie's belly for a minute or so.

"I never knew my own father," Chickie said suddenly, looking up at the ceiling. "Never once saw him. He never even knew I existed."

"I know that, Lovie," Eve said gently.

"I just wanted Nathan to know his baby existed, is all. I didn't want him to do something, I just wanted him to know that."

"I know," Eve said again.

Chickie turned her head to look at the baby. Then she said, "I'm so tired."

Lena covered her up with the quilt and then sat on the edge of the bed. "Your breasts will hurt some for a few days," she told Chickie. "Your milk will come in even if you don't feed her. Bind up your breasts and after a week or so they'll go back down."

"Will I lose my baby fat if I don't feed her? I don't need this belly."

"You're so skinny it shouldn't be a problem."

Chickie hesitated, and then she said, "Evie, do you think Nathan will ever want me again?"

Eve studied her sister. She looked worn out. One of her eyes was still swollen and yellow, but Eve had watched her carefully comb back her hair when Chickie heard that Nathan Cobb was the man waiting downstairs. Shining eyes.

"Lovie," Eve said. "You need to forget about Nathan Cobb."

"He didn't believe the baby was his. But she is!"

"You need to forget about him."

Chickie looked away.

"We should leave soon," Lena told Eve. "It gets dark so early. Can you ask Mrs. Jenkins to make up another bottle of milk?" They had gotten one already; Mrs. Jenkins borrowed the glass bottle and rubber nipple from a neighbor.

"Wait now," Chickie said. She struggled a little to sit up. "Wait. Before you go, I have to tell you something." She looked down at the floor. The room still smelled like her warm, soft body. "Those men who took the money, who beat me up, I think they knew me."

Eve looked at her sharply. "What?"

"I think they knew who I was, Evie, but I promised not to tell. They said they'd hurt me or my baby." Her voice rose and broke.

"All right, calm yourself. Were they Cobb's men? What did they say exactly?"

"No, they weren't Cobb's men. I never seen them before. They were just after the money, said it wasn't mine, said they were going to give it back to the man who lost it."

What man? Eve wondered. Gavin had taken that money from a dead man. Then she thought: some of it. Gavin pulled a fair bit out of his own pocket, money probably meant for Rudy Hardy.

"I promised I wouldn't tell, but what if they hurt her anyway?"

"They won't hurt this baby," Eve said fiercely. "We're going to find her a good home."

"Do you promise?"

Tears stood in Eve's eyes. Outside a bird made a sharp noise, or maybe it was a cat. Fighting for something. "I do promise," she said.

Lena said gently, "We really ought to get going."

"Give her to me," Chickie said.

"What?"

"Give her to me."

Lena looked at Eve. Eve looked back at her, her face open and irresolute. After a moment Lena turned to lift the infant out of her little makeshift crib and brought her over to Chickie, who held out her arms.

The baby shifted as she changed hands but kept sleeping. Chickie looked at her daughter's face. Then she put her nose down and breathed in and out against the skin of the baby's little neck. No one spoke, and there was no noise from outside. After a moment Chickie handed the baby back to Lena.

"All right," Chickie said.

Outside it was colder than it looked, with the lake wind rising and the sky the color of new metal. A winter day, late afternoon. Most people were home making supper. Drinking, some of them, too. Putting a little seed alcohol in a bottle and then filling the bottle with water from the tub, the only place a bottle would fit all the way up under a spigot, why it was called bathtub gin.

The baby looked cold with her little red nose, and Eve watched Lena cover her tiny face with the blanket as much as she could. Eve felt cold, too. And worried. And sad.

"Sadness in birth and joy in death," she heard herself say.

"What?" Lena asked.

"Something Henry told me once. Old saying down where he comes from, I guess. He told me that's how he tries to play his music."

Chickie was back at Mrs. Jenkins's, safely sleeping. The worst was over, Eve told herself: Cobb had found them, fired them, and went on his way. She stepped over a puddle of melting snow. She didn't feel any better.

"This baby will be all right," Lena told her. "I can get a list of orphanages from my hospital. But you have to decide: colored or white?"

"What do you mean?"

"Do you want this baby to be raised colored or white?"

A colored orphanage, or a white one. Eve hadn't considered that. She looked at the baby in Lena's arms. Her soft, light yellow face. Three white grandparents, one colored. Seven white great-grandparents, one colored.

Even so.

"If we asked, they'd probably say she was colored," Eve said.

"*You* get to make the decision," Lena told her.

"You say that like it's a good thing."

They took a tram to the hospital, a large gray stone building four stories tall. Standing outside the colored entrance was a line of people, one of them coughing blood into a handkerchief. Eve followed Lena around to the white entrance where there was no line.

"She'll have more opportunities as a white girl," Eve remarked. They stood by the large double door.

"Is that your decision?" Lena asked.

Eve nodded, then looked away. She said, "Breaks my heart."

Lena gave her the baby to hold, and then ten minutes later she was back on the street, a list of addresses in her hand.

"This one isn't too far. I know them. They come around the hospital sometimes asking for donations. For education, they say."

They walked through the slush until they came to a narrow street with a shoe repair shop on the corner. Lena stopped in front of a rusty-colored stone façade with *Sisters of Charity* chiseled in an arch above the door.

She took the baby from Eve and walked up the steps. Instead of a button the doorbell had a handle to turn, and she turned it. But as she waited, she realized that she didn't know what to say.

The lock scraped back. A nun wearing a long, brown dress belted with a leather cincture opened the door. She saw Lena holding the baby and stepped out quickly, closing the door behind her. She had a long face made longer by her brown and white habit.

"I have a baby here," Lena began uncertainly. "She—she lost her mother."

The woman waited.

"And we need to find her a home. I want to place her here."

"It's not possible."

"You're on the hospital list."

"Did the hospital send you?"

Lena hesitated and then said yes.

The woman sighed. "No, they didn't. Anyway, we can't. Maybe if it was a boy," she said. "We take in laundry but it barely feeds us. We take in sewing. Scraps of jobs—a penny for this, two for that, keeping track of it is hardly—" She shook her head. "Now you want to give me another."

Lena's face grew warm. "I was told you all were about *school*."

"You'd think the good bishop would reward us for our work."

"Your pamphlets talk about how you take in needy children and you train them, you educate them. That's what your pamphlets say."

The nun said, "Take care of your own child; believe me, it's better."

"She's not my own child," Lena insisted.

"God bless you," the woman said, closing the tall door behind her.

Eve and Lena stood looking at the building as if waiting for someone else to come out, someone who would say yes.

"Come on," Eve said. "We'll just go to the next one. Don't you worry," she said to the baby, "I wouldn't hand you over to that dried-up old hen."

They began walking down one block after another, the streets getting even dirtier, lines of small cheap shops and row houses, children playing in shoes tied together with string. At last they came to another orphans' home across from a butter and egg shop, this time without anything carved above the doorway. But the address matched one on the hospital list.

Eve walked up the stone steps and knocked.

Nothing happened.

After a minute Lena said, "Look."

Upstairs there was a face in the window. A boy? He looked down at them, expressionless. After a moment, he put a finger in his nose.

Eve knocked again.

A moment later a woman appeared next to the child up in the window. It seemed to Lena that she saw the bundle in her arms and recognized it for what it was.

Eve stepped up and knocked. She stepped back and looked up at the woman.

The woman pulled the child away. With a shake she drew the curtains.

Eve knocked again.

Lena said, "Do we really want to leave her in a place so dead-set against her?"

They went to a third house, this one only a block away. Here the door opened for them at their first try, and a thin, pretty woman let them in.

She said, "Oh, the poor thing!" looking into the bundle of blankets. Then she looked closer. "I'd stake money she's not over a day old."

The linoleum had buckled a bit under the doorway, and Lena stepped carefully over it, holding the baby. Eve came in behind her. There was a faint smell of cooked cabbage, and they could hear muffled noises overhead. The woman asked them if she could take their coats.

"No thank you, ma'am," Lena said. It was a little chilly inside.

The woman, who introduced herself as Mrs. Teagan, had deep-set brown eyes and small teeth, with one crooked one on the bottom row that was somehow endearing. She looked like a child herself. Lena could see that her dress had been made over several times.

She told them that she'd been running the orphanage almost single-handedly since her husband passed on five years earlier. They got money from the city, she explained, and some money from men who took on the older orphans—fifteen, sixteen years old—as apprentices. Until then, the orphans went to school for three hours every day. Mrs. Teagan was proud of that.

"Not that all of them want to," she said. There were damp circles under her eyes.

She led them back through the house. As they walked along, Lena could see the orphans in various rooms at their chores, all of them dressed in gray dresses with checked pinafores or short gray trousers. The ones she could see close up were a mix—some dirty, some tidy—and they didn't look particularly angry or sad. The older girls seemed to be supervising.

"Of course, I have help. My late husband's aunt, and the cook—she suffers from sore eyes, poor thing, but still does remarkably well."

The orphanage took up three floors, all the beds on the second floor and Mrs. Teagan's room above that— "but we don't call it an attic."

"Had some walls knocked down nine years ago now— no, ten—so the dormitory is airy and light. Two rooms, of course, boys and girls. We left up a wall for that."

They came to the kitchen. In the corner by a large black stove two girls sat washing themselves in a small metal tub. Their dark hair was cut short and the bottom tips were wet from the bathwater.

Lena looked carefully around. The linoleum floor was cracked here too and stained, but not grimy. A small wooden table with shelves stood near the girls, with unmatched dishes piled on the higher shelves, and on the lower ones jars of flour and breadcrumbs and salt. A black squatty-legged pot stood on the floor. Made Lena think of the wash pot her mother used for canning, and sure enough there were some rubber collars and canning jar lids stacked nearby.

The girls in the tub didn't look up from their bath. Mrs. Teagan got out a bottle of milk and began heating it up on the stove. "Coupla the churches help, too," she continued, "from time to time."

She found a clean bottle. The kitchen walls featured a curious mix of wallpaper.

"How long has it been since the baby fed?" Mrs. Teagan asked.

Lena looked at the clock on the kitchen wall. "A little over two hours."

"Best wake her, then."

But she was already awake, blinking her eyes and opening and closing her mouth, getting ready to cry.

"The love," Mrs. Teagan said evenly. "A couple of weeks and her shouts will be deafening. Is your arm tired?"

"Here," Eve said, taking the baby now from Lena. "I'll feed her."

Mrs. Teagan pulled over a kitchen chair, one with arms, and Eve thanked her as she sat. When the bottle was ready, Mrs. Teagan handed it to Eve and watched as the baby began to suck. She sat down on a stool nearby. "That's my only test, that they take a bottle. It's the little ones dying that upsets me."

"Do many die?" Lena asked.

"The influenza, a few years back. That was the worst. No, we do pretty well." She looked at the baby. "Of course, children die." She yawned and put her hand to her mouth. "That happens all over. You done, girls?" she asked the bathers.

"Yes ma'am," the bigger girl said.

"Your towels are there on that chair."

It was hard to get a good reading. The two girls, toweling off and getting into their nightgowns, had the simple look of children living the life they knew. And what choice do we have? Lena wondered.

"I ask twelve dollars for clothes and such, medicine. But if you don't have that, then anything you can spare."

Eve said, "Twelve dollars? That can't get you very far."

Mrs. Teagan smiled. "With an infant, you'd be surprised. All the hand-me-downs. And I'm good with my sewing machine. That was a great gift." She was clearly proud of her household skills. "It's only if they get sick and I need to pay the doctor."

"Do you love these children?" Eve asked her.

The two girls, standing side-by-side, now looked over, curious.

Mrs. Teagan looked at Eve a moment, and then she stood up and went over to the girls. With both hands she stroked each girl's arm at the same time, as if they were two parts to one unit. Then she kissed the tops of their heads.

"Go tell Margaret to put the sixes in bed," she told them. "I'll be along in a minute."

She watched them skip out. She turned to Eve.

"I'll be honest with you. Some of them, yes, I do love. But I'm good to them all."

Eve nodded. She said, "You've done a good thing with your life. I can see that."

So that's that, Lena thought. Her heart dropped in her chest, surprising her.

"Do you have any money?" Eve asked her.

Lena thought: What do I know about a life like this? This is probably the best we can do. It's not bad. Poor is not bad. "I have twenty dollars," she said.

"Give it over to Mrs. Teagan there," Eve said. "All twenty." Mrs. Teagan didn't protest.

The baby had finished most of the bottle and was closing her eyes again. Eve bent over and kissed her little forehead.

"I thank you for your time," she told Mrs. Teagan. "And for the milk." But she didn't hand over the baby. "And now we best go," she said, tucking the baby's little hand into the blanket and getting ready to take her back with them out on the street.

20

THEY WENT OUTSIDE AND stood on the cold sidewalk with the baby.

Lena let out a long breath. She said, "Well, you'd better give her to me now. Your arm is probably getting tired."

"I know what it's like to be raised without money," Eve told her defensively.

"You think we're going to find her someplace with money?" Lena looked down at the baby's scrunched-up face. She understood why Eve didn't leave her there. But what would they do now?

Heavy dark clouds were blowing in fast. More snow coming. In this part of town, the streetlamps hung sporadically on lines strung across the street, some of them with their glass knocked out. In a wind like this, they rocked back and forth, casting their light as if on a whimsy.

They went into a coffee shop on the corner, a colored place called Vetta's. A few customers looked at them twice—a colored girl and white girl together. One woman still wearing her coat made a small ugly noise as Lena passed the table.

Lena ignored her but Eve turned and said, "Excuse me?"

The woman met her stare stonily. "Why you bringing *her* in here?" she said. "They got their own places."

Lena's face flushed and she wanted to turn around and leave, but where would they go? The restaurants around here were not segregated, not officially by law, but as with everything else there was a tacit agreement: We take this, you take that. We'll be here, you be there. Not many places allowed for a mixture. But at least it wasn't like towns in Mississippi where, by law, if you were colored you couldn't buy a new car and you couldn't wear a suit if it wasn't Sunday. For all the unofficial segregation up here, it was still better than that. People like this woman here probably just wanted someplace that was her own place to eat and not be bothered.

Lena knew all this. She knew she didn't belong here. But Eve was tough. "Do you own this place?" she asked the woman. "Are you Vetta?"

The woman said nothing.

"I didn't think so," Eve said. She raised her chin. Then she looked at Lena. "Come on."

Lena followed her to a table in the back, feeling tall and conspicuous. She looked around but everyone had gone back to their eating. "I only have a dime left," she said in a low voice.

"I might have enough for the two of us," Eve told her.

They ordered a couple of ham salad sandwiches and coffee. Eve went into the kitchen and came back with a long wire basket, which she set the baby in after arranging the blankets. She kept the basket on the floor between her feet as they ate.

"Now what?" Lena asked. Her eyes were beginning to feel pulled at the edges, and she wished she could just lie down under the table like the baby and sleep.

"I was thinking," Eve said. "Maybe I could just keep her." She put her two hands around the thick white coffee cup and didn't look at Lena.

"You would keep the baby?"

"I didn't say this before because I didn't want to worry Chickie, but Mr. Cobb fired me and her this afternoon. But that's okay really—his club doesn't pay all that well anyway. Lots of other places pay better, and I'm good, I'm a good piano player. I won't have too much trouble finding something else. And I bet if I didn't go out at night anymore, I mean if I eat in more often, I could cook a dinner on a hotplate—how hard can that be?"

Lena said, "But—"

"Wait. Let me finish. I could save more of my paycheck; I don't have to dress so nice. And I could get a second job, a day job at a restaurant, say. I was meaning to do that anyway. We could make it fine. I know a lot more who have it worse. We could make it fine."

There was a pause. Then Eve said, "Well, that's my piece."

Lena watched her for a moment. "All right," she said. "All right. I can understand—I can see how you'd like to do that. But it's just, well, let's think about it. Who would watch her while you work? You and Chickie have the same schedule. And then if you take another job . . ."

"I could find someone to watch her when we're gone," Eve said. "Someone on the Widow's Pension. Or I don't know."

Lena said, "I think I need more coffee for this." She waved the girl over. Out the window she could see an old man in the wind playing the bones with two flat sticks under a lamppost. It was dark out. The baby would need another bottle soon. She didn't know what to do.

"I'm just about done in," Eve said after the girl poured their coffee and left.

They both needed a good wash and some sleep, and even after the sandwich Lena still felt hungry. She said, "Do you have enough money for pie?"

Eve spilled out the contents of her handbag. Between them on the table lay a couple of nickels and some pennies, a creased cotton handkerchief, a lipstick tube, two sheets of paper folded carefully together, and an empty money clip. Eve pushed the coins to the side and began to count them.

"We could split a piece."

Lena looked at the paper. "What's that, a song? Can I see it?"

It was the song Eve wrote back in Hoxie, "Sea Change." Lena unfolded it on a clean spot next to her plate and smoothed the creases.

"You wrote this?"

Eve nodded.

Lena studied it, a wrinkle forming in the fleshy spot between her eyes. "Is this the piano?"

"Mm-hmm. And that's alto sax." Pointing with her pinkie. "I needed a fourth saxophone but most bands only have three, so instead I used a trumpet with a hat."

"A kind of wah-wah thing?"

"That's it."

Lena moved her finger, following the bass line. When the waitress came with the pie and two plates, she didn't look up. Finally she said, "Will you show me how to play it?"

"You want to play it?"

"I used to take lessons."

Eve had almost forgotten how Lena was that soldier who came up to her after Saturday's show, all hepped up about the music. Talking to her about taking lessons, an accident . . . That's right, Eve thought, she mentioned an accident. Must be how she got lame.

"You hurt your leg going to a piano lesson? That how you hurt it?"

"Funny, I haven't felt it all day. Have I been limping?"

Eve thought back. "I didn't notice," she said. Something struck her. "Is that why you stopped playing? Because you got hurt?"

Lena shrugged.

"But now you want to play again."

It was a question. Lena blushed. "I know this is going to sound foolish, but when I heard you all Saturday night, I just—I suddenly remembered how music made me feel. When I didn't—when I was younger."

"How'd it make you feel?"

Lena shrugged and picked up her fork. "Happy."

Eve watched Lena cut into the pie with the side of her fork like suddenly it was a task that needed all of her attention. She remembered how Lena went to nursing school because that was her mother's dream. She always does what she thinks she should do, Eve thought. Maybe here's something, this music, that's just for herself.

"I can show you how to play it," Eve told her. "If you have a piano."

"My aunt does. She keeps after me to come live with her. She has a spare bedroom downstairs. I probably will one of these days." Lena looked up. "Maybe you could teach piano instead of getting a job as a waitress. Make money that way. I could be your first student."

"If I could take on white students, that would pay more. But who would take care of the baby?" Always they were back to that.

They finished their pie. "We need to tip something," Eve said. Lena stood up and felt inside her coat pocket, pulling out a stiff piece of paper: Rudy's funeral card. A picture of Saint Michael the Archangel, and a prayer underneath: *Defend us in battle. Be our protection against the wickedness and snares of the devil.* Klaus-Rudolph Hardy: June 13, 1898 – January 15, 1922.

An idea struck her. She sat back down.

"What?" Eve said.

21

LENA'S AUNT CLEM LIVED in a small house on the Near South Side of Chicago. Like most of the women in her neighborhood, she sent away for a dozen baby chicks each year, which arrived by train in early spring. Her chicken shed was in the back of the yard, and inside Lena and Eve had to crouch a little to look out the one small window, where they could see the back of the house and the path leading up to the kitchen door. Here they were out of the wind, but of course the shed stank of chicken, although by now the chicks were all grown up and gone.

"I don't know," Eve said. "I just don't know."

They were waiting for Aunt Clem's husband, Uncle Mortie, to go to his Elks Club meeting.

"My aunt's a good woman," Lena said. She tried to work out Eve's expression in the dark but couldn't. "She belongs to the Chicago Women's Club—ever hear of them? They're the ones who started all those classes for new mothers. And the drive for homogenized milk? And nurse visits? I think they got city money for that."

"I've heard of them," Eve said without conviction.

A motorcar started up, a small sedan the color of a conifer tree.

"There he goes," Lena whispered.

The baby was getting hungry again. Her little mouth opened and closed and opened, and her eyes looked wet.

"They're not rich, but they don't have to struggle. And she'll go to good schools."

"It's just . . . it's hard imagining her with a family. I mean, a family that's not me. A white family."

"But we went to white orphanages."

"I know."

Lena waited. There was nothing she could say.

"All right," Eve said at last. She took a long breath and pulled opened the shed door and starting walking with the baby toward the house.

The backyard carried a faint odor known locally as the stockyards smell—an unpleasant smell at times, depending on the breezes, but one that meant work. They were not too far off from one of the largest livestock markets and meat plants in the world: a mile long and a mile wide, with more men and women employed there than anywhere else in Chicago.

But Lena smelled something else as they got closer to the back door—the slight scent of wet bread. Going up the steps, Lena could see Aunt Clem through the kitchen window making something—looked like a Washington pie. That was pie made from day-old doughnuts and stale jellied pastries and just about anything else the baker couldn't sell, all chopped up with a butcher knife and then mixed into a batter and baked. Delicious.

"Lena!" Aunt Clem exclaimed, letting her in. She wiped her hands on her apron and hugged her. She had a round, doughy face with dimples and strawberry-gold hair that was always slightly untidy.

"Well, my, you just missed Pin. He came after supper and ate the last of the butterscotch pie, so I can't offer you any now, I'm afraid. He said you felt sick Tuesday, that's why you didn't come back to the house after—" She stopped, clearly not wanting to say *Rudy's funeral*. "That's why he drove you home."

Nice of Pin to lie for her. "That's right," Lena said. "I'm sorry about that."

Aunt Clem was smaller than Lena but sturdy, like a thick trunk of wood. Her hands and feet were as small as a child's. Although Eve had stepped inside after Lena, only now, turning, did Aunt Clem take real notice of her. She smiled, but a confused expression crossed her face. What was Lena doing with a colored girl? After a moment, she took in the sight of the baby too. Her face softened and she said, "Oh!"

"Aunt Clem," Lena began. "This is Miss Eve Riser. She's a professional piano player right here in Chicago. Can we sit down? Also, you wouldn't have any milk, would you? That we could give to the baby? We need to feed her."

"A little girl?" Aunt Clem said, pushing the blanket away slightly with one finger so she could get a better look at the baby's face. "And she's awake!"

She put on her rubber boots to fetch a pint of milk; she didn't have an icebox but instead used a hole that Uncle Mortie had dug by the back steps, a couple of bricks holding down a plank of wood to keep it covered. Meanwhile, Lena started boiling water to wash the baby bottle. In the corner was the same wooden chair where she used to sit as a girl after her music lesson, her feet up on the wood box drinking hot Postum while Aunt Clem cooked. She always got some hot Postum after every lesson and a slice of whatever cake Aunt Clem had baked that day. Once, when there was a run of lice at her school, Aunt Clem washed Lena's hair with kerosene herself so the children in her building wouldn't laugh at her. She was more than an aunt to Lena. Aunt Clem had had one child, Milton, who died of tuberculosis when he was three.

"Would you like a glass of my apple wine?" Aunt Clem asked as the milk heated up. Homemade fruit alcohol was still lawful, but Lena shook her head. Aunt Clem turned to Eve. "Miss Riser?"

Eve was swaying with the baby. "No thank you, ma'am. Hush now," she said softly to the baby, who was beginning to squirm with hunger.

"Sit down, please. Let me see to that milk," Aunt Clem said, turning back to the stove.

"Aunt Clem," Lena began. She tried to think of what to say. "Aunt Clem, I need to talk to you about this baby. It might be a bit of a shock. But it seems that—

well, it seems we didn't know Rudy as well as we thought."

For a moment Aunt Clem kept herself busy stirring the milk, but Lena could tell she had heard. The smell of the Washington pie rose from the oven, and Aunt Clem took the milk off the burner to let it cool. When she turned around, her face looked fuzzy, like she was trying to catch hold of a math sum she didn't quite have the mind for.

"Rudy had a sort of . . . he had another life," Lena explained. "A secret life. I didn't even know myself until just a few days ago." Well, that was all true.

Aunt Clem looked at the baby.

"And I think that . . . I want to, that is . . . well, I feel that because of Rudy we should take care of this baby." That was true, too. His death started all this, didn't it? And now she was involved. Felt involved.

Aunt Clem cleared her throat. "Are you saying that this little baby is Rudy's?" she asked outright.

Lena stared at her aunt. A good woman. A good woman, who shouldn't be lied to. For a moment Lena looked at the baby, who seemed in her thick white blanket impossibly small and alone. She could feel Eve watching her.

"Yes," she said.

Aunt Clem took in a long breath and nodded as she released it. "Who's the mother?" She asked after a moment. She turned to Eve. "Are you the mother?"

"No, ma'am."

"Who then?"

Lena and Eve looked at each other. Then Eve said, "My stepsister is the mother. But she can't take care of her."

A pause.

"So this baby is colored."

There it is.

"Colored and white," Lena said truthfully.

Aunt Clem nodded again. She still wore that fuzzy look. "Colored and white."

After a few moments she turned back to the stove and, holding the pot by a dishtowel, began pouring milk into the clean bottle that Lena had set on the counter. When the bottle was nearly full, she affixed the rubber collar and nipple.

"Well," Aunt Clem said, testing the milk's temperature, "I worked with a lot of colored girls in the yards. I don't have anything against colored girls."

She had met her husband, Uncle Mortie, when they were both working at the local stockyards—Mortie was the manager of the pork trimming room where Clem worked. The room was really a cooler, which was always wet and cold and slippery, and like all the other girls Aunt Clem wore wooden shoes while she worked. Only problem was, to go to lunch they had to climb down two flights of iron stairs in those wooden shoes, and one day Aunt Clem slipped and twisted her ankle. Though he didn't have to, Mortie saw her home. Two months later they married, and she went back to work in the canning section, which was run by the only colored supervisor in all of the yards: a straight-backed, no-

nonsense woman named Bernadine Sparks. Best supervisor I ever had, Aunt Clem always said, next to Mortie.

The bottle was ready. Eve had taken off the baby's hat and was stroking her sparse, light brown hair. Aunt Clem held out her hands. "Let me," she said.

For a while the baby just drank the bottle resting comfortably in Aunt Clem's arms. Aunt Clem sat in the wooden chair by the stove looking down at her. The stove hissed, needing more coal, but Aunt Clem did nothing. After a moment she said, "Well, you can't tell by looking at her. Looks as white as could be."

Lena glanced at Eve. Her face was taut, resigned. Tired.

Eve said, "Yes she does."

"Fact, she looks just like Rudy," Aunt Clem said fondly. After a moment she added softly, "And just like my brother too."

It was settled without really talking about it. Aunt Clem didn't mention Uncle Mortie, and Lena didn't ask what she would tell him. After the baby finished her bottle, Aunt Clem helped Eve swaddle the baby in her thick blanket on the clean kitchen table.

"When are you going to move in with us, then?" Aunt Clem asked Lena.

"Soon," Lena promised.

Eve tucked in the last piece of blanket and put the baby in the little makeshift cradle that Aunt Clem had made out of a wooden crate. Then stood there looking down at her. Lena couldn't tell what she was thinking.

"My pie's coming up in a few minutes," Aunt Clem said. "Why don't you both stay for a piece? Oh, and I wanted to tell you, Lena, Pin asked about you earlier."

"Pin?"

"Tonight. When he came to visit." Lena could tell that Aunt Clem still harbored hopes for her and Pin as a couple. She tried to think of something mildly discouraging to say, but Aunt Clem went on, "As he was leaving, he asked if I'd seen you. I could tell he felt bad about—well, Rudy, that whole business."

Outside a few snowflakes were at last beginning to fall. Lena's thoughts turned to Eve, who, as strong as she seemed, was still recuperating from a bullet wound. Could she ask to borrow money for a taxicab? She found her glance straying to the tea tin where Aunt Clem kept spare change.

"Also he asked about a friend of Rudy's. He wondered if Mortie or I knew him. I suggested he ask you." Aunt Clem glanced up at Lena. She looked almost mischievous. "A good pretext for a visit. You could make him that nice tea you mix up, maybe have a sugar cake waiting."

"Who was he looking for?" Lena asked idly, angling a hatpin into her hat.

"Man named Shugs," Aunt Clem told her, raising her eyebrows at the strange name. "Shugs Burroughs, he said."

22

SHUGS BURROUGHS. THERE WAS no mistaking a name like that—the name in Gavin's letter. But what did Pin want with him? As soon Aunt Clem told her that Pin was looking for Shugs Burroughs, a gap seemed to open up between the world as Lena understood it and the world as it was.

"Who is he?" she asked Henry later, back in Eve's room, when Henry dropped by to check on them. "What's he do?"

"Oh, well," Henry said, looking around the corners of the room as if that was where you might expect to see a man like Shugs Burroughs. "Shugs, he's a kind of a rough man, I guess you'd say. He does jobs softer men don't want. Imposing fellow. He can walk into a club that requires a tie and collar and not wear either one, but no one dares to say a thing."

Usually he had a regular job somewhere, but after hours he was always on call. A man for hire.

"You think Pin found him already?" Lena asked.

Henry shook his head. "No way of knowing."

"What could he want with him?"

"We'll find out if Shugs has a mind to tell us."

But Eve said, "Must be part of this business."

For many years Shugs worked at the Crow's Nest, an after-hours club open from midnight until six in the morning. But now, Henry heard, he was working for some gangsters down at the Weatherford. They had a room in the back of the club where at any time of the day or night there were little games going on, set up nicely with drinks and sandwiches and enough chorus girls to persuade a fellow with money to stay put. Smooth-voiced men with slick hair rolled dice for the house, and the blackjack dealers knew every spot on every card. Like the Oaks Club, the Weatherford kept its own stills running in the basement.

Prohibition was over a year old, and yet people drank as much as ever. New clubs were opening every day. Many of them offered gambling and whores as well as liquor, and men like Shugs Burroughs found themselves in demand. Shugs was hired to see that no one became too unruly or too drunk or too rich. He loved throwing men in shiny suits out into the snow.

Henry caught up with Shugs early Thursday afternoon in the lunchtime mix of drinks, gambling, and girls that the Weatherford offered. Right outside the door, a streetcar lay on its side—its brakes had failed going around a curve, and it left the tracks and tipped over. Some kids were standing around trading broken-off scrap metal for penny candy, but otherwise business went on as usual.

The Weatherford's gambling room had only one high, long window looking out at the street at shoe level, and today most of the view was blocked by that streetcar. Still, from the fixed expression on Shugs's face, Henry thought that maybe Shugs had known he was coming.

"Man with the magic," Shugs said by way of greeting.

"How you doing there, Shugs?"

Shugs had a fresh scar on his chin and he pointed it out. "Little kid did it, must have been about six. Never more surprised in the whole of my life. Look at it!" He was proud. "That kid had some aim."

"What was it, a tin can?"

"Lucky I didn't duck—he'd a gotten my eye."

Shugs was tall, thick-limbed, and muscular, with a flattened-out face and fingers like half-smoked cigars. Not a man to be approached incautiously. At one time he was married to a woman named Bertha Allen, who looked like she was a man dressed as a woman, but she left him to work as a cook on a merchant marine ship. This afternoon he was with a skinny moll wearing an emerald green dress and green eye shadow, who shimmered when she moved like a jewel catching light.

"Move over, Kittens," Shugs said to the girl. They were sitting at the long bar by the game tables. Behind the bar was a parrot cage with a dark green parrot that said "Shirley" occasionally in a high falsetto, or "You give me my money."

Shugs motioned Henry to sit. "Got a game for you," he told him. "Called Pay for the Pot. Ever hear of it?"

Henry caught the barkeep's eye and ordered a drink. "Can't say I have. But I'll play it with you." The room was lined with wooden boards and a low wooden ceiling, and the game tables—seven or eight of them stretching to the back of the basement—were covered with bright green baize. Henry could smell fresh coffee as well as the faint scent of hops, and at the end of the bar a table was set up with sandwiches cut into triangles, more butter than meat.

"Here are the rules," Shugs told him. "Rule one: there are only two players, you and me. Five dollars antes in. Rule two: We both bid on the pot, and the pot goes to the one that bids the highest. With me?"

Far down at the other end of the bar, a couple of cops were discussing the Dempsey fight, their drinks on cork coasters in front of them. Henry glanced their way, but they had no interest in him. "I'm with you."

"Then where's your five dollars?"

Henry found a five and put it on the bar counter.

"Okay then," Shugs said. "Kittens, lay a bill down there for me."

Kittens said, "All right," in the softest voice imaginable, and fetched him a bill from her green silk purse.

Shugs looked at the two bills on the counter. "I'll bid five dollars for it," he said.

Henry saw how this would go. "I'll bid six."

"Six? That all? There's ten dollars there."

"You have another bid?"

"Nah, I'll let you take it for six. Give it over."

Henry hesitated only a moment before he pulled six dollars from his money clip and gave it to Kittens.

"I'll take this one, Kittens," Shugs said, and swept Henry's money into his palm. "Go on, take the pot," he said to Henry. "You won."

Henry picked up the bills from the bar top. "I'll take the pot, but you're the one who won."

Shugs fixed him with a stare. "What do you mean by that?"

"You put in five and got back six. I put in eleven and got back ten."

Shugs was still staring at him. Henry let himself smile a little, casually, like they were friends, like he wasn't afraid Shugs would haul him off and sock him a good one for the least little infraction. "Unless you want to play again?" Henry asked, smiling still but looking him straight in the eye.

"You want to play again?" Shugs asked. Challenging.

"Only if this time I bid first," Henry said, calm as he could, not shifting his glance. Shugs didn't say anything for a moment. Henry waited. The parrot behind the bar cried, "Shirley!"

Shugs kept staring at him, and then, surprisingly, he laughed. "You're all right," he told him.

"I'll even up the ante," Henry said. "Ten dollars buys you in. Long as you bid first."

Shugs shook his head and kept smiling. "Most people don't even know they been taken, the fools. The one percent that do, they get themselves in a fight with me. Always a mistake." He downed his whiskey. "You a cool customer," he said to Henry.

"Have to know how to lose sometimes." Henry drank his own shot.

"I'm telling you."

"Called sportsmanship."

Shugs ordered two more drinks and nodded at Henry. "Now what can I do you for?"

Henry looked around the room, but since he wasn't a drink or a card or a girl, no one was paying him the slightest attention. Still, he lowered his voice. "I'm hoping you can help me sort out a little complication," he began. "Friend of mine was asked to deliver a note to Rudy Hardy. But Hardy died before that happened, and the note, it kinda . . . disappeared. Only thing we know is it had your name in it, connected with a shipment coming into town."

Shugs nodded. "All right."

"Reason we're coming to you is, my friend was supposed to deliver some money with the note, too, but the money was stolen."

"The note disappeared," Shugs asked, "and the money got stolen?"

"I know, a bad business. My friend's worried that someone might be looking for the money and the note, both of which we just don't have. Don't mind telling you it makes me nervous not knowing whose money that was. We was hopin' you could help us with that. Might all be connected to Hardy's . . . to his accident."

Shugs took off his hat a moment and pressed it to his chest in a sign of respect, and then put it back on his head. "Man had it coming," he said.

"That may be so, that may be so," said Henry. "But my friend is worried. We want to play it straight. How much you owed?"

"Nothing," Shugs told him. "Not a dime until I unload a freight car and store some items. After that I get fifty dollars. But the deal fell off when Hardy died."

"Fifty dollars!"

"Mm-hmm."

"What items did he ask you to unload?"

Shugs glanced down the bar at the cops. He said, "Here, Kittens, why don't you go off to those gentlemen there and see if you can't entertain them."

Kittens blinked and then pulled a little girl face. "Let me have a cigarette?"

He gave her a cigarette and lit it for her, but as she bent over the flame her eyes were on Henry. "Off you go," Shugs said. "Come back when you're hungry."

His thick fingers rubbed his whiskey glass absently, and the barkeep came around with another shot and a fresh Coca-Cola chaser. Didn't take Kittens too much time to have the cops take notice of her. Most of the police officers in this district answered only to Big Bill

Thompson, the mayor, and it was rumored that Thompson had an understanding with the clubs. The understanding was simple: money and free drinks for his men in exchange for turning a blind eye.

Shugs lit a cigar for himself and then he turned back to Henry. "They was guns," he said in a low voice. "A load of guns." He took a sip of Coca-Cola. "Hardy hired me to unload them and store them in a warehouse down around 62nd and Cottage."

A lot of warehouses there. "Anybody else know about these guns?" Henry asked.

"Matter a fact, a man came to see me late last night about it. Tall skinny fella."

"Man they call Pin?"

"Didn't say. Just told me the deal was on again—all he was waiting for was a set time. Said could I unload and store the merchandise same as I was asked to before. Sure, I told him. But this time I wanted to know a little more than what Hardy told me, so I asked him who the buyer was. Know what he said?"

"I'm guessing the fellow with the scar they call the Walnut. Victor Rausch."

"That's right!" Shugs looked almost impressed. "How did you know that? The Walnut wanted the parcel of guns unloaded from a train car and stored. My guess is the money that got stolen from your friend was his."

"I see," Henry said, and in his mind he began to run a line between the dead man, Travis, and the Walnut, and poor, beat-up Chickie.

"Now," Shugs went on, "I have to tell you, I did wonder a little bit about why he wanted the guns just to store them. You have to be on top of things in my business. So I nosed around some. Know what I found out?"

Henry tilted his head.

"Walnut has ties to the Sicilians, everyone knows that. Torrio and the new guy, Capone. But what I also found out is that he has ties to the North Side Gang, too. You know them—mostly Irish. Dug a little deeper and I found something interesting about Walnut's daddy, name of Thomas Rausch. Thomas Rausch was killed in the circulation wars between the newspapers here, when was it, maybe ten years ago now. You remember that business?"

Henry nodded, though it happened in the time before he'd come to Chicago. Rival newspapers—the *Tribune* and the *American*—got petty gangs to pressure vendors into selling one newspaper and not the other. Called it bootjacking, but it was really plain old thuggery. By the time it was over, thirty street vendors had been beaten, stabbed, or shot, and the gangs involved grew even stronger. Now, with Prohibition, it was rumored they were eager to carve up the city again.

"Walnut's pop was one of the vendors got stabbed to death for carrying the wrong paper," Shugs said. "Course he didn't tell me this himself."

"What do you think he wants with the guns?" Henry asked.

"He's selling them to either one gang or another, is my guess."

"Making himself useful."

"That's right, making himself useful, getting in good in case there's another gang war coming on, which everyone says there is. That's one possibility." Shugs tapped cigar ash onto the bare bar top. "Or two, he just wants to protect himself. Or three, he's starting his own rival gang, but I find that unlikely. I just think he don't want to end up like his daddy."

Down at the other end of the bar, the cops were getting more rowdy with Kittens. She was laughing, but also looking over at Shugs. Shugs ignored her. He said, "And by that I mean dead."

So the Walnut had ties to both gangs. Henry thought about that. Maybe he was still trying to decide which one he should back, not wanting to end up on the wrong side.

"The guns are his bargaining chip. Funny thing," Shugs went on. Briefly, his eyes swept the room for the subtle signs of trouble he was paid to notice. "I was with him and Rudy Hardy the day Hardy died. Just that afternoon."

They had a meeting, Shugs said, and that was strange, too—usually he met with Cobb when there was anything to discuss, like if someone was behind in their corn sugar payment. Shugs said that the Walnut told Hardy at this meeting that he wanted an exclusive from Hardy, but Hardy wouldn't have it.

"Well, at the time I thought they was talking about the sugar. Hardy said he was goddammed if he was going to tie his own hands. He said he could sell anything to anyone he wanted to in this city. Wasn't going to have an exclusive with the Walnut or anyone else."

Henry nodded thoughtfully. "Then the man died," he said.

"Then the man died," Shugs agreed. He took a draw from his cigar. "I don't know if the Walnut had him killed or somebody else did, but I want in on this deal whoever it goes to. Something is coming down."

"But why not just buy guns right here in Chicago?" Henry asked. He thought of all the pawnshops, all the gun stores, all the men you could approach on the sly, some of them even here at the Weatherford. "Easy enough."

"Don't I know it! Listen now, I'm telling all this to you as a favor, and because I know you'll do the same for me. But I find out something goes down I don't know about, well, let's just say I'll be looking for you. Nothing personal."

All over the room men were losing money. Someone sometime tonight would get beat up or thrown out by Shugs, his cigar still fixed in his mouth. He had scars all over his body, not just the one on his chin, and a shoulder he could dislocate at will.

"Just don't go for my mouth," Henry told him.

"What's that?"

"My lips," Henry said with a straight face. He liked Shugs. He probably shouldn't, but he did. "I need them to play my horn."

Shugs looked at him and gave a short laugh. He tipped another knuckle of ash on the bar top. "I'll keep that in mind," he said.

23

THURSDAY AFTERNOON WAS AS gray as dusk with
heavy clouds overhead, but at least the snow had
stopped falling. Cobb passed a group of men shoveling
the street snow by hand, piling it into a horse-drawn
wagon. When the wagon was full, they would take the
snow to an empty lot, dump it, and then start all over
again.

The sun felt very far away. He pulled his chin in toward the collar of his coat. On the next block over, a
streetcar lay on its side just outside the Weatherford
Club, and Cobb almost took a moment to go look at it.
But just then he spotted the building he was looking
for, and he decided against any sightseeing.

Colored and white musicians belonged to different
union locals, and the colored union in Chicago was in a

three-story building with long windows and a small front door. On the sidewalk in front, a ragged-looking man was playing a mouth harp with an upturned felt hat by his feet. Cobb tossed in a penny as he passed.

He walked up the shoveled path and then stamped the snow off his boots. As he made his way to the office at the end of the hall, he passed a line of men and women waiting to pay their dues. A dense smell of perfume and cheap cigarettes filled the hallway.

Inside the office, one young man was arguing with an older man about a temporary work card, but everyone else in the room took a moment to look at Cobb. He was the only white man in the building, but he didn't care about that.

"Care to look up a musician for me?" he asked a man with rectangular glasses and a closely shaved head, who was pecking away on a typewriter.

"Not my department."

"Gavin Johnson's the name. Also called the Saint." Cobb stepped closer and put a folded bill next to the typewriter.

The man looked down at the bill, glanced at Cobb, and then let out a sigh as he took it up. He rolled his fingers into a fist and cracked the joints.

"Johnson, you say?"

While Cobb waited he pulled off his gloves, although there was only one small stove in the corner and the room was cold. Faintly, from upstairs, he could hear the sound of a piano plunking out single notes like an exercise. "I'm going to give you just one note today," his old trumpet teacher Mannie sometimes told him. Mannie, again. Why was he thinking so much about him? Just an old colored man from Georgia who happened to know more about the horn than anyone Cobb had ever met. "Just one note, and you see how many ways you can play it," Mannie would say. "Growl it, sharp it, make it angry. That's how you find the feeling."

Cobb moved closer to the stove. Above him, a trumpet started playing with the piano, and the piano went from exercise notes to a proper tune. What was it? Cobb tilted his head and listened. "Ukulele Lady." After a couple of minutes, the man with the rectangular glasses came back holding a manila folder.

"Gavin Johnson, you say?" He looked at a page in the folder and adjusted his glasses. "Looks like he's with the Syncopaters now. Jimmy Blakeley's band."

"Where?"

"On the Toby. Let's see. Last week in Hoxie. This week a little uncertain, either Maryville or Farmington." He closed the folder. "I believe Earl Sims is upstairs— why don't you go ask him? He just came back from Hoxie. Trombone player."

Cobb took the steps two at a time, looking at his watch as he did. At the top of the stairs there was a large lounge with oak wainscoting, the walls above it painted dark green. A few card tables were arranged on one side of the room, and along the other side were some easy chairs, a crooked music stand, and an ancient piano in the corner. Some Dapper Dan in a pressed blue suit was the one playing the piano, while the trumpet player sitting next to him adjusted his valve.

Cobb looked around for Earl Sims, whom he knew by sight. He spotted Sims playing cards—hearts, it looked like—and talking about the Dempsey fight like everyone else was these days. Smoke floated up in wisps above his table.

"So Willard's running away," Earl was saying, ordering his cards with long slim fingers.

"He's a guffer," the man to his left said. "A goddam coward."

"We—will—see." Earl passed three cards to his right, one on each word.

"Earl Sims?" Cobb asked. Earl looked up. "Speak to you a moment?"

Earl picked up his cigarette from the ashtray and put it out. Then he followed Cobb to the doorway. Probably thought Cobb wanted him for a job at the Oaks, but instead Cobb asked about Jimmy Blakeley's band. If Earl was surprised, he didn't show it.

He thought for a moment. "Yeah, they were going on to Farmington, what day is it, Thursday?" He touched his chin. "They should be there by now. They got a gig at the Palace Theater there on Drake Street for tonight and tomorrow night."

Cobb gave him a bill. Earl played a good valve trombone and was an easy-going man, though it was said he liked his tonk games a little too much. A gambler. Well, that was better, in Cobb's view, than a drinker. Cobb thought maybe he could find a place for Earl one of these days at the club—he'd talk to Henry about it. He said as much to Earl.

"And if you hear anything more, let me know."

Earl touched his forehead like there was a hat there. "I certainly will," he said. He was a first-rate improviser—just like Mannie. How often did Cobb copy Mannie's fingering, trying to get his sound? But one morning Mannie's heart gave out after a good breakfast, with his trumpet in his lap. Sometime after that, Cobb admitted to himself that he would never be as good as Mannie. Nowhere near as good. He was better than a lot of the musicians he played with, but even Mannie couldn't make him great. It took Cobb about six months to break into management, and even though he told himself he was moving on, for a long time it felt like he was giving up. That was a period in his life he didn't like thinking about.

Earl went back to his hearts game and Cobb went down the steps, out of the building, and back into the sunless day feeling like he was getting somewhere at last. On the sidewalk he put on his hat and looked up and down for the nearest telegraph office. The snow removal men and their horse had gone only a little way up the street; it was slow work, what they did.

You have to finish one idea before you begin the next, Mannie would tell him. Cobb spotted a shingle for a telegraph office up the block. As he walked toward it, he composed in his mind the telegram he would send to Mr. Gavin Johnson, the Palace Theater, Farmington: "Send Rausch shipment earliest train. Payment to come."

Finish one idea, start the next.

That was what he aimed to do.

24

LENA NEVER HAD DREAMS about her mother or father or Rudy, but in the days to come she would dream about Pin. His long frame resting against an old hitching post, holding a letter that he asked her to mail. He was so close she could see the chip on his bottom tooth. When she reached for the letter, he pulled out a gun and shot her.

On Thursday, while Henry was hunting down Shugs Burroughs, she packed her suitcase and said good-bye to the girls at the rooming house, none of whom were her friends. She made her way to the hospital, where she asked for another week's leave, and they agreed to it. But instead of going to Aunt Clem's, she went back to Eve's.

Eve had moved her things down to two rooms on the first floor, one of which used to be the back parlor, and in fact there was still an old upright piano in the corner. It was Mrs. Jenkins who suggested it, saying there was enough space for both Eve and Chickie this way: two bedrooms, or a bedroom and a parlor if Eve preferred. More rent money for her, of course. The far room had formerly been a back porch, weatherproofed now, though the walls looked as thin as nail files. Lena would stay there for a few days, maybe a week, before moving to her aunt's.

The rooms were cold but comfortable. This was to be her first lesson. Before they began, Lena stretched, clasping her left wrist with her right hand. She pulled her arms to the right and then to the left. After that, she did some deep breathing exercises like her old piano teacher, Mrs. Fenstraker, always recommended.

Chickie was sitting in the corner of the room hemming a pair of Henry's old trousers, and Eve stood beside the piano thumbing through some music. Lena clenched her fingers, relaxed them, and then looked at Eve. "I'm ready," she said.

They had a plan. And in this plan Lena had to play jazz piano like she'd been playing jazz piano for years. It was Lena who came up with it. She had to find out what had happened to Rudy and what was Pin's part in it. Maybe it was crazy but she had to know. She was tribal, her mother always said, *stammesgefühl,* and maybe because of this Lena couldn't let go. She owed it to her little brother to find out why he was shot, even if there was a simple explanation. Was there ever a simple explanation for death?

"All right," Eve said. "For this music you need to strike the keys differently. Your hands should be flatter, more like sticks. Hard loud chords, that's what you're after." Eve moved Lena's fingers into position. The piano was pale brown, old but polished, with yellowing keys. "Nothing dainty. How a man would hit the keys. You've got large hands, that'll help."

"My father's hands," Lena said, looking down at them. "I always hated them."

"My father's hands were like thin hard planks of wood, ain't that right, Chickie?"

Chickie had her head bent over her sewing, and for a moment she didn't say anything. Today she was able to stand without help and even move around the room, and the swelling on her face was going down. But something was different behind her eyes, like she was looking for something but she didn't know what. Lena studied her anxiously. This was the time women fell dangerously ill, after a heartbreak; she'd seen it so many times at the hospital.

"Had pretty fingers, though," Chickie said finally. "Tapered. Why don't you try her out on 'Pineapple Rag'—that's a good one."

Eve must have seen Lena watching Chickie, because she said, "You got to concentrate on yourself and your fingers. Nothing else matters right now."

"Pineapple Rag" was complicated. Twice Eve changed Lena's fingering, and then she made her go through it by herself three times alone before they moved on.

"Bring out your left hand more," Eve told her. "That's where the feeling is."

The kind of piano they were playing was stride piano—Lena didn't even know it had a name. It came out of ragtime music rather than the blues, and was based on a motion in the left hand—a note played by the pinky finger followed by one played by the thumb ten notes higher. For a while Lena practiced just that motion like it was a drumbeat. As far as she could tell, she had three things going for her: her sight reading (excellent), her ability to pick out a tune by ear if she'd heard it before, and all those years of piano lessons. Also her large hands. Four things.

The room had windows facing the side yard where Mrs. Jenkins kept her big black washing tub and her scrubbing board—they could see her now through the window stirring sheets around in the hot water with a long stick. Although the day was wintry and gray, Lena felt just the opposite. She held the beat with her left hand while trying to play around with her right. When her mother was ill, Lena used to play the piano for her every afternoon; they had their own piano by then. Once she played a song she'd gotten from Rudy, "Mexicana Rag," not sure if her mother would like it. When Lena finished playing, there was a pause, and then her mother's deep, accented voice: "You would play that last again, please?"

Ragtime jazz, jass, hot music—there were so many names for it. "Don't drop your wrists below the keyboard," Eve said. She moved Lena's hands again. "Flatten those fingers. Now lean your body forward; get some weight pressing on those keys. Let's try a two-beat."

Chickie said, "You kinda jump up with your hands."

"Keep the rhythm going in your head," Eve told her, "even if you don't play on it. Emphasize your left hand. Bring out the feeling."

Lena played a few tenths and then alternated with some chord and single-note figures.

"That's it. Be open to it," Eve said. "You're a horse or a train—let it ride along on you. And stretch those fingers. Come on, you can make that E." She told Lena about a famous piano player who, it was rumored, cut the webs between his fingers to increase their span. "A white man's rumor," Eve said, as if Lena were not white.

Chickie said, "Let her go through a whole number again." She finished Henry's trousers and now was sorting through thread to alter his shirt. "And remember not to play so loud the singer can't hear her ears."

"That's a singer talking," Eve said, and Chickie smiled for the first time that day.

Lena played through "Stoptime Rag" twice, varying it a little on her own toward the end. After that, Eve set before her another song, and then another. Finally, at the end of two hours, Eve brought out the score of one of her own songs, the first one she'd ever published. "Try this," she said.

"A lot of broken tenths in this one," Lena commented, looking at the score.

"You can do it. Just stay with the beat."

It began slowly with a two-bar introduction and then a twelve-bar chorus. Lena leaned over the keys. A repeated bar and then a chord progression. The story, when it came to her, was a surprise. She always heard stories in music, or sometimes just scenes: fat women eating pastries in a pastry shop, girls walking along a path carrying picnic baskets and getting caught in the rain. Usually there was an outing, or horses, or dancing and food.

But the story that came to Lena with this song—it was called "Then and Now"—was simply a woman in her kitchen doing her chores. Heating her iron on the stove, wrapping her hand in a rag to pick it up, and then doing some ironing. A man comes in; she gives him food. She takes her iron off the stove again and irons. Lena tried a variation of her own.

Chickie said, "That was nice."

The musicians Lena heard at the Oaks Club played as if they had something to say about life, and it might not be good, it might not even be true, but it sure wasn't pastry shops and picnics and horses. Eve's song had the same kind of grit. She had something to say, too.

Henry came in just as she was finishing up the second ending. Eve said, "Now try varying it a little more. Change your fingering. Put your own self into the music." So Lena went through it again.

"Don't rush the beat," Eve said.

Lena leaned over the keyboard. Suddenly, she felt a surge of power.

"That's it," Eve told her.

Now Lena pushed her left hand harder as if slapping the keys into place. At the same time she felt something in her had uprooted. This is what it feels like to fly, she thought, like the music was air supporting her body. She kept the rhythm going with the chords, and she laid the melody along top, strong and sure. But it was her left hand, the rhythm, that spoke to her. She thought of her mother before she was ill, when she was working in the kitchen trying to stretch a little bit of meat into one more meal. When Lena finished the coda, Henry and Eve and Chickie all clapped.

"That was fine!" Eve told her, and Chickie said, "I felt that one!"

Henry looked at her with his sad eyes, but he was smiling as he spun his hat around on one finger. "That was all right. I think you'll do all right." He nodded and Lena felt a rush of pride. She brought her hands to her lap and rubbed her fingers.

"So I stopped by to tell you it's all set up," he said.

"They're expecting me?"

"I have a few pointers I thought of on the way here. How to get in good with the man."

Lena turned to look at Eve. "Do you really think I can do this?"

She still felt high from her playing. She wished she could always be here, in this cold back room, with Chickie and Henry and Eve. Especially Eve. Chickie put down her sewing and looked at her sister as if she, too, wanted to know.

Eve said, "Yes I do."

25

THE NEXT MORNING, LENA went to a barber and had her hair bobbed, and then she put on pants and went to a different barber, who cut it like a man's. He showed her how to comb it back with petroleum jelly.

Back at the house, Eve helped her bandage up her breasts to flatten them, and then pinned the bandages in place. Lena was glad she'd inherited her mother's deep voice. She wore Henry's trousers and shirt and jacket, which Chickie had hemmed for her. But she had to wear a pair of little boy's shoes, since her feet were too small for Henry's.

"You don't have to do this," Eve said as they stood side by side before the hallway mirror, looking at Lena's reflection. "We can just leave well enough alone."

"He was my brother," Lena said. Her heart was beating fast and light, like a bird's. She adjusted the derby hat that Eve got for her. "I have to find out."

Henry was waiting for them by the front door. "Remember, you don't need to hotdog it," he told her. "Just keep the beat. Better to play a wrong note twice than drop the beat even once."

"In your opinion," Eve said.

Henry grinned. "Evie, of course, never plays a wrong note."

They smiled at each other, and for a moment standing between them Lena felt like a neighbor or the friend who introduced them, though of course neither was true. Eve said she'd go with her as far as the club. Outside Lena pulled on Henry's old leather gloves, which were a little too loose in the fingers. Her bandaged breasts felt curiously itchy and her overcoat cuffs were too long. In spite of herself she was excited, more excited than when she had worn Rudy's uniform. Less nervous, was that it? One thing was true: she certainly did not feel like a man, however that might feel. She felt like herself, wearing pants. She liked that.

Henry walked them to the tram stop, and then Lena lifted her gloved hand in farewell in what she hoped was a masculine way. On the tram no one looked at her twice. She and Eve rode uptown without talking or sitting next to each other, and then got out a stop early because Eve mistook another building for the building they wanted. Out on the street a couple of little boys ran around wearing their daddies' vests, opening them up to show some picture postcards they had pinned to the lining—"Only two cents!" they cried.

"See that music store?" Eve pointed out a narrow storefront near the corner. "That's where I got my first job when I moved here—I was demonstrating sheet music for them. Got three dollars a week."

"You could live on three dollars a week?"

"Me and Chickie did, both of us," Eve said.

They waited for a coal wagon to cross the street, pulled by a couple of skinny horses covered with matching green blankets. When a motorcar sputtered by, both horses skittishly lifted their heads, and Eve and Lena had to wait to get into the alley behind them as the coal man struggled to get the horses moving. Lena pulled out her pocket watch. She felt warmer and stronger in long pants. Also a sensation she hadn't had since she was a girl—that she could break out in a run and leave everything behind. No one looked at her twice.

In the alley, a couple of men in gray coveralls were standing in front of a stack of crates listening to a news report on a homemade radio: for the first time since the war, the price of milk had fallen back to thirty cents a gallon. "Better days are here at last," the announcer said. It felt like a long time coming.

"My brother Kid once made a spark radio out of old spark plugs," Eve remarked as they passed. "That was the first time I ever heard music that wasn't played out in front of me. It was the Coon Sanders band, you ever hear of them? From Kansas City."

"I've heard of them."

"Listening to that radio, I'll never forget it. It felt like a door had cracked open and suddenly I could reach out to all the people in the world."

They came to an unmarked door with a long brass peephole. Eve nodded. "That's the one."

Lena stepped up and knocked. All at once her mouth felt dry. After a minute the peephole door slid open an inch and she saw a dark iris like a marble. The iris waited for her to speak.

She wet her lips. "Darby couldn't play today. He sent me along. Name's Finch."

Nothing.

"Freddie Millard knows I'm coming."

A tense moment, but then the door opened. It was dark inside and she could barely make out the man who had let her in. He looked her over. Then he saw Eve.

"Go around to the side for the laundry," he told her brusquely.

Eve frowned. "I'm not here for the laundry."

"She's with me," Lena said.

"Son, anybody ever told you to leave your whores in bed where you can find 'em again?" Leering.

"This is Eve Riser," Lena told him. "She plays piano at the Oaks. She was just showing me—"

"What's wrong with your voice?" he interrupted. She was whispering.

"Nothing's wrong," Lena said, startled. Then, "I'm not here to sing."

At that the doorman laughed, though she didn't mean to joke, and he looked Lena over again. "Don't eat the oysters," he said in a low voice. "They've turned."

Was he joking? He was a short, stocky man with a series of scars down one side of his face, the result of which made one eye seem like it was caught in a wink.

"Name's Squint," he said. Then he said to Eve, "You run along back home, now, sugar."

Lena turned back to Eve, but Squint closed the door between them before she could do anything but see Eve's frown deepen. She wanted to tell Squint how good Eve was, how gifted, how very soon everyone would know her name—she didn't know what she could say that would make him pay attention.

"Here's a young fella playin' for Johnny," Squint called out. "Voice still changing, looks about twelve, so be nice to him, gents. And don't give him nothin' to drink!" Now he turned and winked with his good eye. "Give 'em hell," he said.

Lena walked around the small square tables toward the stage, glad the weather was milder and she wasn't limping today. There was a smell of salt and leather and stale smoke, and she could make out potted plants along one wall. This was a noontime club open only from eleven till two, a casual place that offered a little background music for businessmen to drink by. No one was making musical history here. It took some time for Lena's eyes to adjust to the darkness.

The band played on a little raised platform in the back of the room and the musicians were all as white as the clientele. Lena felt thankful that it was so dark. When he saw her coming, Freddie Millard, the trumpet player, hopped off the platform and introduced himself, shaking her hand. He was the bandleader.

"Henry didn't tell me you were so young. How old are you?"

"Eighteen," Lena said.

"That's what kids say when they're sixteen."

"I was born in 1903."

"Well, you got your math right. Come on and I'll introduce you to the rest of the band." He was a tall, lean man with a disorganized manner and thick hair that was barely kept plastered down. "Hope you're warmed up, we're starting in a minute. Doors already opened. Afterwards we'll feed you a meal, ham sandwiches today. You a fruitarian?"

"A—?"

"Crate of grapefruit came in this morning from Florida. Make sure you get one. Old age comes from waste, you know, in the cells. Dr. Oldfield."

Lena had heard of the man, famous for claiming that with the right diet any man could live to be one hundred and five. Recently it came out that, during the war, fully one-third of all the men drafted were rejected as physically unfit, and now people were beginning to talk about diet and nutrition and vitamins, and everyone had an opinion about what people should eat.

But if Freddie was a fruitarian, then Lena thought she would stick with meat—he was as skinny as a whip with waxy pale skin. Up on the platform he introduced her to the band: alto sax, tenor sax, clarinet, trombone, bass, and banjo.

The banjo player was called Moaner. He was one of Nathan Cobb's men, a friend to Travis Pitts. Lena was hoping that he knew something about Travis's death. Maybe even Rudy's. If not, then all this dressing up was for nothing. The trick was to get him to talk to her.

Moaner grinned, showing a row of stained teeth. "Johnny liked me on his right," he said, "but I can stand on the other side if you want."

"The right's fine with me," Lena said uncertainly, trying not to look at him too long but also wanting to get his measure. A country boy, Henry had told her. Likes music and horses and stories about natural disasters, in that order.

Lena's flattened breasts itched a little and she pulled at her celluloid collar, which was pinching her neck. Her fingers felt strange too, like tiny pine needles were pricking them. Nerves. The piano was a polished black upright and, still standing, she ran her hands lightly over the keys. Recently tuned, that was good.

"We start off with some Tin Pan Alley," Freddie was saying. "But we don't have the scores for those, too expensive, and besides everyone knows 'em. Just keep the beat and you'll be fine. We got scores for the rest of our numbers, mostly."

After he gave her a handful of sheet music, he reached into his pocket to pull out some eyeglasses, which he unfolded and fitted onto his nose. Lena wiped her sweating hands on her trousers and started to sit down. But someone had put three upended tacks on the stool.

"Oh!" she cried, springing up and swiping at the back of her trousers.

Moaner and the trombone player laughed.

"Just testing your cool, kid," Moaner said.

Lena felt her face grow warm. Had she yelped like a girl? No one looked at her strangely.

"Enough of all that," Freddie said. He stood in front of his music stand, ready to begin. "Crowd's starting to come in."

A few gentlemen had already been served drinks at their tables, newspapers unfolded in front of them, their collars unbuttoned. A girl went around taking coats and offering cigarettes from a long silver-plated box. No one looked up when the music began, a slow number. The clarinet carried the melody while Freddie gave a gentle explanation on his trumpet. Although her mind felt blank, Lena put her fingers on the yellowing keys. Below her, the voices of the businessmen as they chatted and drank their lunch had the cadence of a babbling brook.

Freddie nodded at her and without thinking she found her way in. An easy couple of chords, then the clarinet came back and the trombone stepped in and the trumpet added what it could. All the while the drums sadly supported the horns, agreeing with whatever they said.

Lena couldn't hear the story on that one. When the number was over, the babbling brook rose up and gave a little applause, but Freddie plunged right into the next. This one was faster and Lena moved her fingers hard, remembering what Eve had said about the beat. She tried to concentrate her attention on her left hand.

By now her heart had quieted a little. She was beginning to feel it. By the time the third number began, she forgot the men at the tables, and by the fourth number, another slow one, she forgot everything else. Moaner started off on one note on the banjo, and then the clarinet player, a young man with wild red hair, put his instrument to his lips and began to tell his story.

After a couple of bars, Lena moved in, saying don't exaggerate, and the clarinet said no this is how it really is, and the trombone said all right. Lena stuck to the upper registers, and she found herself swaying slightly over the keys. She picked it up suddenly as the clarinet moved in again. The trombone posed a question, the clarinet suggested a change, and suddenly, as she moved down the register, Lena heard the story.

There was a boy in the snow and he was dead. There was another boy behind him leaning against a brick building. The dead boy in the snow could talk but all he said was: listen. The other boy was not afraid, but he could not listen.

The snow started falling.

And that was the story.

When they finished, Lena looked around and saw men clapping but she couldn't hear them. Freddie held up two fingers and tapped his nose, and then pointed to the redhead, who began a rag on his clarinet.

Her heart was beating fast again, but not in fear. It was like falling in love. While she waited for her cue from Freddie, Lena thought about how in German there are two words for musical: *musikantisch*, technically proficient; and *musikalish*, artistic and passionate. She never really understood the difference until now.

They went through "Prince of Wails" and "Bugle Call Rag" and "Farewell Blues," and all the while Lena alternated chords and single notes. She felt like a different person. It didn't make sense, but she felt as though finally she was getting to do what she'd always wanted to do, only she hadn't known before what it was that she wanted to do.

Of course, the music was nowhere as fast as the music Henry and Eve could play, and she couldn't improvise like they could. Still, she tried to concentrate on her left hand, and whenever she did, she felt it. Twice Freddie looked over at her and nodded sharply: good run.

She felt it. That was all she could say.

When the last set was over, Freddie congratulated everyone. "Good show, fellas," he said. "Now don't leave anything on the stage. Mel, don't forget your cloth there."

Moaner grinned at her. She grinned back.

"Know why a possum ain't got no hair on his tail?" he asked. "Cut it all off for banjo strings." He picked up his banjo and gave it an affectionate strum.

Lena followed him and the other musicians off the raised platform and downstairs for her ham sandwich and grapefruit. Like everyone else she was smiling. She felt wonderful. Her hands hurt and her breasts underneath the bandages had gone from itchiness to numbness to pain, but she was elated. The businessmen went on drinking and talking to each other, although a few of them left when the music was over.

The kitchen was just a modified root cellar—the building used to be a narrow, private house—but it was clean with a red-and-black tiled floor and the largest icebox she'd ever seen. A barrel of fermenting sauerkraut stood in one corner, and stacks of wooden fruit crates lined one wall. All the musicians got plates from the cook and then leaned against the counter as they ate. Lena angled to get a spot near Moaner. A few men took beer bottles, Moaner among them, from an open crate on the floor. He passed her a bottle, and she opened it but only pretended to sip.

"Oyster?" Moaner offered loudly.

"No thanks," Lena said.

The men laughed.

"What is it?"

"You passed the test," the red-headed clarinet player said, but didn't explain further. Lena looked around. She could see no oysters.

For a few minutes everyone just ate without speaking. Then the cook came around with another round of sandwiches and took an apple cake out of the oven. Finally Moaner put down his plate and unbuttoned his collar. His shoes were shined, but old. He eyed Lena curiously, wiping his sleeve across his mouth. "Say," he said to her, "you hear what they're saying about the fire in '71?"

One of the sax players groaned. But Lena thought, here it is. Her heart started pounding hard again in her chest. She tried to remember just what Henry told her—the name of that town. How Moaner was always on about it.

"You mean," she said casually, "that it was started by a comet?"

At that Moaner looked genuinely surprised. Lena took a sip of beer, a real sip, but tiny. Now she remembered. "I have a cousin in Peshtigo," she went on. "Same comet hit there too, and a coupla other towns along the way."

Moaner swallowed. He lowered his voice and said, "Government conspiracy."

"That's exactly what I think," Lena lied.

Not ten minutes later, Lena took her bottle of beer and a slice of apple cake and followed Moaner out to the alley. Moaner lit a couple of cigarettes and gave her one, and for a while he kept talking about the comet. Eventually, though, Lena was able to steer the conversation toward Travis.

Moaner was surprisingly eager to talk about him. It was true, he said, that Travis worked for Nathan Cobb. But he also had another job on the side with a fellow who wanted in on the bootlegging business. A tall, lean fellow; Moaner saw him once or twice. As far as Moaner knew, Travis was just passing along information to him and getting a little extra cash.

"He did that with a lot of people," Moaner told her in a low voice. "But the tall fellow was different—I think Travis hoped that eventually this fellow would set up his own operation and need a right-hand man." He took a drag from his cigarette and thought. "Travis had ideas and plans, he wasn't like me. I get to play my banjo a few times a week, get some money in my pocket, play the horses some, well then I'm all right."

"What was the tall fellow like?"

"Nice enough, but sometimes only halfway here, know what I mean? Thoughts somewhere else. Gassed once too often, maybe," he suggested.

Pin.

"Travis hated Germans," Moaner went on. "Hated them. He was in a war camp, you know, for over a year. I think the tall fellow felt the same way."

"Rudy Hardy was German." Lena's throat tightened, and she tried to swallow but her mouth was too dry. "Didn't I hear that Travis did some work for him?"

"Rudy Hardy," Moaner said, looking carefully away, "that was a bad business. Yeah, Travis hated that one, too. Not to speak ill of the dead." He crossed himself.

She threw the end of her cake into the trash bin, cloth napkin and all. "Know who killed him?" She couldn't look him in the face. Sounds from the street beyond the alley grew suddenly loud as people shouted at someone and a couple of horns sounded in unison.

"Well . . ." Moaner hesitated. "Word on the street has it that Hardy was killed by someone sending a message—they just wanted to hurt him, not kill him, but the bullet went astray."

"Was it Nathan Cobb sending the message?"

Moaner slid his eyes away. "Dunno. Maybe."

"And maybe the tall man, the one who got gassed—
you say Travis was working for him, too? Maybe he had
something to do with that bullet going astray."

"Could've." Moaner took another sip of beer. "Now I
didn't say it was Travis driving the truck, mind," he
added. But he spoke like this was just a formality; he
was no rat, understand. He had principles.

Half an hour later, as Lena walked back to the tram
stop, she went over what Moaner had said. Her mouth
felt sticky from cigarette smoke. He more or less told
her outright that Travis had killed Rudy. But was it a
mistake, or did Pin hire him to do it? Did Pin say to
Travis, "Let's set up our own operation once Rudy's
gone?" If so, why then did Travis get killed?

Something didn't fit. What?

"Lena!"

She turned. Marjorie, Pin's rich friend, was walking
toward her with a broad, knowing smile.

"I saw you crossing the street," she said. "I recognized you at once!" She looked down at Lena's trousers
and shoes. Marjorie was wearing a pair of yellow harem
pants and had been shopping downtown from the look
of the bags she was carrying. Lena felt a rush of embarrassment, but Marjorie was delighted.

"And you cut your hair! Wish I'd stayed with you
that night. Pin got sick and we never got to hear Carol
Tanner sing. He dropped me off without even a night-

cap." She pulled out a long cigarette holder. "Man can't hold his liquor," she said evenly.

Lena stared at her. What had Pin called Carol Tanner when they were at that restaurant together, after Rudy's funeral? A real sapphire. That's what he'd said. But in fact he never went to see her that night.

Something else he had lied about.

Marjorie walked with her to the tram stop and then took her hand. "I'm sorry I didn't go to your brother's funeral," she said. She hesitated, and Lena saw her decide not to make an excuse. Lena liked her for that. "I should have," Marjorie just said.

Watching Marjorie walk away, a thought struck her. After a moment something seemed to crumple inside her. She thought of Rudy's expression that last night. The surprise of the hit was still on his face when he fell, blood like a spray of mud on the snow bank behind him. The right side of his head.

The tram, when it came, could not go fast enough for her. When at last she reached her stop, Lena jumped out, glad for the trousers she was wearing, and ran down the block to Mrs. Jenkins's house, taking the steps up to the front door two at a time.

She found Eve in the back room sitting with Henry. Lena didn't stop to order her thoughts. "I was thinking it was the man in the Kokomo truck," she told them, with no introduction, trying to catch her breath and talk at the same time. "I thought it was the driver, someone Nathan Cobb hired, probably Travis."

"Lena, what . . . ?" Eve said.

"You all right?" Henry asked.

"Here, sit down," Eve told her. "Calm yourself."

"But I was stupid," Lena went on, still standing. "I didn't think. The bullet was on the right side of Rudy's head. That means the shot came from his right."

"Get me that water glass over there Henry, will you?" Eve asked. He handed it to her and she filled it with water from the white pitcher on the dresser. "Here."

Lena took the glass. "The bullet came from the other side, do you see? Not the street side, the club side."

"Sip your water," Eve told her.

"Also, Pin lied to me about where he'd been that night."

Eve said gently, "You're not making sense."

It took all three of them the rest of the afternoon to sort it out, and even so there were holes. Chickie was in the other room sleeping, so they kept their voices low. At one point Mrs. Jenkins came in with some coffee, and Henry went outside to find a little boy to bring them back sandwiches, but that took him less than five minutes.

Lena tried to demonstrate, showing with her hands the street, the club, the truck, and where everyone was standing.

"Your wound is on the right side," she said to Eve, "but you were facing Rudy, so the right side for you was the street side. Rudy got hit from the other direction."

The man driving the truck got Eve. But someone else, maybe someone standing alongside the club, got Rudy.

"Travis talked a lot. That's what Moaner told me this afternoon, that Travis sort of sold information, and the man he described was Pin. My guess is that Cobb ordered Rudy to be shot at, and Travis passed that information along to Pin, and Pin . . . when Pin found out, he decided to . . ." Lena stopped.

After a moment, Eve said, "Let's get you some of this coffee."

Lena watched Eve pour it out. She took the cup and wrapped her hands around it. By now she was sitting on the piano bench, while Henry and Eve sat on a couple of straight-backed chairs. Every once in a while, one of them stood and paced the room.

"I think Pin knew Cobb was planning on scaring Rudy. So he used that as a cover to really . . . he wanted to . . ." Lena's throat was closing up again, but she didn't want to cry.

"You think Pin took matters into his own hands?" Henry asked. His voice was very gentle. "You think he shot your brother?"

Lena nodded. She didn't say anything for a moment.

"But why?" Henry asked.

"Lena," Eve began.

Lena swallowed and shook her head. "No. It's all right. I can finish." She took a sip of the coffee. "Pin went back to the club, waited for Cobb's man to make the false hit, and as that was happening he shot Rudy for real." She looked at Eve. "But that's not all. You remember I saw Travis at Rudy's funeral? I think what happened was that Travis went to the funeral to give Pin the letter Chickie had given him. The letter from Gavin Johnson about the gun shipment. Travis probably thought he'd get some extra cash for that."

"Did you see them talking together?" Henry asked.

"No. But I left the church a few minutes after he did. And Travis was the first one out the door, as I recall. I remember wondering who he was."

Henry nodded. "They could have had a few words while people were still inside. Even exchanged money; that doesn't take long."

"So that means Pin is the one who has Gavin's letter," Eve said.

Lena nodded. "But at the funeral Travis would have seen Rudy's body . . . he might have noticed that Rudy's wound was on the wrong side. He could have put two and two together just like I did."

"And even if he didn't, Pin might worry that he would," Eve said.

"That's right."

"A man who sells information."

"That's right."

"So Pin kills him too."

"Like he killed my brother." She made herself swallow. Eve leaned forward, took a handkerchief out of her pocket, and handed it to Lena.

"You're both guessing about an awful lot here," Henry put in. "Let me be the voice of reason."

"I know I'm right. I know he shot my brother."

"But why?" Henry asked. "Weren't they friends?"

Lena shook her head. "Maybe the police can figure that part out."

"You thinkin' of going to the police?"

"They can send a detective—" She raised her eyebrows. Right?

But Henry just pinched his lips. After a moment he said, "The police ain't gonna help you on this one."

"Why not?"

"All of them in the pockets of the club owners, least in this district. Paid off to look the other way."

"But this isn't about bootleg whisky!"

A small pause.

"Well, you can try them," Henry said.

Lena looked around the small room with its piano, its long windows facing the yard. The snow outside was streaked yellow from the neighborhood dogs, who ran in packs behind the houses looking for something to chase.

She pulled her fingers through her newly cut hair. She was still wearing Henry's clothes. Soon she'd go back to her own life, to her job at the hospital and Aunt Clem and the baby. Maybe that would be all that she had now. Everyone she once saw in her future had disappeared one by one—her father, her mother, Rudy, now Pin. But *I never really had ideas about Pin*, Lena told herself. *Not really.*

She was on the brink of something. A powerful feeling.

"I have to do something," she said.

26

THAT NIGHT, LENA WENT over to Rudy's apartment for the first time in a week. It was no surprise to her to find that, although the door was still locked, someone had already been there looking through his things.

Pin.

She was aware of something new in her heart, a kind of resolution. First she looked in the coffee can where Rudy kept his money. Nothing. Next she looked through his mail. Two circulars from the drugstore downstairs and a gas bill.

His bedroom was neat, the bed made. A stack of books stood on the floor by the armchair. She looked at the covers: Booth Tarkington's *The Magnificent Ambersons* and an inspirational tract by Dale Carnegie. There were no bankbooks, no receipts, nothing tucked under his mattress.

It wasn't as though she was expecting a diary. One by one she put everything he owned into a large wooden packing crate: his cambric shirts and starched collars, a gray wool winter suit, two tight-fitting vests from before the Armistice, and a looser, more stylish vest he must have recently bought. She wedged in the books and his gooseneck reading lamp. In the kitchen she wrapped all the dishes in newspaper and then fit those into the crate, too. When she was done, the crate was only half full. Lena looked around. All his possessions.

She stood in the middle of the room and thought.

It was nearly midnight when she left. As she was locking up, the woman in the apartment across the hall opened her door a crack.

"Evening, Mrs. Sweers," Lena said.

The next day was Saturday. When Lena got to Rudy's apartment in the morning, she found a telegram under the door, and she read it with the door still open. She waited for Mrs. Sweers to peek out again from the apartment across the hall, but she had some luck—Mrs. Sweers must have gone out. Lena locked Rudy's door and left, the telegram folded in her pocket.

Three hours later she came back wearing new harem pants—not yellow, like Marjorie's, but a more somber brown—and a white blouse. She carried in two full string bags. First she sprinkled a handful of salt over the living room rug, and then she swept it from corner to corner. After that she tackled the kitchen floor.

She had brought along everything she needed, even an apron, which felt a little strange over pants. In no time she had a chocolate cake in the oven and was boiling water for tea. Like her mother, she stored her tea leaves in an old salt box, the different leaves separated into marked envelopes.

Passionflower, chamomile, poppy seeds, some dried lemon peel. She wouldn't use all of them, of course. Originally her mother had brought many of the seeds over from Germany when she migrated. She was a practical woman, her mother, although she came from a family of gamblers and one horse thief—Lena's grandfather Rudolph. After nine successful thefts and one unsuccessful one, Rudolph was kicked out of the country and moved to America with his wife and daughter, Lena's mother, who was only fourteen. But old enough to think of seeds, which she hid from the customs officials.

Lena took a pail of warm water and began to wash the windows. Everyone said she looked just like her mother, although she always thought of herself as the tamer version. Now she wondered if she might be crafty like her grandfather as well, but she had never had an occasion so far to test that. When the window glass was dry, Lena rubbed it with a cloth dipped in fuller's earth to make it shine. Outside, low heavy clouds moved slowly between buildings, and sure enough, when she went back to the kitchen, she could feel herself start to limp. She took off the apron and, using the teakettle as a mirror, she applied Chickie's dark lipstick to her mouth. It looked strange and exotic, too dark for her probably. She liked it.

There was a knock on the door. Lena stood still, holding her breath. "Telegram," said a young voice. She waited. She didn't open the door. Soon afterward she heard light footsteps going down the stairs.

They had to try three times before leaving the message under the door; that was the rule. Lena could picture the boy in his short green pants, his knee socks, a little cap that the telegram company provided. After a moment she heard a soft click as another door closed on the floor. Mrs. Sweers was back.

Lena began wiping down the living room furniture. The apartment lost its closed, stale odor and instead smelled like ammonia and lemon polish. After a long while she heard what she was waiting for: the sound of a key scraping into the door lock. A man walked into the apartment like he owned it.

"Pin," she said.

For a moment he looked—what? Embarrassed? Sly? Certainly surprised.

"Lena?" For some reason he glanced down at the dark key in his hand. "What are you doing here?"

"The landlord contacted me," she lied. "Someone is moving in next week."

He looked at her. "You've cut your hair."

"Do you like it? The barber went a little beyond what I'd intended."

His face didn't seem any different to her. She couldn't imagine him hurting anyone. But he had been in the war, she reminded herself. He knew how to kill.

He smiled gently. "Smells good in here."

"I've been cleaning."

Pin looked around and then shut the door behind him. By now it was late afternoon. The last of the sun's light angled in through the front windows.

"No," he said. "Something else. Are you baking?"

"Oh. Yes. I thought I'd give the woman across the hall a cake for looking after Rudy's mail and things this last week. Mrs. Sweers."

"Actually," Pin said, holding up the key, "that was me. Rudy gave me a key a long time ago. I try to stop by on my way to work to check on things."

Lena smiled lightly. "Then I suppose the cake is for you."

He followed her into the little kitchen, where she mixed tea and set the water to boil. The cake was cooling on a wooden shelf near the oven. She shook out her apron and tied it again around her waist, trying not to look at Pin too closely, afraid that her face might give something away. She had gambled that Pin was paying Mrs. Sweers to watch Rudy's apartment for him, and she had been right. He would stay until the telegram came, she figured. What he was waiting for? She felt a slight elation, like a tickle or a long breath, the feeling of winning a bet, of getting away with something. Maybe I am like my grandfather, she thought.

When the water was ready, Lena tipped the kettle into the teapot she'd brought with her, her mother's

teapot. Next she went back to the crate in the bedroom
to get cups and plates; she didn't want Pin to know
she'd been expecting him, so she packed them up like
everything else. When she returned to the kitchen, Pin
was looking through the mail.

This time he did not look embarrassed.

"Are you expecting something?" she asked. She knew
that he was. He was expecting the telegram from Gavin
Johnson saying when the gun shipment would arrive.

"I feel I should take care of Rudy's bills," Pin said.
"Any money he owed."

"Why?"

"You might not have known this, but I had a little
hand in his business."

For a moment she couldn't trust herself to speak.
Then she said, "How is that?"

"Oh, I helped him with some of his runs," Pin said
easily. "Of course, if I had known he might be someone's target . . . we thought of it as a game."

"A game?"

"Playing bootlegger."

"But you didn't make any liquor." The tea had been
steeping for three minutes by the kitchen clock. Gingerly, she strained the seeds out, poured the liquid into a
clean cup, and brought it to Pin. "I thought you only
transported the corn sugar."

"What's in this?" Pin asked, bringing the cup up to
sniff it. For a moment he sounded suspicious.

"Tea. I mixed it myself. It's mostly lemon verbena
and water. Also caraway seeds."

"Are you going to have some?"

"Of course." She poured some for herself and, still standing, she brought the teacup to her lips. The rim was hot. Pin watched her take a sip. "Are you afraid I might poison you?" she asked.

"Ha-ha," Pin laughed weakly. "No, I just . . . no."

She took another sip. "Why would I want to do that?"

"I was only having some fun." He tasted it. "It's good," he said, surprised.

There was no caraway in it; she'd lied about that. Just poppy seeds that had been steeped in warm water and lemon juice. The poppy would infuse the tea with morphine. Not as strong as other ways of getting the drug, but strong enough. You had to be careful, though. A few years ago there was a scandal in an Illinois town when five women attending a "poppy seed tea party" drank too much and died. One had been the wife of the mayor.

She didn't want to kill Pin, she just wanted to get him to talk. The tea made you feel relaxed and, as her mother would say, *gesprächig*. Talkative.

Lena sliced two large pieces of cake and put them on plates. Pin took a bite of his and then wiped his mouth with a folded handkerchief.

"So you come here before work?" she asked. "You must be on the late shift. Where are you working?" But as soon as the question came out, she had a prescient feeling. Of course.

"Actually, the union steward at the station gave me Rudy's old job," Pin said.

Setting it all up. Very clever.

"I think Rudy would have wanted that, don't you?" he asked.

Lena sat down across from him at the white metal table and sipped her tea carefully. She didn't want to become talkative, too. Say what she thought of him.

The water was bubbling gently on the stove, staying hot, and Lena refilled Pin's teacup twice. She kept listening for a knock at the door. Once Pin poured whiskey into his cup from a flask in his pocket when he thought she wasn't looking, and after that he really did relax, stretching his long legs out to the side of the table.

"I was excited to work with Rudy," he told her. "But Rudy was cautious. Not sure if the business could support three people."

"You're talking about the corn sugar."

"He had that partner in the country but we didn't need *him*. I told Rudy that." Now Pin seemed almost maudlin. "I could have saved him. There was a message . . ." He glanced up at Lena and seemed to reconsider. "I learned about something just a little too late, more business, a venture I really could have helped him with! He didn't have to die . . ."

Lena finished the thought: Didn't have to die *yet*.

Just then the knock came. "Telegram," said a young voice.

"Ah," Pin said, getting up quickly to go answer. Then he seemed to recollect himself. "That is . . ."

Lena stood also. "I'll see what it is," she said.

She opened the door. But instead of a messenger boy there was a girl standing there in the olive green uniform of Western Union.

"Telegram, miss," the girl said.

"I didn't know Western Union hired girls," Lena said, smiling in spite of the fact that her heart was racing again.

"Yes, miss," the girl said. She was dark-haired with a serious round face, and wore the Western Union cap and jacket over a skirt. "There's a few of us. Have to be fourteen, like the boys. Got my working papers last week."

"They pay you well?" Pin asked.

"Not as well as the boys."

Lena took the small, khaki-colored envelope between her fingers. She saw Pin eyeing it. "Just a minute," she said to the girl. She went into the kitchen and came back with a penny and a piece of cake wrapped in newspaper.

"Thank you, miss," the girl said, touching her cap.

When the door shut behind her, Pin began to laugh.

"Shh," Lena said. "She'll hear you."

"I don't care, she looked ridiculous. A girl delivering telegrams."

"She probably needs the money."

For some reason that made Pin furious. "Money! It was the war, that's what it was. Gave 'em ideas. Now what do we have? We have little girls with jobs while their fathers and uncles, good men who fought for their country, can't find anyone to hire them! That's right. Women have the jobs these days, and colored folks, and krauts." He leaned in close as he said this. His breath stank. He was standing very close to her.

"Pin." She tried to sound calm.

"Some of 'em, they didn't even fight. Yet here they are, making money hand over fist. Partnering with colored men who should be back home pulling plows!"

He was thinking about Rudy and Gavin, Lena realized. "It's the horses that do that," she said coldly.

He wasn't listening. "Came up here and stole our jobs while we were fighting for them. I told your brother, I told him he should get rid of that partner. It wasn't natural. Choosing him over me, the same as it's happening all over Chicago! This is what we were fighting against over there."

"I thought it was the Germans."

"They're even worse!" He turned and looked at her, and then, just as abruptly as he began, he stopped. "Not you," he said, his voice dropping. "You're not . . ." He took a step toward her. "I'm sorry you cut your hair," he said. "And you shouldn't wear those pants." He touched her throat with his thumb and index finger. His hand was cold, as though coated with something. She stepped back. Tried to think of something to say.

But Pin's eyes had strayed to the envelope. "Here I am keeping you from your message. Would you like me to open it?"

"No. Thank you," Lena said. Her fingers were trembling, she noticed, as she tore the paper. She read the telegram through. It was exactly as she had written it. *We're on Saturday 11pm.* Followed by a siding and a train car number. Signed: G.J.

Gavin Johnson. But Gavin Johnson hadn't sent this telegram; she had sent it herself. The real telegram from

Gavin Johnson was folded up in her pocket. The one she'd found this morning.

"What's it say?" Pin asked. He ran his fingers through his hair casually, but his voice sounded strained.

"Nothing. I don't know," Lena told him. "It doesn't matter. Someone who doesn't know Rudy is dead."

She crumpled the telegram without showing it to him and threw it into the dark oval wastepaper basket by the front door. "If you give me a moment, I'll pack up the rest of the cake for you."

For the next few minutes she busied herself in the kitchen. She could hear Pin moving around. A few coughs. When she came out again, he was holding his coat and hers. She looked around for the last time.

"A man will come for the crate tomorrow," she said.

"What about the furniture?"

"Came with the apartment."

If she let herself, she could see Rudy standing in front of the windows, tapping an unlit cigarette against his thigh in his nervous, excited, boyish way. He was so energetic; he was so young.

"Everything is ready," Lena said, but there was a catch in her voice. That surprised her.

"You'll make someone a good wife someday, Lena."

She handed him the cake. She didn't trust herself with words.

"Lena, listen, I hope you'll forgive that outburst—I probably sounded more upset than I really felt. Sometimes it all comes rushing out." He gave a short laugh and looked at her sideways. "Don't mind me. Once in a while I get a little . . . troubled."

She made a small noise with her lips pressed closed.

"Since the war," he explained. He pulled the apartment key from his pocket. "Here. I won't be back."

Lena looked at the key. "I won't either," she said, but she took it. Pin went out to the hall before her, and she took the opportunity to glance down at the wastepaper basket by the door. Rudy's telegram was gone.

"Ready?" Pin asked.

He held her arm as they walked down the short flight of stairs and then out of the building and onto the street. The wind blew at her hard, and Lena felt conscious again of her limp. Worse when you're nervous, a doctor once told her, but she didn't feel nervous. She felt calm and full of purpose. A tram was coming, its brakes screeching as it adjusted for a turn. When it stopped, Pin saw her in and then put a hand in his overcoat pocket.

"Good-bye, Lena. Stay well."

The crumpled telegram was no doubt in that pocket. She stood just inside the open car door watching him as the tram started up again. He still held the remains of the cake. For a moment, nothing seemed to move.

Lena stayed by the door. He would take the bait, she was sure. Still, at the very next stop she got off the tram. Half a block away she could see Pin's back. He was walking slowly. As she got closer she saw him go up to a garbage pail near the curb, open the lid, and throw in her cake. After that, he stopped at a telephone booth on the corner and began to make a call.

27

ON SATURDAY AFTERNOON EVE went with Henry to see
Arkie White at a former saloon—now officially called a
café—near State Street, hearing that Arkie might have
a job for her. It was a place well known to musicians,
with an old baby grand in the corner and famous fried
sandwiches.

They got there early on purpose, before the show. A
couple of men were sitting at a round table in the back
with two girls and what looked like twelve or so bottles
of beer. One man, Arkie's sax player, was playing a
Bach suite on someone's guitar, varying it a little here
and there since it was originally written for the cello.

His name was Howland Freed. Eve knew him a little.
He played his tenor sax like it was an alto sax and dec-
orated it with glued-on pictures of women.

"Eve Riser," he said, standing up and handing the guitar back to his friend. "I have heard you play. You play like a man. You do, you play like a man."

"Well, thank you."

"I didn't say a good man."

"Then you haven't heard me play," she said.

At that he laughed, and he looked her over with more interest. Eve explained how she wanted to see Arkie about a job, was he around? Howland said, "Sure, wait just a minute," and went along to the back. Henry and Eve sat down at an empty table, and Eve drew off her gloves. When Howland came back with three bottles of kitchen beer, she didn't say no.

After a bit, Henry got out his trumpet and Howland wiped his sax, and pretty soon Eve was at the piano setting the tempo. Arkie came out and sat at a front table to listen. Eve was wearing a nice pale pink suit and a new cloche hat—when you were asking for a job, you had to look good. For a while they just messed around, and then Henry began a blues number with a dominant B minor chord, sad and steady, while Howland's sax floated in and around the trumpet as if belying its worries. Four bars in, Eve started the melody and the trumpet backed her up, both of them progressively falling to lower notes.

This was all she wanted sometimes. To play her music and forget about everything else. Worry followed her like owed money; there was no relief from it. Lena was going to do what she was going to do, she told herself. She was a grown woman and she had made her choice.

After the third song, Arkie stood up and shook hands with her, telling her she could have a job with him come Monday when Carl Hill, the man playing for them now, left for Kansas City.

Afterward they had another drink with Howland, catching up on the gossip, and then Henry said he'd see her home.

"Don't you have to get to the Oaks?" Eve asked.

"Marvin'll cover for me," Henry told her. "He owes me one."

"He does not!"

Henry smiled. "Well, he think he does."

It was dusk now, and they walked along the cold wet streets under the elevated train. Eve smelled a fresh earthy smell on the lake breeze like spring was coming on, though she knew it was not. She could feel Henry glance at her.

"Played well back there," he told her. "You get this music right in your heart."

Eve liked that. "You do too, Henry."

They were both tall and walked fast. A handsome couple, a couple that other people looked at as they passed. Henry took Eve by the elbow to guide her around a slushy puddle.

"I was just a little child about six years old when I first heard this music," he said. "It was at a church where at night they played ragtime—just covered up the altar with a cloth, and four or five men sat in front with their instruments. It wasn't ragtime really; it didn't even have a name yet. Everything was looser

back then. When the men heard two knocks, they started playing."

The wind began blowing harder, and at the corner
they had to put their heads down against it.

"My Uncle Les taught me everything he knew. Let
me tell you, that old man had some tricks. Never used
sheet music. Couldn't tell me what key the number was
in, but his fingers moved so fast they made mine look
like they was dipped in molasses. One night a little fire
started in a place we were playing at. We all rush out,
and then the bass player, a friend of my uncle's, he tries
to sneak back in. 'My baby's in there!' he kept saying.
Come to find out he was talking about his instrument."

Henry laughed and Eve laughed with him. It felt
good, hearing someone laugh, and Henry's laugh had a
nice full ring.

A moment later his face became solemn. "You have
to take it serious," he told her. "You have to be serious
about it, you have to play it like it's your way out. Like
you'd go into a burning building to save it."

Eve looked up into his face. Those long, sad eyes.
"Are you talking about music or something else?" she
asked.

He took her gloved hand in his. "Did you know my
mama once told me I would fall in love with a tall girl?"

"Whatever happened to your wife anyway?"

"Went off to Cleveland with Charlie Crane, you
know that. She wasn't tall, was Delia. Medium, I'd say.
Maybe even short. But I did love her, yes I did, before
Charlie Crane came around. That man sure could sing a
love song."

Eve watched his face. He was telling the truth. "And you have a voice like a rooster," she said. They both laughed, and she took another moment to look him over, his broad shoulders, his serious face. A sensation rippled over her skin like a light wind in summer. She wanted to feel what it felt like to be in his arms.

"You've been doing a lot of running around these past few days," she said. "Helping Lena. Nice of you, Henry."

"I'm not doing it for Lena."

She looked at him, not sure what to say.

"I'm doing it for you," he said.

They were standing on a corner. Henry took off one of his gloves and then took off one of her gloves, too. He laced their bare fingers together. The traffic light changed and they crossed the street without speaking, hand in hand. Her thumb moved to the sweet spot in the middle of his palm, the place where a gypsy might cross it with silver. In front of Mrs. Jenkins's house, they stopped. Eve turned her head and looked at him. Then she closed her eyes and he bent forward and kissed her.

After a while Henry drew back and looked up the sidewalk. A drunken couple was walking up the stoop across the street, leaning in toward each other like a pair of shoes on a pigeon-toed man. Eve took Henry's hand and led him up Mrs. Jenkins's front steps and into the house, both of them careful not to make noise.

She unlocked the door to her rooms. Chickie was asleep in the bedroom, and Eve just poked her head in to make sure, though she didn't want to leave Henry's side or stop touching him even for just that one moment.

For a while they kissed on the hard horsehair couch, spinning that along. Then Henry circled her wrist with his fingers and drew back a little. "That's a tiny little wrist for such a powerful hand," he said.

Eve smiled. Henry stroked her collarbone with his long forefinger as if drawing a line, and a shiver passed through her. Sometimes it seemed to her that she'd constructed this life, her life, out of paper—one crumple and she'd have to start all over again. Or go back to Pittsburgh and get a job packing crackers. That was what happened to her cousin Vanetta, who used to play the piano, too.

The room felt suddenly small, shrunken down to the size of their couch. Henry ran his finger along the curve of her shoulder and then bent to kiss her neck. After a moment she reached up and pulled at her hatpins. His hat lay on the floor by their feet. They didn't switch on any lamps, but there was some light from the moon coming in through the window. Everything felt serious, even the moon. Henry stood and pulled the curtains shut. His long body against the window frame. No amount of hardship, Eve thought fiercely, would make her leave this. Pittsburgh was another life, and she didn't want to worry that she and Chickie were heading that way. Henry came back to the couch and kissed her and started to unbutton her blouse. After that she forgot about Pittsburgh.

There were times when Eve was playing the piano when she had an almost prescient feeling, when she could tell what notes the other musicians were going to play before they played them. A sort of quickness of mind and hearing, which seemed to happen without thought. That was when she played her best.

Once or twice she'd felt that way outside of playing. Like that time in Hoxie when the man got killed, starting all this in motion. And now, lying naked on the floor with Henry.

She was curled up at his side with nothing keeping her warm but his skin. Most of Henry's large, muscular body was covered by a womanish black-and-tan throw blanket, and she almost could laugh at him for that. His arm came out from underneath it and spread some of the blanket over her.

The knitted wool made her skin itch but also was curiously warm.

"*C'est si bon,*" Henry said.

"Yes it is," Eve told him. She turned onto her back. "Yes it is." The ceiling looked farther away than it was, with specks and dark cracks like some beautiful mystery in the night sky. It felt good just lying there.

Henry said, "I been wanting that ever since you came back to Chicago." He paused a moment. "Maybe not while you were in my room bleeding out of your head, but a little bit after that."

She laughed, and then shook her head. "You brought me back to your own room when I was hurt."

"That's right. Almost scared me to death."

They were silent for a while, and then Henry said, "I saw you come to life."

She thought about that. Yes, that was what it felt like.

"Like you was being born. First your face was like a little innocent child's. Then I could see the memory come back, the bad stuff and the good." He paused, thinking. "Sometimes I wonder if it isn't just memory that's the original sin."

"What does that mean?"

"We can't be scarred if we wake up fresh every day. Like Adam in the morning."

Eve touched the tender spot above her ear where the bullet had shaved her. "We can be scarred," she said.

"Only on our outside."

His long eyes looking at her were dark and kind. She thought about how careful he was with his lips, how soft they were.

"We can be scarred and we can be killed," Eve told him. "I was almost killed. That boy next to me, he wasn't as lucky as me. Dead before his sister could say good-bye."

Henry fiddled with the fingers of her hand. "She's important to you," he said finally. It was a question.

"She helped me and Chickie out when we needed it." Eve let out a breath. "Now she's got some crazy plan."

"She's just setting it up."

"I'm worried she might go out there. She might follow him out there."

Henry stopped playing with her fingers and squeezed her hand.

"I guess I've grown fond of her," Eve said. And right then there it was: that prescient feeling.

Outside, a dog started barking. She pulled at the blanket a little. "I'm afraid, Henry," she said. She didn't mean about him.

Henry said, "I know it."

"That girl is in over her head."

"Nothing you can do. She needs to do this for her brother. Maybe for herself."

There was a scuffling sound at the window, and something or someone pushed against the glass.

"Henry!" Eve whispered.

Henry got up, pulling on his trousers. "I hear it," he said quietly. "Just stay there." He lifted the curtain. "Who's out there?"

The sound of something in the bushes.

"Maybe just a rat or raccoon or something," he said to Eve.

Eve stood up too and found her blouse, which was luckily long. She looked around for her skirt. Just as she spotted it, a man's face appeared at the window. She gasped and stepped back almost to the door.

"Hi! Hiya!" the man said, slurring his words. "Can I get in?"

"Who is that—Gavin?" Henry asked. He opened the window and held the man by the forearm as he climbed inside.

The man brushed off some snow from his pants. Then he pulled in a suitcase.

"Why, Gavin Johnson," Eve said. Her heart was still racing. She didn't know whether to be angry or relieved or embarrassed.

"Whew. Well, that wasn't too hard to find you," Gavin said to Eve. He put down his suitcase and looked at Henry, naked from the waist up. Then he looked back at Eve a little unsteadily. "And see," he said, holding something up in a bag. "I brought up that new dress I promised."

It took a little time to get the story started, seeing as how Gavin was three sheets to the wind.

"You want some water?" Eve asked him.

Gavin held up a flask. "I got this."

"Maybe I better make you some coffee instead."

"Coffee! No, you can hold off on that. Tonight I'm celebrating."

"Well then, you better tell us," Henry said calmly, "what the celebration is about."

It was a little convoluted. After Eve left Hoxie, Gavin went on playing with the Syncopaters like before, wondering how Rudy Hardy was faring and worried that Victor Rausch might be so angry about the gun shipment falling off—seeing how the point man had been killed dead by Gavin—that he might send someone

after him. "Lord knows I didn't mean to kill the man,"
Gavin told them. The whole thing was an accident.

But he had some luck: the dead man's brother knew
where the guns were and could sell them to Gavin just
the same. Good thing the man didn't know Gavin was
the one who killed his brother; like everyone else, he
thought it was the Black Hand Society, that secret or-
ganization, pursuing some vendetta of its own.

One problem: the money to pay for the guns, of
course, was what Gavin sent back with Eve. But then
Gavin got a telegram from Nathan Cobb saying to send
along the guns immediately with payment to come. So
he gave the gun seller all of the money he had—what he
was supposed to use for buying corn sugar up and down
the county—with the notion he'd get it all back and
more from Cobb.

As he told Eve and Henry the story, Gavin drank
repeatedly from his flask. At one point he knocked over
his suitcase and Eve checked on Chickie in the next
room, but she was still sleeping soundly, her soft face
turned away from the door.

"Why did you have me bring that money to Rudy
Hardy?" Eve asked, coming back into the room. She sat
down on the couch next to Henry.

"Like I said, that man I shot, he was our contact for
the guns," Gavin told her. He was sitting on the floor
facing them, leaning against the far wall with his knees
up and holding the flask on top of one kneecap. "I wasn't
sure I was going to be able to find another, and I didn't
want to hold the Walnut's money. Not a good idea to
make that man worry, wondering if he's being cheated.

But it all worked out, didn't it? Only this time he'll pay for the guns after he gets them instead of before."

"How do you get the guns past the inspections?" Henry asked.

"We got a good hiding place for them," Gavin said with a little smile.

The guns were here now, in Chicago. They were going to be unloaded that night. When Eve heard this, she put her hand on Henry's arm in a worried gesture.

Gavin misunderstood. "Don't worry, I don't need to be there. Nathan Cobb's the man now. And I sent a telegram along to Hardy."

"To Rudy Hardy?" Henry asked. "Why, don't you know, Rudy Hardy's dead."

"Dead?" Gavin put his flask down on the floor.

"Gavin," Eve said. "Listen. This is important. When did you send your telegram to Rudy?"

"Early this morning," Gavin told her. "Just before I boarded the train."

Eve turned to Henry. "I wonder which telegram Pin found. Gavin's real one or Lena's."

"Maybe Lena got the real one in time and threw it away," Henry suggested. "Anyhow, Evie, it's out of our hands."

"That may be so." Eve looked around for her coat and hat. "But I'm going to the station."

"It's all right, don't worry, Cobb's there!" Gavin said a little too loudly for Eve's liking. "He'll take care of it."

"Hush, now. You don't know what you're saying. Nathan Cobb's gonna get himself killed," Eve said.

28

THEY WERE AT THE FREIGHT yards in less than an hour. Although there were many ways in—holes in the wire fence, scrub and garbage made into climbable piles—Eve and Henry came in through a proper gate since Henry knew one of the guards. They made their way slowly, stepping over disused rails that were half buried in snowy dirt, and looking for the car they wanted by the lights on the telegraph poles, only half of them working. To their left stood dark warehouses with loading docks stretching out over the water, and Eve caught the strong scent of river. Not surprisingly, Gavin decided to stay behind.

"She might not have come here," Henry told Eve again.

"What was that number Gavin said?" She meant for the train car, the one with the guns hidden inside.

"8481. If she's not there, we go back how we came."

They walked behind a line of orange train cars on a rip track, empty but with their doors wide open and a smell coming from them like rainwater and rust. Up ahead, Eve could hear the grind of train cars being uncoupled and men shouting orders. The yard was like its own little city, with lights and wooden shanties where the gandy dancers—the track workers—took their breaks. All sorts of things were being unloaded, even at this time of night: plows, cases of fruit, a dead body in a casket coming home to be buried.

"Busy night," Eve commented.

Most of the action was on the other side of the yard, and they stayed well away from the laborers.

Henry said, "Always is."

Another hundred yards up they reached a spot with trucks backed up to a siding. Beyond that an open wire gate led to a long brick factory built all the way out to the edge of the water. Eve just wanted to find Lena, if she was here, and get her out. Would she ever be done with all this business? she wondered. A rock on her back.

"It's somewhere around here," Henry said. "According to Jones." That was the guard he knew. "Course Jones is a fool," he added.

A light engine moved down a lead track, and Eve could see someone's arm jutting out of the window making a signal. Henry scanned the cars. "Wait a minute. You stay here," he told her.

A moment later he was back.

"Got it. This way."

He led her up a few feet and then pointed. There was a piece of machinery between them and the train track, with a cluster of men nearby. Henry and Eve inched closer, and then Henry pulled her over behind an empty car. Probably good enough cover if no one flashed a lantern their way.

But she saw it. 8481. White letters on a brown car.

Two men stood together near the approach signal on the other side of the lead track, which connected to the main track a few hundred yards down. Eve looked for Lena and was relieved not to see her. But then a movement caught her eye—something behind a small tin-roofed shanty near the tracks. Lena? The men by the signal looked up suddenly at the sound of a shout. Another man was walking toward them.

"That's the Walnut," Henry whispered.

The wind whipped over from the water and Eve could feel her hat pulling away from her head. She pushed her two hatpins more firmly in place. The wind carried some of the men's conversation her way.

"I got two calls tonight," the Walnut was saying. Some of his words were lost. ". . . Surprised . . . thought . . . to check out . . ." A screech of brakes, and another shout from down the yard. A smell of smoke and hot metal.

Eve took a tiny step forward to look more closely at the shanty. She felt Henry's hand on her arm. There *was* someone there. Someone crouching.

"Look." Eve pointed, keeping her hand close to her body. "I think she's there. Lena. Behind that little hut."

Henry frowned. "Can't hardly see . . ."

"I'm going to fetch her."

"Wait."

But suddenly the men all moved back as the Walnut pulled a gun to hip level, not exactly pointing at the men but also not pointing away. While everyone was looking intently in that direction, Eve took the opportunity to cross the track. She sidled over to the shanty trying to make herself skinny, as if she could do that by just thinking it. Holding her breath, moving fast. If the men looked over, they might have seen her, but they didn't look over.

She got behind the shanty and flattened herself against it. Lena, who was squatting down next to the shanty wall, looked up at her with a startled expression. "Eve!"

Eve bent down. "You all right?" she asked in a whisper. She was wearing pants, Eve noticed, which were smeared with soot. When she turned, Eve saw her head wobble a little. Something about her seemed too fluid, not quite balanced, like she'd been drinking.

"Why are you here?" Lena whispered.

"What do you think? To get you," Eve said crossly. "What's wrong with you? You don't look right."

"I'm fine. I'm a little bit—I had to drink some of the tea."

"The tea?"

"The poppy seed tea." Quickly Lena explained what that was. "I wanted it to slow him down. Pin."

"You're drugged?"

"I think it's starting to wear off."

Eve shook her head. "You're hoping he gets killed here."

Something ugly crossed over Lena's face. "Yes I do."

"Let's get you away," Eve told her.

"No. I want to see it."

That's the drug talking, Eve thought. "How did you get in here, anyway?"

Lena stared at her. She worked her mouth a moment. Finally she said, "I don't know."

"Henry is over there waiting. Come on back with us now." She touched Lena's arm.

Lena pulled back. "No," she whispered again.

"You think you can't get hurt, but it's just the drug in you."

"I know. I don't care." Now Lena was looking at the cluster of men. They were arguing, one of them waving his hands. "That's Pin," she told Eve. "The tall one."

"Whose the little short fella with him?"

"I'm not sure."

A light flickered. Now that she was closer, Eve could hear more of the men's words. Pin was pointing to another train car. "That's where the shipment is. And I got a fellow here who can open it up." He looked around, held up his lantern. "Shugs!" he called out. No answer. "Maybe he already unlocked it." He leaped up on the train car and pulled at the door: unlocked. With a heavy thud he hauled it open a crack and stuck his head in. Opened it further and got the lantern in there, too. After a moment, he was able to turn his body and slip in sideways.

Eve watched him disappear inside. "Henry told Shugs there'd be trouble tonight. Left it up to Shugs whether he wanted to be part of that or not. Guess he chose not to stick around." She paused. Then she said, "You were lucky to pick another train car so close to the real one."

"Not luck," Lena told her. "I came here this morning." She put a hand on the shanty wall to steady herself. Nearby, something rustled in an empty ventilator car—a rat probably. Lena stood up a little uncertainly. Eve noticed again how tall she was—with those pants, if you didn't see her up close, she did look just like a man. "I found an empty train car nearby and wrote down its number," Lena went on. "That's the number I put in my telegram." It seemed to take her longer than usual to finish a thought.

"How did you know where the real train would come?"

"I got a telegram. Came this morning. From Gavin Johnson."

So she had known. Eve felt impatient with herself, impatient with Lena. Why put herself in this danger? Why not just let the men kill each other like they always did?

"You should leave," Lena told her.

Pin jumped down from the train car, stumbling a little against the wheel flange. He looked like he'd just been hit over the head with a lead pipe.

"Well?" the Walnut called out to him.

"I don't understand it," Pin said. His voice sounded unsteady. "The car's empty."

The Walnut turned, disgusted. "Let's check this other one then."

It was an old car, not meant for cargo. A passenger car. Something about it looked familiar. Eve drew in her breath. "That's the Entertainers' car!" she whispered. "I rode in that car!" It was the car where she'd had her rendezvous with Gavin in Hoxie.

Later she learned a hole had been cut underneath the last seat, and a large container was screwed to the underside of the car—a metal box about three feet long. Now Eve noticed there was someone leaning against the wheel of that train car, someone so still she hadn't noticed him at first in his brown coat and hat. When the figure moved to open the door, he paused beneath one of the tall pole lights.

Nathan Cobb.

"I was wondering when he'd show up," Eve said.

The four men stood facing one another: The Walnut, Pin, Nathan Cobb, and a short man with a dark, stiff hat. Hard to tell who was allied with whom. A pack of wolves.

Cobb turned and went into the Entertainers' car. For a moment there seemed to be silence in the yard, like all the energy got sucked in with him. Someone tapped Eve on the shoulder and she jumped and covered her mouth.

Henry.

"How'd you get here?" she asked.

"Shh," he said. "Went round that way. Took me a while."

There was a clatter, and then all at once Cobb jumped down out of the train car with an enormous—what was it, a club? Something thick and partly metallic but with a wooden handle. The middle section glinted when he swung it, but it didn't swing far since it was obviously heavy.

"A gun," Lena whispered.

It was the biggest gun Eve had ever seen.

"Thompson's new submachine gun," Cobb was saying loudly to the little man in the dark hat. "Just off the factory line. The company's trying to sell it out West to ranchers. There are five more of them in there, market value two hundred fifty dollars apiece."

"A *sub*machine gun?" the little man asked. He had an Irish accent. "What's that then, like those machine guns they were using in the war?"

"Multiple rounds without reloading. You can feed the ammo yourself."

"Let me see that, now," the little man said.

"Like the army's machine guns, except made for one person," Cobb told him, handing it over. "See the circular magazine built right in? Thompson wanted a single man to be able to go across enemy lines with this beauty and sweep their trenches with bullets. Problem was, he was just a little too late. War ended before he was finished."

So. A machine gun that didn't need three men to operate. Now Eve could understand why so many people were interested.

"See that little man there?" Henry whispered. He pointed to the Irishman. "I recognize him. Member of the North Side Gang."

"What could they want with that gun?"

Henry pulled at his hat. "What any of them want. Gang stuff. Do away with Johnny Torrio, maybe, and his second-in-command, Capone." He shook his head. "Guess the Walnut made his choice who to back, and it's not the Italians."

"Look at Pin," Lena whispered.

He had his hands at his sides but something about him looked ready to fight. All at once with one quick movement he leaped forward and snatched the gun from the Irishman's hands.

"Hey," the Irishman shouted. "Hey!"

With another swift movement Pin knocked the Walnut's gun out of his hand and looked meaningfully over at the Irishman, who raised his arms up in the air. Pin examined the submachine gun, turned it over once to check the mechanism, and then pointed it at Cobb.

"I'm going to be the man in this operation," Pin said to him.

"Are you now?" Cobb stepped forward.

Pin fired the gun.

Nothing happened.

Cobb stepped forward again. "Do you think I would come out with it loaded?" He sounded as if he were smiling.

But faster than Eve could think, Pin flipped the rifle over and hit Cobb solidly in the head with its butt. A soldier used to the turns of battle. With a groan, Cobb fell to his knees and put his hand on his ear. A few men working nearby heard the noise and looked over. When they saw Pin's gun, they quickly jumped over the siding and skirted away.

Pin handed the unloaded submachine gun back to the Irishman. "You'll be working with me now," he said. He put his hand in the pocket of his overcoat and pulled out a pistol, ridiculously tiny compared with the submachine gun, but probably loaded.

He aimed it at Cobb's head.

"You were close," he said.

"No!" Lena whispered. She started to move, but Eve lay a hand on her shoulder and Henry took hold of her other arm. Eve was thinking: Only a few seconds more, and then Cobb will be dead. In the confusion we can get her away from here.

This was what she was thinking while she watched Lena. But the sound of a gunshot didn't come. Instead she heard Henry say, "What in the—how'd she get here?"

Eve looked up and saw Chickie.

She was standing between two rail lines in her old purple coat holding a white-handled pistol, some silly lady pistol she'd gotten from God knows where. Pin was still aiming at Cobb's head and she was aiming at Pin.

"Chickie!" Eve screamed. She started to go, and Henry let go of Lena to take hold of her. Eve felt her mind spin. Had Chickie followed them? She must have followed them. She must have heard everything— everything about Cobb and the gun shipment. She must have been only pretending to sleep. It was Eve's own fault—what had she said? That Cobb was going to get himself killed.

"That's the father of my baby," Chickie said loudly, to Pin. Cobb raised his head and looked at her. "Don't you hurt him."

She fired off a shot and Pin flinched. Was he hit? He didn't pitch forward. Chickie took a few steps back and looked down at her little pistol, trying to work out how to make it shoot again. But she couldn't. Was it jammed? Eve wondered. Pin was still holding his gun.

"Well," he said evenly. The shot hadn't killed him, hadn't even made him drop his gun. It had missed him entirely. Meanwhile Chickie was shaking her little pistol desperately. Pin took a step toward her.

"Run, Chickie!" Eve screamed.

Pin didn't even look over at the shout; he just kept walking slowly toward Chickie like he was enjoying this. What was the matter, why wouldn't Chickie run? Eve didn't know what to do—this was a nightmare, every-thing warped and slow like a harmonium losing its air. Beside her, she was aware of Lena running from the shanty. The Walnut and the Irishman—where were they?

Pin was slow but Lena was fast. There was a small truck between their shanty and Pin, and Lena got into it and released the handbrake. It was as small as a go-cart, probably used to haul coal.

Henry said, "Look."

The truck was slightly uphill, and all at once Eve understood what Lena was doing. A light from one of the posts lit her briefly; she was struggling with the steering wheel, trying to direct the truck toward Pin. Pin was staring at Chickie, who was staring back, standing stock-still like she had tried and failed and this was the consequence. She wasn't going to fight it.

The little truck gained speed. Its wheels turned slightly. Pin was intent on Chickie. He could raise his gun at any moment and kill her, he was that close, but all at once the truck's movement caught his eye and he turned to the side and jumped—not soon enough.

Lena jumped out just as Pin started to shout. The left headlight made contact with his body and his voice went up in pitch. The truck wasn't going terribly fast but fast enough to push him back over a rail and against the Entertainers' car, pinning him at his thighs. Eve ran to Chickie, and Henry was right behind her. The Walnut was on his hands and knees looking around for something in the rails, probably his gun. The Irishman was nowhere to be seen.

Chickie leaned on Eve. Eve tried to hold her up but Chickie sank to the ground on her knees. Her face was very pale.

"Chickie, you fool, you're such a fool," Eve was saying. She couldn't even cry yet.

"My daddy never knew I existed."

"I know that. I know."

"I wanted him to know at least that his daughter existed."

She was talking about Cobb. On the other side of the siding the Walnut stood up. He had his gun now. He turned to Cobb and helped him to his feet.

"Because why else would I save him?" Chickie went on. "Father of my child. Why else would I save him? He'll never love me again. Do you think?"

"It's done now, Lovie. He knows."

Chickie looked up at her, and then she looked over at the truck and at Pin.

"He's trying to do something," she said.

Pin was struggling, pulling at part of his overcoat, trying to get it unstuck. Eve was on one side of Chickie, Henry on the other.

"He ain't going nowhere," Henry said.

Lena was watching Pin, too. She was standing only a few feet away from him. "You never went to see Carol Tanner that night," she told him.

Pin was still struggling with his coat.

"You knew Cobb's man was going to scare Rudy with a false hit. You decided to make it a real hit. You went back to the club and killed Rudy yourself."

Pin spit. "He was a kaiser-lover just like you."

"I planned all this, I want you to know that. The cake, the telegram. I wanted you to come here and get yourself killed."

"You little bitch," Pin said. "Didn't have the guts to do it yourself."

"There's still time," she told him.

"Not much." He brought his arm up quickly and Eve could see something in his hand. Something he'd been struggling to free.

It was a knife. But before she could move, Pin threw it at Lena with the precision of a Boy Scout, and the blade pierced her neck and hung there.

"Lena!" Eve screamed. She let go of Chickie and ran over. A gunshot sounded and Pin slumped against the hood of the truck. Another shot. Then another. Or maybe that was her heart. Somehow Eve got to Lena, who was now leaning back with her hand at her throat.

Lena whispered, "Stings."

Without thinking, Eve pulled the blade out and put her handkerchief over the wound, which was bleeding more than she could believe possible. She looked into Lena's eyes and Lena looked back into hers with a question. They were sitting together on the ground but Eve didn't know how they got there. Her arms were wrapped around Lena, and there was no noise anymore in the yard, no work being done, no men, no prescient feeling. Her mind was a stone.

"Don't die, don't die, don't die," she whispered to Lena, rocking and holding her like she was her child. "Don't you die."

29

SHE STOOD IN THE RAIN outside the church under a cotton umbrella that Henry had given her. She wondered if this was the same church where Rudy had had his funeral. A white church; she couldn't go inside. On the corner some kids were playing instruments in the rain— a washtub with a string, a drum made of hubcaps. Her shoes were getting wetter and wetter because the wind kept changing direction, blowing raindrops under her raised umbrella.

She watched the casket get carried in.

It was a simple brown box carried by men who were paid to do it. Behind them, women in dark coats stepped gingerly over the black puddles on the path. Eve recognized Aunt Clem on the arm of a man, probably her husband, Mortie. The baby was not with them, and Eve told herself that was for the best. After a while she thought she heard music start up inside the church, and a white man stared at her as he walked by. I can stand here, Eve thought sullenly. She raised her chin. I can stand here on the sidewalk and pay my respects.

A song kept running through her mind, "Si Tu Vois Ma Mere"—"If You See My Mother"—with its melody that started low and fell progressively lower. Nothing about the day felt right; not the weather or what she chose to wear or what she ate that morning for breakfast. A half hour later the church doors opened and people starting coming out, shaking their umbrellas open. Eve waited for Aunt Clem to recognize her, but she never looked Eve's way. She wore a hat with a black veil over most of her face, and she got into a motorcar with her husband and left.

Only then did Eve turn to go back to Arkie's, where Henry had said he'd meet her. Her cheeks were wet, but she thought that must be from the rain.

"Play 'Si Tu Vois Ma Mere' for me?" she asked.

He looked over at her with his long, shadowed eyes, reading her face like a musical score. "I can do that." Just that morning, he'd told her he was planning to break off from the Oaks Club and get together his own band to go out West and play the circuit all the way to Los Angeles. He asked Eve and Chickie to come with him—it was something he'd been wanting to do anyway, he said. They were planning to leave the following week if they could find a tenor sax and maybe another drummer if Baby Diggs couldn't persuade his wife to go. But if everything worked out, Eve would be back on the

circuit come Tuesday, this time with Chickie along so
that she could keep a good eye on her.

They sat at one of Arkie's back tables, and Henry
played the song twice over while Eve did something she
almost never did: she drank two shots of whiskey, one
right after the other.

"That help?" Henry asked, pulling his horn away, his
sad eyes looking kind.

"Not really," Eve said.

But she was a professional: that night, when the time
came, she put her dense, low mood aside and played the
show. She put everything she had into it—joy, love, sor-
row, whatever the music called for. She had it all and
she put it all in. In her mind she pictured Lena sitting
there at one of the back tables, listening. It was only
after the set was over and Eve was back in her room
pulling the shade down that she let herself cry.

It was all so senseless. Lena died in Eve's arms with
her eyes half-open and looking up at Eve as if to say: So
this is what happens next. Pin had died immediately
after being shot in the head and in the chest twice by
the Walnut, who left before the police got there. He and
Cobb and the Irishman would sort out the guns however they might. More would be dead because of those
guns, that was for sure, before too long. Lots of people,
maybe. They were made for a war. But Eve didn't care
about any of it. What she cared about was Lena. Seeing
her die. Knowing she was gone.

She wiped her eyes with her shirtsleeve. It was late,
after two, and she could hear Chickie snoring in the
next room. She was just sitting down on the piano

bench to unroll her stockings when, just like that, it came: a two-bar walking bass rising in her mind like an engine chugging across a field.

Eve stopped. Sure enough, there was a song there.

A train ride. Two high chords like a whistle, then a break in the beat, then a third whistle. She had to get it down on paper. Her notebook was in the other room, but she found a pencil and an old laundry bill with a blank back side. Outside, the rain had turned to snow and she knew she had to write fast: when it comes it comes quick. An AABA chorus. Now the bridge. The snow against the window became snow on the train and the train was moving west. Alto and tenor sax together, a cornet interjecting. She wrote a notation for a mute. Now the clarinet, now the trombone. She got the piano right hand and turned the paper over and wrote over the bill's printed side. A harmonic progression here with room for variation. The brass weren't quarreling in this one, they were all agreed: there was a better place ahead.

Eve wrote the coda. "Sugarland," she would call it. She knew what it would be like out on the circuit: some places they love the music and some places they don't. You get into a groove, then a waiter drops a tray and you lose it. Can't get your dresses cleaned properly, the man stiffs you on your pay, you take a break to eat lunch and can't find a restaurant that will serve you. She knew what the life was like, but she was going to do it anyway. She had to, and she wanted to. She thought about Lena's face when she was playing the piano, when she got it right. Like a light shone behind it. That better place. Lena was part of her song, now.

Eve made a change to the second ending, and when she looked up, Chickie was standing in the doorway in her robe.

"You comin' to bed?" Chickie asked, half in a yawn.

Her face was soft and young. Eve hoped she was taking care of her throat. In the morning she'd fix Chickie a lemon gargle, or maybe one of those teas Lena liked to make, something good for you that tasted like dirt. Eve could almost smile, thinking of that tea.

"Go back to sleep, Lovie," she told Chickie. "We're packing up tomorrow."

59459811R00173

Made in the USA
Charleston, SC
04 August 2016